THE UNCOMMON APPEAL OF CLOUDS

RANDOM
HOUSE
LARGE
PRINT

BOOKS BY ALEXANDER McCALL SMITH AVAILABLE FROM RANDOM HOUSE LARGE PRINT

IN THE ISABEL DALHOUSIE SERIES

The Sunday Philosophy Club
Friends, Lovers, Chocolate
The Right Attitude to Rain
The Careful Use of Compliments
The Charming Quirks of Others
The Comforts of a Muddy Saturday
The Lost Art of Gratitude
The Uncommon Appeal of Clouds
The Forgotten Affairs of Youth

IN THE NO. 1 LADIES' DETECTIVE AGENCY SERIES

A Full Cupboard of Life
In the Company of Cheerful Ladies
Blue Shoes and Happiness
The Good Husband of Zebra Drive
The Kalahari Typing School for Men
Morality for Beautiful Girls

IN THE PORTUGUESE IRREGULAR VERBS SERIES

Portuguese Irregular Verbs
The Finer Points of Sausage Dogs
At the Villa of Reduced Circumstances

IN THE 44 SCOTLAND STREET SERIES

44 Scotland Street
Espresso Tales

The Girl Who Married a Lion and Other Tales from Africa

THE UNCOMMON APPEAL OF CLOUDS

Alexander McCall Smith

RANDOM HOUSE
LARGE PRINT

These are works of fiction. Names, characters, places, and incidents either are the product of the author's imagination or are used fictitiously. Any resemblance to actual persons, living or dead, events, or locales is entirely coincidental.

Published in the United States of America by Random House Large Print.
In association with Pantheon Books, New York.
Distributed by Random House, Inc., New York.

Originally published in Great Britain by Little, Brown, an imprint of Little, Brown Book Group, an Hachette UK Company, London.

Excerpts from the poems by W. H. Auden appear courtesy of Edward Mendelson, Executor of the Estate of W. H. Auden, and Random House, Inc.

Cover illustration by Bill Sanderson
Cover design by Linda Huang and Brian Barth

The Library of Congress has established a Cataloging-in-Publication record for this title.

ISBN: 978-0-307-99080-8

www.randomhouse.com/largeprint

FIRST LARGE PRINT EDITION

Printed in the United States of America

10 9 8 7 6 5 4 3 2 1

This Large Print edition published in accord with the standards of the N.A.V.H.

This book is for Edward and Maryla Green.

THE UNCOMMON APPEAL OF CLOUDS

CHAPTER ONE

❖

MOZART," said Isabel Dalhousie. And then she added, "Srinivasa Ramanujan."

From his side of the kitchen table, Jamie, her husband of one year, lover of more than four, looked up quizzically. "Mozart, of course, but Srini . . ." He attempted the name, but decided he could not manage it and trailed off into a liquid melt of **vee**s and sibilants. Indian names, mellifluous sounding though so many of them may be, can defeat even those with a musical ear. Jamie was accustomed to the stocky sound of Scottish names, redolent as they were of an altogether more forbidding and windswept landscape—those Macdonalds and Macgregors, Macleans and Mackays.

"Srinivasa Ramanujan," Isabel repeated. "He was, like Mozart, a child prodigy. A genius."

"I used to be so discouraged by Mozart," said Jamie. "I suspect he has that effect on any child who's interested in music. You hear about how he was composing complicated pieces at the age of five, or whatever, and you think, **I'm already twelve—which is ancient by comparison—and I haven't written anything**. And it makes you ask yourself whether there's much point in making all that effort." He paused. "But what about this Srinivasa?"

"He was a brilliant mathematician back in his day," said Isabel. She made a gesture that indicated the earlier part of the twentieth century—or at least did so to her; to Jamie it was no more than a vague movement of the hand. "He died when he was barely into his forties."

"Like Mozart. What age was he when he died? Thirty-five, wasn't he?"

Isabel nodded. "Which prompts the usual thoughts of what might have been."

"Of music lost," said Jamie. He had noticed that people invariably said something like that when the shortness of Mozart's life was mentioned. What he could have done if he had lived another ten years, another twenty . . . the symphonies, the operas . . .

Isabel reached for her teacup. "Yes. And in the case of Ramanujan, of problems unsolved. But that's not what interests me. I've been thinking of the parents and of their role in their children's lives. Mozart's father spent a very large part of his time on his children's musical education. Teaching him to compose, taking him on those long tours. A pushy father, if ever there was one."

"And Srinivasa . . . what about his parents?"

Isabel smiled. "He had a mother to contend with. She doted on him. She said that he was the special gift of the household's private god. She was a mathematician too."

"So the best chance of being a prodigy is to have an obsessive parent?"

Isabel agreed, but only to an extent. She believed in nurture, but she gave more weight to nature. "You have to have the right genes in the first place. Mozart's sister had the same upbringing as he did, with the same musical attention. She became a very competent performer but she was not a musical genius."

Jamie looked up at the ceiling. "Imagine being Mozart's sister . . ."

"Yes, imagine. That bit—the genius bit—has to be there somewhere in the brain. It's probably a matter of brain design, of neuro-anatomy. Mozart had it; his sister clearly didn't."

Jamie called that the **wiring**. Badness, he thought, was usually a question of faulty wiring;

Isabel was not so sure. "I read about a rather interesting case of mathematical genius," she said. "Nabokov."

"The author? The one who wrote **Lolita**?"

"Yes," said Isabel. "Nabokov was a mathematical prodigy as a child. He could do elaborate calculations in his head, within seconds."

Jamie was interested. Musicians were often competent or even more than competent mathematicians—the **wiring**, perhaps, was similar. At school his best subject, after music, had been mathematics, and yet he had always had to approach it slowly, even ploddingly. "How do they do it? I just can't imagine how it's possible. Do they have to think it through, or does the answer come to them automatically, just like that?"

Isabel said that she thought they had their tricks—systems that allowed them to make seemingly instantaneous calculations, just as people with exceptional memories had their mnemonics. "Some of it, though, comes to them instantly because they just **know** it." She took a sip of her iced tea, and looked at Jamie. "You wouldn't have to think, would you, if I asked you what number multiplied by itself gives you nine." She smiled encouragingly. "Would you?"

"Three."

"You didn't have to work that out?"

Jamie replied that the answer had simply been there. He had, in fact, seen the figure 3.

"Then perhaps it's the same for them," said Isabel. "The work is done at a subconscious level—the conscious mind doesn't even know it's being done." She returned to Nabokov. "He was capable of amazing calculations and then suddenly he became ill with a very high fever. When he recovered his mathematical ability had gone. Just like that."

"The fever affected the brain?"

"Yes. Burned out the wiring, as you might say."

"How strange."

"Yes. Very."

They looked at one another wordlessly. Each knew that the other was thinking of their young son, Charlie, now an energetic three-and-three-quarter-year-old; energetic, but currently asleep in his bedroom on that summer morning that was already growing hot. An uncharacteristic heat wave had descended on Edinburgh and the east of Scotland. It brought with it not only a summer languor, but the scent of the country into the town—cut hay, baked hillsides, heather that was soon to flower purple, the sea at Cramond . . .

Isabel broke the silence. "So what exactly did he say?"

Jamie's reply was hesitant. "I think it was something like this. You know those bricks of his—the yellow ones?"

Isabel did. They had on them bright pictures of ducks engaged in various pursuits—driving a train, drinking tea, flying in small biplanes—and Charlie adored them, even to the extent of secreting one of them under his pillow at night. One could love anything as a child, she thought; a teddy bear, a security blanket, a yellow brick . . .

"There were twenty bricks," Jamie went on. "We counted them. And he counted with me, all the way up to twenty—which is impressive enough, if you ask me. But then I said, 'Let's take half of them away.' I don't know why I said it—I hadn't imagined that he'd be able to cope with the concept of halves. But you know what he said? He said, 'Ten.' Just like that. He said, 'Ten.' "

There was more. "Then I said, 'All right, let's put eight bricks here and take half of those away.' And he said, 'Four.' He didn't even seem to think about it."

Isabel was listening intently. Had Charlie ever done anything similar for her? She did not think so. He had asked some perceptive questions, though, and one or two of them had startled her. The other day, apropos of nothing, he had suddenly said, "Brother Fox know something? Know not a dog?" She had been momentarily taken aback but had replied, "I think he knows that." Then she had quizzed him as to why he had asked her this, but his attention had been caught by something else and he had simply said, "Foxes and dogs," before moving on to another, quite different subject. For Isabel's part, she had been left with a question that had become increasingly intriguing the more she thought about it. Brother Fox presumably instinctively understood that dogs were not part of his world, but did that mean that he had some concept of **foxdom**? Probably not.

"So then I tried something different," Jamie continued. "I took nine bricks and asked him to put them in three piles that were all the same. And you know what he said? He said, 'Three.' He said, 'Three bricks, here, here, here.' "

Isabel looked thoughtful. "Division. It sounds impressive, but is it all that unusual?"

Jamie shrugged. "I asked them at the nursery school. They said children of four should be able to add and count up to five. They said nothing about division, or multiplication. Just counting."

"Or the piano," added Isabel.

"Or that. I told them that he can do a C major scale and they said something about his hands still being quite small and it must be difficult for that reason. They didn't seem all that interested."

Isabel imagined that there were numerous parents who believed their children to have prodigious skills and boasted to teachers about it. She did not want to be one of them; and yet if the child was really talented, then shouldn't the nursery at least know?

From upstairs there came the sound of a high-pitched voice—something between a chuckle and a shout. Charlie was awake.

"I'll go," said Jamie.

Isabel nodded. "We'll need to talk about it. About what we do—if anything."

He gave her a searching look. "Do about what? About his being good at numbers? You think we should ignore it rather than encourage it?"

"I'm just not sure that it's in his interests. Would he be any happier if we encouraged him to be a mathematical prodigy?" And there was something else that worried her: being a pushy mother. All mothers were pushy to an extent: one did not have to look far in the natural world to see mothers being pushy for their offspring—any self-respecting lioness would make sure her cubs got their fair share—but there were limits . . . "I don't think we should push him too much."

Jamie frowned. He encountered pushy parents in his work, and one in particular came to mind. She had written to him recently asking whether her son's innate musical ability was being adequately recognised and whether he was ready for a public performance. Jamie did not want the stage of the Usher Hall for Charlie, although if it came to that, he and Isabel would of course be in the front row. And Charlie would come onstage and need a box to stand on to climb on to the piano stool; or perhaps have his teddy bear carefully seated on the stool next to him while the conductor raised his baton to bring the accompanying orchestra to order. The frown became a smile. "Can one ignore something like that? Wouldn't that be to waste it?"

Isabel did not have time to answer. Another cry came from Charlie, more urgent now, followed by a rattling of the bars at the top of his bed. Jamie began to leave the kitchen but turned at the door and said, "Mozart was quite happy being Mozart, you know. He liked billiards. He kept a canary—and a horse. He enjoyed practical jokes."

Isabel reflected on this while Jamie was upstairs. To play billiards, to keep a canary and a horse, and to enjoy practical jokes—were very ordinary things like that the recipe for an enjoyable life?

THAT CONVERSATION WITH JAMIE about mathematical ability took place on one of Isabel's working days. Jamie, who was a musician, kept irregular hours, and frequently had days when not only did he not have any rehearsal or performance commitments, but he also had no teaching. He taught bassoon at the Edinburgh Academy and had a number of private pupils too, but he managed to cram all his teaching into two mornings and one afternoon a week, which left three weekdays for other things. Those days might easily have filled up with session work or preparation for concerts, but times were hard and there seemed less and less of that work around. "Perhaps the music's stopped," he remarked to Isabel. She had assured him that music seemed to continue in the face of every difficulty, just as philosophy did. "We imagine our crises are unlike all other crises," she said. "But they aren't. There's always been uncertainty. There's always been danger. It's the human condition—the normal one, perhaps."

On Jamie's free days, he took over responsibility for Charlie, allowing Isabel to attend to her job as editor, and owner too, of the **Review of Applied Ethics**. Charlie now went to a small nursery school round the corner, and Jamie would take him there at eight-thirty in the morning, deposit him in the classroom with his neatly packed tiffin box, and then return for him five hours later. After lunch, while Isabel worked in her study on the latest issue of the **Review**, Jamie would often supervise Charlie's afternoon rest, read to him, play the piano with him, or take him for a walk by the canal or, as a special treat, to Blackford Pond. That pond, inhabited by a tribe of over-fed and demanding ducks, could keep Charlie amused for hours, and Jamie knew every inch of its muddy shore quite as well as an experienced mariner knows the bays and inlets of his native waters. He had also come to know the personalities of the various ducks and could identify where each stood in order of precedence. Size, it seemed, was the sole determinant of that.

Even though she had made an early start while it was still comparatively cool, already the weather was making it difficult for Isabel to work.

She had opened her study windows, but there was only an intermittent breeze and the air inside was heavy. Her study had a particular smell to it—the smell of paper, she had decided—and for some reason this oppressed her. Perhaps it was not a day on which to sequester oneself inside; perhaps it was simply not a day on which to do philosophy. Her friend, Julian Baggini, who, like her, edited a philosophical paper, seemed to be able to do his thinking in all sorts of circumstances—in the car, in a train, in the bath—but it was different for Isabel. It was true that thoughts came to her at the oddest of moments, but what she called **organised thinking** needed the time and place to be right; and the thinking she was trying to do that day—assessing submissions for a future issue of the **Review**—was definitely organised thinking.

She got up from her desk, putting aside the paper she had been trying to read. There was nothing wrong with the paper itself, which was a discussion of responsibility to future generations; there was no reason why it should not see the light of day. The author was a post-doctoral fellow at the University of Toronto and needed publications for the next stage of her career. Isabel knew just how competitive the academic world could be and just how easily people could fall at any of the fences that stood between them and a career as a philosopher. She was aware that the author would be waiting anxiously for her verdict, and that a positive answer would lead to the popping of champagne corks, real or metaphorical, in some apartment in Toronto. All that was required was a one-word email: **Yes.** One word, three letters, that would bring such joy to somebody she had never met and probably never would. And by the same token, **No** would have the opposite effect.

She had found it difficult to concentrate on the author's argument. We obviously can owe duties to people we do not know. **Yes, of course we can**. So what is the difference between people who do not yet exist (future generations) and people we do not know? Well, thought Isabel, one set of people exists and the other does not. So, the author continued, the essence of the problem is whether one can harm the non-existent. **Or is it?** Isabel asked herself. Surely the non-existence of the victim at the time of the harmful act is not the real issue: the real issue is future harm to people **who will exist**.

Eating fish, the author wrote, **is a good example.** We know that if we eat fish now, fish stocks will be depleted and there will not be enough for the people who follow us. So does our current hunger—or current taste for fish—justify using up fish stocks that would otherwise be enjoyed by people as yet unborn? **Do we owe any fish to those who follow us?** the paper asked.

Do we owe any fish to those who follow us? The sentence struck Isabel as vaguely comic, as if it might have been lifted from some music-hall song; it was redolent, perhaps, of "Yes, we have no bananas."

She put the paper down and moved across the room to the open window. From where she was standing, she could see her neighbour's contract gardener digging in a flower-bed. He was a hard-working man who had once told her that he looked after twenty gardens and was thinking of taking on several more. He had been a coal miner before the mines closed—digging, in one form or another, had been his life. And thinking of that made Isabel wonder whether the work she did—thinking about responsibility to future generations and such problems—could really be described as work. Work usually made something happen in the world, and she was not sure whether she did that at all. There was a physical product—several hundred copies of a journal once every three months—but did that actually change anything?

She looked at her watch. She was due to relieve Jamie of Charlie duties in two hours' time, but if she stopped work now she would have time to go to her niece Cat's delicatessen and buy something for lunch. Cat had a supplier who delivered freshly made onion tarts in the morning, which people picked up during their lunch break or on their way home from work. If she left now, she would be able to have her choice of the tarts, and still have time to finish reading the responsibility-to-future-generations paper—and make a decision too. It would be yes, of course; she already felt that.

She closed her study windows, collected her shopping bag from the kitchen cupboard and let herself out of the house. It was even warmer outside than indoors, though tucked inside the shopping bag was her light jacket; the weather in Edinburgh was notoriously fickle, and even a day like this could suddenly turn hostile. There would be room for the onion tart too, and for some salad things—the bag was copious.

She made her way into Bruntsfield. Halfway along the road, she saw a large **For Sale** notice on the railings of one of the houses. She stopped and looked up at the windows of the property. It was a large Victorian house that had been divided into flats, and it was one of these that was now on the market. She paused; she had been expecting its sale, as the owner, a quiet man whom people rarely saw, had died six months before. He had lived by himself, and it was thought that he had met somebody one evening who had stabbed him to death in his own hallway.

Isabel stared up at the windows. Places where unhappy events have taken place are no different from anywhere else. The physical world—the world of stone and brick—is indifferent to our suffering, to our dramas, she thought. Even a battlefield can be peaceful, can be a place for flowers to grow, for children to play; the memories, the sadness, are within us, not part of the world about us. And yet this house, as she gazed at it, seemed bereft, seemed tragic and loveless, a reminder of the dark thing that had happened there.

"Isabel?"

She gave a start.

"Sorry to give you a fright."

She turned and saw Martha Drummond. In Isabel's life, Martha was one of those people who occupied that awkward territory between acquaintanceship and friendship; she saw her relatively infrequently, and they were not on dropping-in terms. If she had been pressed, Isabel would probably have confessed that she found Martha slightly irritating, and felt bad about this feeling. It was hard to put her finger on it: Martha meant well—whatever that meant—but had the habit of making intrusive remarks. There were some people, in Isabel's view, who lacked social judgement, not picking up quite the same social cues as others did. "They don't quite get it" expressed the notion exactly. They didn't.

Martha lived several streets away, in a house surrounded by a large rhododendron-filled garden. And the rhododendrons were a case in point: a few months ago, when Isabel had bumped into Martha in the supermarket, there had been an exchange that had left Isabel thinking distinctly uncharitable thoughts. Martha had let drop the fact that she had recently walked past Isabel's garden and noticed her rhododendrons. "They don't seem to be doing all that well," she said casually. "My own rhododendrons are much more—how shall I put it?—luxuriant."

Isabel had stared at her mutely. "There's nothing wrong with my rhododendrons," she had eventually said. It was extremely tactless, she thought, to criticise another person's rhododendrons and, anyway, such criticism in this context was objectively wrong.

"They don't look very healthy to me," Martha persisted. "Perhaps you've got the wrong sort of soil."

Isabel smarted. That was another serious accusation: to suggest to somebody that they have the wrong sort of soil.

"There's nothing wrong with my soil," she said coolly. "Or with my rhododendrons, for that matter."

It had been a ridiculous exchange, but it was typical of the direction in which a conversation with Martha could go. And it was for that reason that Isabel found it difficult to consider Martha as a friend, although she knew that friendship did not depend on seeing eye-to-eye.

Martha, who was in her early forties and divorced, shared her rhododendron-surrounded house with her elderly mother, who, in her heyday, had been one of Scotland's best-known artists. Isabel liked her work, and had one of her smaller paintings in a corner of her study.

"Not the best of Mother's works," Martha had said when Isabel had shown it to her. "In fact, barely recognisable as one of her works at all."

That had led to another pointless exchange. "Others might not agree with you," Isabel suggested through clenched teeth.

"But others are not the painter's own daughter," retorted Martha. "I imagine that people don't dismiss too readily the opinions of Paloma Picasso."

Isabel had quickly planned her reply to that. A painter's family, she would suggest, were probably the last people to be asked for a judgement on their relative's work—they were simply too close to it, too emotionally involved to be able to give an objective view. But she stopped herself, mainly because it would not be true. Members of the family were often the best of judges, just as her friend, Guy Peploe—to think of only one example—was the best judge of the paintings of his grandfather, S. J. Peploe. So she had said nothing.

Now, standing in front of the **For Sale** notice, Martha asked after Charlie. "Where's your little boy?"

"Jamie's taken him to nursery," Isabel explained. She pointed to the notice. "I was thinking about this . . ."

Martha sighed. "Very sad. Did you know him?"

"I think I saw him," said Isabel. "But no, I didn't know him."

They were both silent for a few moments. Then Martha asked Isabel whether she was going to Cat's delicatessen. "I thought you might be," she said. "Something easy for lunch?"

Isabel smiled, and nodded.

"I'm headed there too," said Martha. "I can't be bothered to cook in this heat. And Mother eats like a bird. A couple of lettuce leaves and a slice—a very thin slice—of smoked salmon, and she'll be complaining about being bloated."

"How convenient for you," said Isabel.

"I'm very lucky with my aged parent," said Martha cheerfully. "But listen, I need to talk to you about something. About somebody I know who's in difficulty."

Isabel looked up at the sky. People asked her to do things for them. She had no idea why they did, but they did. What did they think she was? A private detective? An agony aunt? Or simply a friend? And because of her particular sense of moral obligation, she felt that she had to do something, and that led to Jamie's accusing her of not minding her own business. But I cannot do otherwise, she thought. I am no saint; I am no heroine; but how can anybody say no to a request for help?

"Do you mind?" asked Martha. "We could have a cup of coffee and I could tell you about it." She looked at Isabel enquiringly. "But only if you don't mind."

Isabel shook her head. "I don't mind," she said.

"Good," said Martha. "Because I promised my friend I would speak to you and he was very relieved. He said 'Thank God.'"

They began to make their way together down the road. As they walked, Martha told Isabel about her latest letter from her former husband. "Do you know, he said that if he could turn the clock back, he would. Can you credit it?"

"He wants to come back to you?" asked Isabel.

"So it would seem."

"And how do you feel about that?"

"It's the last thing I want," she said. "I've gone right off men."

"Altogether?"

"Yes." She paused. "Except for your Jamie. I would willingly have him on my mantelpiece. Just to look at him, of course."

Isabel smiled. "Not possible," she said. "Sorry."

"If I had somebody who looked like that," mused Martha, "I would spend all day just gazing at him, drinking it in. Do you do that sometimes, Isabel? Do you just sit there looking at Jamie and . . . and purring?"

CHAPTER TWO

◆

CAT'S DELICATESSEN WAS unusually busy when they arrived and it was a good ten minutes before Eddie, who was single-handed behind the counter that morning, managed to serve them. Eddie had recently returned from a trip across the United States he had made with his uncle and his uncle's girlfriend. The trip had been extended to include a four-month stay in Canada, during which Eddie had worked—underpaid, and illegally—as a waiter in a ski resort in Alberta. North America had changed him profoundly, boosting his confidence and pasting a healthy tan over his normally pallid Scottish skin. The tan was now fading, but the same could not be said of the traces of an affected American accent that Eddie had somehow miraculously picked up on his travels. His conversation was now littered with "sure thing"s and "you bet"s, so much so that Isabel had found it difficult to conceal her amusement. Eddie had noticed this, and had looked injured. Isabel was mortified; she was fond of Eddie and had always done her best to encourage him. Now she had hurt him.

If offence had been taken, it was not long-lasting. Eddie greeted Isabel cheerfully and went to some trouble to select for her the best of the onion tarts.

"I know you're going to get the best tart," Martha said over Isabel's shoulder. "But could I at least have the second best?"

Isabel drew in her breath. There was so much she could have said, including an observation that people got the onion tarts they deserved in this life; but that would have been childish. Martha simply did not know that virtually everything she said was inappropriate, and so there was no point in remonstrating with her. Isabel remembered the discussion with Jamie about the **wiring**. This was much the same issue. Those important brain circuits, the ones that enabled most of us to avoid saying the wrong thing, were simply not there in Martha's case; or fired in the wrong order; or were short-circuiting. In other words, Martha Drummond was an electrical problem. And understanding people as electrical problems undoubtedly helped one to tolerate them.

Once they had purchased their tarts, alongside one or two other things needed for their respective meals, Isabel and Martha sat down at one of the tables Cat kept for the serving of coffee. The customers were thinner on the ground in the pre-lunchtime lull, and Eddie had time to prepare and bring to their table two large, steaming cappuccinos.

"Here we are, ma'am," he said as he placed Martha's cup in front of her. The intonation was contrived American, overlaid with a heavy dose of Scotland.

Martha looked at him. "You from Glasgow?" she asked.

Eddie looked down at the floor, humiliated.

Martha smiled at Isabel, and winked conspiratorially.

"Eddie has just spent quite a bit of time in America," said Isabel quickly.

"Yes," said Martha, still smiling. "I suppose it must rub off eventually."

Eddie went back to the counter in silence.

"That wasn't necessary," Isabel said quietly. "That young man has had a lot to put up with."

Martha looked towards Eddie on the other side of the counter. "Seems robust enough to me. And I was only joking."

Isabel wanted Martha to know the implications

of her casual tactlessness. "Something bad happened to him some time ago. Something traumatic."

Martha looked interested. "What? What happened?"

"I'm not absolutely sure."

Martha shrugged. "Dreadful things have happened to just about everyone," she said. "It's called growing up. You know the statistics . . ."

Isabel decided to change the subject. She was not sure that she wanted to spend too much time with Martha—time that could be better spent making up the salad that would go with the onion tart. "You wanted to talk to me about somebody?" she said.

Martha looked at Isabel over the rim of her coffee cup. "I did. Of course I don't want to impose . . ."

Isabel cut her short. "Don't worry."

Martha lowered her cup. "You're very good, you know. Everybody knows that you help people in all sorts of ways. Where does it come from?"

Isabel squirmed with embarrassment. "I'm no better than anybody else," she said. "I have all the usual faults and flaws."

"And you're modest too," said Martha.

Isabel said nothing, waiting for Martha to continue.

"So," said Martha. "This problem: Do you know somebody called Duncan Munrowe?"

She did not give Isabel time to answer. "You might have read about him. He crops up in the **Scotsman** from time to time. He does a lot for charity." Martha paused, but only briefly. "He's the sort of person everybody hears about but doesn't really meet very much. That's not to say that he hasn't got any friends. He has quite a few actually."

Isabel waited until it looked as if she would be allowed to speak. "I've heard of him. I get him mixed up, though, with those other Duncan Munroes."

"They're Munro with an **o**. He's Munrowe with a **w** and an **e** at the end. Not to be confused with all those Munros that are mountains over three thousand feet."

"I see," said Isabel. She decided to be brief; sometimes people like Martha, who spoke at excessive length, eventually exhausted themselves. The problem then was that they lacked the energy to listen to what you had to say.

Martha continued. "These Munrowes—Duncan's lot—are originally from Wigton or somewhere near there. I've always thought of that part of Scotland as being virtually Ireland, it's that close." She looked at Isabel with sudden interest. "Have you got any Irish blood in you?"

"On my mother's side there was some, I think. Irish and Acadian. They drifted down to the South generations ago. The Acadian part of the family was from Nova Scotia, I believe." She thought: My sainted American mother, who would have been patient even with somebody like Martha. And I must try.

"You've probably got a temper then," said Martha, almost to herself.

Isabel sipped at her coffee. Martha was impossible—risible, really.

"Not that I'm one to talk," Martha went on. "There are some things that make me see red. I have to watch myself."

"We all do," said Isabel. **Watching yourself,** she thought. It was the essence of the moral life. Watch yourself; evaluate. The examined life; the watched life. "Duncan Munrowe? You were telling me about him."

It was as if Isabel had introduced an entirely new topic of conversation. "Oh yes," said Martha. "Duncan would very much like to meet you."

"Why?"

"Because something has happened up at his place." Although there was nobody near them, Martha lowered her voice. "Duncan's family used to be pretty well-off. They had rubber plantations in Malaya. And they were something to do with Hong Kong—I have no idea what, but they were. So when they came back to Scotland there was plenty of money."

Isabel remarked that this was not an unusual story. The Scots had profited greatly from the British Empire; they did not always like to admit it, but they had. There were numerous families that had done well out of things like jute in Calcutta or wool in Australia and had returned to Scotland to buy landed estates. It sounded as if the Munrowes were in this category.

Martha leaned forward. "They were discreet about it, but one of them, Duncan's grandfather, had a very good eye. He was rather like that shipping man in Glasgow—what was he called?"

"Burrell?"

"That's him. He put that great collection together, didn't he? Well, Duncan Munrowe's grandfather had the same sense not only of what was what in the art world, but also of what **would be** what. He anticipated fashions."

This began to sound familiar to Isabel. "And he lent paintings to the Scottish National Gallery?"

Martha nodded. "Yes. You might have seen some of the Munrowe collection there. It's not quite as impressive as the Sutherland collection, but it's still pretty good. He was particularly strong on the Post-Impressionists. Bonnard and so on. He picked those up by the dozen in Paris, as you could in those days."

Isabel had seen them. She remembered the wording on the labels: **On loan from the Munrowe Collection**. The galleries, with their tiny acquisitions budget, increasingly relied on such generosity. She tried to bring to mind particular Munrowe paintings, but could not. There were the Titians, and that whole roomful of Poussins, but they belonged to the Sutherlands. Was there a Bonnard of a woman sewing, or was that Vuillard? And was it part of the Munrowe collection?

"They still have some of the paintings in the house," Martha continued. "They live near Doune. It's a rather **shy** house. I call it shy because it's tucked away and you'd not know it was there until you turn a corner and there it is next to some woods. And a hill. It has a hill directly behind it—straight up. It's an odd place to put a house, but there we are."

Isabel was keen to hear what had taken place. "You said something happened. What was it?"

"They have all these paintings in the house, as I've said. Maybe they're not quite as good as the ones in the Gallery, but they're still pretty special. There's a whole room of seventeenth-century French and Italian paintings, and the dining room has got a Toulouse-Lautrec in it—not a big one—and a Vuillard, I think."

"They're very fortunate," said Isabel. "Imagine being able to look at paintings like that over your boiled egg in the morning."

Martha laughed. "There's a small Degas drawing in one of the loos."

"Loos, too, can be made beautiful."

Martha frowned. "Have you heard of the open gardens weekend that they have round here?"

"Yes. It arranges for private gardens—"

"To be open to the public on a particular day. Exactly. And Munrowe House—that's the name of their place: somewhat unimaginative, but accurate, I suppose—was opened to the public. The house too."

Isabel could tell what was coming. "And some of the paintings were . . ."

"Stolen. Not some, just one. But, as it happened, it was the most valuable painting in the whole house. Duncan had been thinking of transferring it to the Gallery, where it would be safer, but he hadn't got round to it."

"What was it?"

"A Poussin. One of the relatively few in private hands in this country. And a rather nice one. It was worth about three million, they thought. Possibly more."

Isabel asked what the subject was, and Martha explained. It was a painting known as **Time Reconsidered** and bore some relationship to the artist's great **A Dance to the Music of Time**. Martha began to describe that painting, but Isabel told her that she had visited the Wallace Collection in London and knew the picture well.

"It was insured, of course," Martha said.

Isabel said that she was relieved to hear that. An insurance payment was not always full compensation for loss, but it undoubtedly dulled the pain. "I assume that what he really wants is to get the painting back."

"Yes. He does. They picked the one thing he didn't want to lose."

Eddie appeared at the table to collect their empty cups. He took Martha's wordlessly, but at the same time gave Isabel a look of gentle reproach. Isabel mentally sent him a message: **Yes, I know what she's like, but we can't . . .**

"Anything else?" he asked Isabel.

Isabel shook her head, and Eddie went back to the counter.

"There's something lost about that boy," Martha said. "Odd."

Isabel did not engage. "Duncan Munrowe?"

"Oh yes, Duncan. It's the reward, you see."

Isabel looked puzzled. "The reward?"

"I gather that many of these art thefts are really ransom attempts," Martha explained. "They can't sell these very well-known paintings—or at least not on the ordinary market—and so they use them to extort money from the insurance companies."

Isabel had read about this. "That must be difficult," she said. "If you pay the Dane to go away, he always comes back. So perhaps you should make a point of never paying ransom."

Martha frowned at the mention of Danes.

"Danegeld," said Isabel. "It's what people used to pay the Vikings to stop them destroying things. You paid your Danegeld and the Vikings went away. Until next time."

Martha shrugged. "I suppose there is a general issue about paying ransom. But that's not the problem here—or at least it's not the problem that's worrying Duncan. His difficulty is the attitude of the insurers. They've suggested one thing and he's wanted to do the other. They've argued about figures too. The insurers say that the market is depressed at the moment and this means they need to pay less. They also don't want to pay a ransom until it's clear that the painting won't be recovered."

"Insurers are like that," remarked Isabel. "As a general rule, if they can avoid paying, that's what they'll do."

"And yet we can't be late with our premiums," said Martha sharply.

Isabel agreed. People were always very keen to have their bills paid promptly but were not so willing to reciprocate.

"So that's where you come in," Martha announced.

Isabel frowned. "I don't see . . ."

"Duncan wondered whether you might help him deal with this. In particular, he wants help in dealing with any approach from the people who have the painting. They'll be in touch, he thinks. They might even have already contacted him—I'm not sure about that."

Isabel's surprise was immediately apparent. "But what possible assistance can I give? I know nothing about this sort of thing. Nothing at all."

Martha laid a hand on Isabel's forearm. "But everybody knows how helpful you are. That's why I recommended you when he asked me about you."

"You recommended me?"

"Yes. Poor Duncan: he so wanted somebody to talk to about it—to advise him. Somebody had mentioned your name. I said that you had quite a reputation for helping people in a tight spot and that he could talk to you. I hope you don't mind."

Of course Isabel minded; it was very easy, she thought, to offer the services of others. But then she remembered her sainted American mother and asked herself how she would have reacted to such a request. She knew the answer. "Never turn your back on another," her mother had said to her when she was a girl. "The person you're turning your back on might die that night." It was not, Isabel realised, the sort of thing one should say to children, who could feel unreasonably anxious about death anyway. And if somebody died, the child could well blame himself or herself; children often did that, the psychologists told us; they felt guilty about things that happened, even if they had nothing at all to do with them. **I turned my back on her, and she went**

and died! But it was advice that had stuck, and came back to Isabel now, years later, in this difficult encounter. She stared at Martha. "I will, if you want me to," she said. She almost added, "Though I can't say I'm overly enthusiastic," but decided against it. There was no need to be churlish.

Martha looked at her gratefully. "Even if you just talk to him," she said. "Listen to his tale of woe. Even that would help."

"I'll try," said Isabel.

"Tomorrow?" asked Martha. "Duncan's coming into town. Could you see him then? Lunch—just the three of us. Unless you'd rather I didn't come."

Isabel hesitated. There were times when one had to act self-defensively, even if it caused disappointment. It went against the grain, but one had to.

"Just him and me, I think," she said. She tried to speak gently, but even then felt she had to explain. "It's sometimes easier for people to talk if there's nobody else there."

"Do you think so?" said Martha.

"I do," said Isabel.

Martha shrugged. "Odd," she said.

It was true, thought Isabel, that none of us ever imagined that people might **not** wish to be in our company. We assumed that people found us good company, would like to be with us. But they might not. They might find us opinionated or dull or irritating—as poor Martha undoubtedly was; all of which qualities we would be the last to discern in ourselves.

Isabel swallowed. It was so easy to forget the needs of others, and to allow irritation, boredom or sheer indifference to get the better of us. She would not do that; she would make an effort. It was very easy to build people up, to make them feel better about themselves: a few words of praise, an appreciative comment or two, and people felt better. Martha clearly took pains to look her best; perhaps a remark about that would help the situation.

"I must say," Isabel began, and then searched desperately for a suitable comment. "I must say that you're looking really . . . really attractive. That top suits you, I think. Your colour."

She drew in her breath. The top was beige: she had just suggested that Martha's colour was beige.

"Beige?"

"No," said Isabel quickly. "I wouldn't call it beige. I'd say **oatmeal**. I've got a carpet that colour in the upstairs bedroom and . . ." She trailed off as it struck her that she had now compared Martha's top to a carpet.

Martha stared at her for a moment before smiling wryly. “It’s kind of you to say that, Isabel, but I’m sure you don’t really mean it.”

“I did mean it,” Isabel lied. And she thought, more than a little ashamedly: Kant would never, **never** have given that answer. He would never have paid an insincere compliment in the first place. Kant would not have noticed the way a woman was dressed; Hume might have, and Voltaire certainly would. **What the Great Philosophers Would Say About Your Wardrobe:** that would be an amusing book to write—and it might even prove rather popular, as Robert Pirsig’s **Zen and the Art of Motorcycle Maintenance** had become.

She became aware that Martha was shaking an admonitory finger at her. “Not really, but thanks anyway. It’s good to be told nice things, even if they aren’t true.” She paused. “And it’s very kind of you to say it, especially when you’re so . . . Well, you’re much more glamorous than I am. And your life . . . your whole life is so much more—how shall I put it? Intense? And . . .”

“Please,” said Isabel, reaching out to touch her gently. “That’s a generous thing to say, but you’re wrong, you know. My life isn’t really any different from anybody else’s.”

Martha shook her head. "But it is! You've got money. You live in that fantastic house. You've got that man of yours. Everything. You've got everything."

Isabel looked down at the floor. It made her feel uncomfortable to hear her blessings enumerated—nobody welcomed that, least of all those who, like Isabel, were aware enough to know that all the good things that we have in life are on temporary loan, at best, and can be taken away from us in an instant. The borderline between good fortune and disaster, between plenitude and paucity, between the warm hearth of love and the cold chamber of loneliness, was a narrow one. We could cross over from one to the other at any moment, as when we stumbled or fell, or simply walked over to the other side because we were paying insufficient attention to where we were. It was well to remember one's good luck, but it was not always helpful to be reminded of it by one who was not equally blessed. Or to be reminded of it in public, when Nemesis, whose radar is said never to be switched off, picks up the echo and begins to take an interest.

CHAPTER THREE

MARTHA LEFT THE DELICATESSEN, telling Isabel that she had other shops to visit before returning home to her lunch of onion tart. Isabel said goodbye to her but remained at the table; she had decided that she would read the newspaper, even if the only paper she could see on the rack was what looked like a three-day-old copy of the **Corriere della Sera.** Cat had the Italian newspapers passed on to her by a friend who bought them religiously to keep her language up to scratch. Isabel was the only beneficiary of this generosity; she had never seen anyone else reading the papers, although she had observed some customers examining them in puzzlement, trying to stretch their restaurant Italian or to make sense of the reports from the pictures. But their presence seemed just right: it went so well with the smell of coffee and the sight of the salamis that

Cat hung above the counter, almost over the heads of customers; the salami of Damocles, she thought . . .

The **Corriere** would give her half an hour in the opaque realms of Italian politics; a world of Byzantine intrigues and endless feuds, operatic in its intensity. She scanned the front page and noticed a trailer for an interview on an inside page. A well-known politician, now disgraced, was speaking about his fall from power. It was a bad decision, he said, to replace him; the country needed him more than ever, and the attempts to prosecute him were symptomatic of the ingratitude for which the country was becoming so famous. Isabel smiled. She never ceased to be amazed by the antics of politicians. It was as if politics were all about **them**, and not about ordinary members of the public who were, after all, the people whom politicians were meant to serve. People like me, she thought—sitting here drinking coffee, waiting to be served by politicians . . . She closed her eyes and imagined the Prime Minister, in a waiter's apron, serving coffee. Martha, curiously, came into the picture, shaking her head and saying disapprovingly, "They'll do **anything** for votes, won't they?"

She opened her eyes a few seconds later to see

Eddie standing in front of her holding a replacement cup of coffee.

"I assumed you wanted a refill," he said. He spoke normally now, the attempt to affect an American accent being abandoned.

Isabel smiled at him and took the proffered cup. Eddie hesitated, glancing around the shop to see if there was anybody needing attention. But, seeing that there was nobody waiting to be served, he sat down on the chair recently vacated by Martha. "That woman you were with looks familiar. Who is she?" he asked, nodding his head in the direction of the door.

"She's called Martha Drummond."

Eddie made a face. "I didn't like her. Sorry, I know she's your friend, but she behaved like a real cow just now."

"That's possibly a bit unfair," Isabel said. "She's not all that bad."

"I can tell you don't think that," said Eddie. "Your eyes looked different when you said it."

I'm a bad liar, thought Isabel. That was twice in the last few minutes that she had been accused of insincerity. "All right," she confessed. "I'll admit it: she gets on my nerves a bit. A lot, sometimes. I feel guilty about my attitude towards her. I'm not proud of it. But you know how it is? We all have people in our lives we don't really choose as friends but with whom we're, well, lumbered, I suppose. Heart-sink friends. Have you heard that expression?"

Eddie had, and yes, he knew a few people like that. There had been a boy in his year at school, he said, who smelled of fish but who always wanted to sit next to him in class. "He had this condition, you see. It wasn't that he didn't wash—he did—it's just that he smelled of fish. It was a medical condition, see."

Isabel said she had heard of it.

"One of the teachers told us about it," Eddie went on. "Apparently people who have it can't break down some sort of chemical and that's what makes them smell. It's not their fault."

He looked at Isabel as if to challenge her to refute the proposition that smell has nothing to do with fault. And that was right, she thought, though only in respect of smells we could not help; those we could help were our responsibility; soap was readily available, and water too. A paper in the **Review**, perhaps? Responsibility for the body? Do we have a moral obligation to look—and smell—as good as we can manage? In one view, this could be a Kantian duty to the self, but in another it could be part of our duty not to offend those around us—one of those items of good social manners that strayed into the scope of morality proper. Of course, that had all sorts of ramifications. What about wearing clothes that offended other people—clothes that revealed bad colour coordination, for example? Was that wrong? Surely not, although wearing scanty clothing in sensitive settings was another matter. When important women went to see the Pope, they dressed conservatively out of respect for . . . for what? Now it became even more complicated: the following of a dress code that treated women as potential temptresses revealed an acceptance of a whole attitude towards women that some did not condone. So had the Pope any **right,** Isabel wondered, to expect women to dress in a particular way when they called on him? That raised the question of whether the hosts could dictate the dress of their guests—and they could, Isabel considered, because people were always telling their invitees what to wear: **black tie**, **casual-smart** and all the rest of the signals were everyday examples of precisely that. So the Pope had the right, if he wished, to expect a certain sort of dress on the part of his visitors. And so did everybody else, it seemed. She smiled; that sorted **that** out.

Eddie could tell that Isabel's mind was elsewhere. It was chronic, he thought. She's always thinking about all sorts of really **stupid** things. He continued, "The teacher said that we needed to know about it because she didn't want people saying anything to him. He was called Julian, which was bad luck too, because that's not a name that many people have where I come from."

"I'm sure you were kind to him," Isabel said. "It must be a pretty difficult condition."

Eddie hesitated. "Some people tried to be kind," he said. "Not everybody, though. There was this boy called Derek who was a real thug. People hated him. He used to call out 'Look out, rotten fish!' whenever Julian came near."

"Children are like that," Isabel said. "We were tremendously cruel. All of us." She took a sip of her coffee. "What happened to Julian?"

Eddie stared at her. It seemed that he had not been prepared for the question or had not understood it.

"I mean, what did he go on to do after he left school? Do you ever see him these days?"

Eddie frowned, and looked away. Isabel waited.

"He topped himself," he said quietly.

Isabel sat quite still. Perhaps she had misunderstood. "You mean he—"

Eddie interrupted her. "Yes. He put himself in the bath and then he got one of those electric fires and dropped it in. That was it."

Isabel said nothing.

"I felt bad."

"I'm sure you'd done your best. You said he liked you. That must have been because you'd been good to him."

"Not good enough," muttered Eddie.

She decided not to argue with him. "I'm really sorry to hear that story," she said.

"He had an older brother," said Eddie. "He's a DJ in a club on Lothian Road, I still see him now and then. He's got long greasy hair. It's quite disgusting, actually. He's called Daniel. He doesn't really know who I am, but we still say hello to one another in the street. He has a girlfriend who rides a big Harley-Davidson."

Isabel listened to these almost random facts. They were the ordinary details of life, all of them quite unexceptional: the disgusting greasy hair, the club on Lothian Road—except perhaps for the Harley-Davidson-riding girlfriend—and yet it was these same mundane facts that were the background for the poignant story of Julian.

For a few moments they were both silent. Then Eddie shrugged. "These things happen," he said.

Isabel inclined her head.

"And we shouldn't think about them too much, should we?" Eddie went on.

No, agreed Isabel, we should not; and Eddie, she thought, had had enough difficulty in his life without dwelling on additional tragedies. She made an effort to brighten up. "I've been reading about an Italian politician," she said, pointing to the newspaper.

Eddie glanced at the photograph accompanying the interview. "Oh, him. He's the one who liked parties."

"He was very outgoing," Isabel agreed.

Eddie looked more closely at the picture. "Has he had cosmetic surgery?" he asked inconsequentially. "By the way, I've got some photographs I want to show you some time. I took them in Alaska—on the trip. You wouldn't believe it. The mountains. They make ours look tiny."

Our tiny mountains, thought Isabel. We are a small country with tiny mountains.

"I'd love to see them, Eddie. Maybe you could bring them round some time. Jamie would like to see them too. Have supper with us."

Eddie liked Jamie, she knew, because Jamie had always been kind to him. Eddie was used to being looked through—a shy young man behind the counter. Jamie smiled at him.

"All right. I'll bring them round. And . . ."

He looked at Isabel hesitantly.

"Yes?"

"Could I bring somebody with me?"

Isabel nodded. "Of course you can. Who is it?"

Eddie blushed. "There's a girl I've met."

Isabel waited for him to continue.

"She's called Diane. I've been seeing her for six weeks now." He moved his right hand to rest it on the table. She saw that his nails were dirty. Cat had spoken to him about washing his hands thoroughly before handling food and had equipped the small washroom at the back of the shop with a stiff nailbrush, which Eddie had evidently not used, or used to inadequate effect.

"It's serious, Isabel. We're going to live together now."

Isabel caught her breath. In her mind, Eddie was still very young, even if he was twenty-one.

"That's quite an important step," she said.

"I know that," said Eddie. "But it's what we want to do. If it works out, we're going to get engaged."

Isabel's smile was very tentative. "That's . . . well, that's also a big step, isn't it, at your age?"

Eddie looked at her searchingly. "What age were you when you first fell in love?"

She had to think. Most of us first experienced love in our teenage years, sometimes when we were barely into our teens. The passionate friendships of those years were really love affairs even if they remained innocent. And they often focused on friends of the same sex—a rite of passage to heterosexuality, for some people, not all, of course. If people were honest with themselves, they would remember such friendships, but then people were far from honest when it came to things like that.

She had fallen in love with a boy when she was sixteen. That had been her eye-opener. She had felt elated, excited and miserable in roughly equal measure. She had never dreamed that love could be painful, but it was. She had loved him so much that it hurt, and when it ended, as was inevitable, the pain had been even more intense—for three weeks. Then she had suddenly woken up one morning and realised that he was just a boy and that she no longer wanted to spend the entire day thinking about him. That was her cure.

"I loved somebody when I was sixteen,

seventeen," she said. "And then again a few years later I fell badly for somebody whom I eventually married. It was a bad mistake on my part. I think I told you once, didn't I?"

Eddie remembered. "Yes. What was he called again?"

Isabel had to make an effort: the uttering of names can be potent—and painful. "John Liamor. He was not a good man, I'm afraid to say."

"Then you're best off without him," said Eddie. "He's history. Forget him."

"I did," said Isabel, and felt, as she uttered the words, a pang of regret. "I had to teach myself not to think about him. It wasn't easy."

"Then let's talk about something else: Diane."

Isabel smiled at him. "You're obviously head over heels in love with her. You're lucky." She paused. Eddie's face had broken into a grin of sheer pleasure.

"Yes," Isabel continued. "You're really lucky, Eddie. Love transforms everything, doesn't it?"

She assumed that he might be embarrassed by this talk of love, as any young man might be. But Eddie seemed to relish it. "Everything's really great, Isabel. I feel really great."

She leaned forward, across the table, and kissed him gently on the cheek. He was surprised, and she heard his breath come sharply; but again he did not seem embarrassed.

"I'm happy for you, Eddie," she said. "Stay head over heels in love. Buy her flowers. Give her lots and lots of kisses. Worship her. Diane, Diana: they're the same goddess, you know. Diana, the Huntress."

Eddie looked at her wide-eyed. "She's a nurse."

Isabel laughed. "Don't be too literal," she said. "Being in love allows a certain poetic hyperbole."

Eddie remained wide-eyed.

"What I mean by all that," said Isabel, "is: go for it."

The translation was effective. Eddie beamed. "Thanks, Isabel."

WITH CHARLIE STILL at nursery school, Isabel and Jamie ate their lunch on the lawn, shaded by the large oak tree that dominated one side of Isabel's garden. They sat on green canvas deckchairs that were nearing the end of their life but were still the most comfortable garden furniture that Isabel had ever known. The fabric, rotted in places by summer after summer of not being put away promptly enough when rain began to fall, had now ripped in several places, and it was only a matter of time, Isabel thought, before it would give way altogether and deposit the person sitting on the chair unceremoniously on the grass. She would not mind if that happened to her, or to Jamie—it seemed as if deckchairs were designed to humiliate their owners, to trap their fingers, to dump them on the ground—but she did not want it to happen to a visitor.

Now, sitting in the shade on that particularly hot day, Isabel struggled to eat a slice of onion tart without distributing flaky crumbs of pastry or fragments of onion all over her clothes. Jamie did not have that problem. He had disposed of his shirt and had only an old pair of jeans to worry about. She glanced at him, and then glanced away. There was no spare flesh on him, she thought; just muscle. She had always felt that somehow it was unfair: Jamie never went to the gym. So did one get like that, she wondered, just from playing the bassoon? She glanced at him again; his skin was brown from exposure to the summer sun, and he was perfect. She wanted to touch him. But did not, and instead looked up at the sky, which was empty.

"Do you believe in angels?"

He had not been paying attention; a bee had landed on his foot and he had leaned forward to flick it off.

"Do I believe in eagles? Of course I do. Who

doesn't? You can see them flying about in the Highlands."

"Angels."

"Oh, that's another matter."

Isabel looked back up at the sky. "There is no evidence for the existence of angels, and I suppose we must reluctantly conclude that they don't exist. It's a pity, I think, because I can just imagine them floating across a sky like this one."

Jamie looked up.

"What's that poem you quoted to me once?" he asked. "Something about Italy."

Isabel closed her eyes. " 'Angels in Italy.' Al Alvarez wrote it. He's in Italy, in the country . . ."

"Tuscany, of course."

"Of course. And suddenly he sees angels. He says something about how they make no sound, although their wings move. That's how it starts."

Jamie was intrigued. "Their wings make no sound? That's what he says?"

"Yes," said Isabel. "And then he goes on to say that people down below are doing all sorts of ordinary things—like cutting wood with a buzzsaw. And the leaves on the vine rattle like dice. All while the angels are crossing the sky, until the clouds take them."

Jamie whispered again, savouring the words. "Until the clouds take them."

Isabel was silent for a moment. Then she turned to face Jamie. He was watching her. His eyes were kind. She reached out and laid a hand against his cheek and then let it slip down to his shoulder. His skin was smooth. If he had wings, they would sprout here, perhaps, right here; great wings; angel, angel.

For a few minutes nothing was said. She felt Jamie's shoulder move slightly as he breathed; she felt, she thought, his heartbeat. She willed him not to say anything, not to disturb the moment. They looked at each other. His lips moved almost imperceptibly into the slightest, the faintest of smiles.

And then it seemed right to speak. "I saw Eddie this morning," she said.

He sounded drowsy. "Oh yes?"

"He wants to get engaged to a girl he's met."

Jamie smiled. "Good. Poor Eddie."

"He's still very young."

Jamie thought that did not matter. "He thinks he's old enough to set up home with her. That's what he wants."

"Perhaps." She paused. She had taken her hand away from his shoulder now. There had been a moment, an extraordinarily intense moment, but it had passed and they had begun to talk about Eddie. What had happened?

The deckchair canvas protested—a tiny, ripping sound as a bit more gave way. And then it came to her: Auden's poem. She had been thinking about "Angels in Italy" while all the time she might have been remembering Auden's "A Summer Night." Was that not about sitting outside, at night, in a deckchair in the company of friends; and with Vega "conspicuous overhead"? Auden had later described how during those few minutes sitting under the stars with his friends he had experienced a mystical understanding of **agape**, that non-sexual love of others. He had been vouchsafed a glimpse of **agape** and it had stayed with him for some time before it had faded. Had she felt something similar?

"And I met somebody else," Isabel said. "Martha Drummond."

Jamie raised an eyebrow. "That rather odd woman? The one who lives round the corner?"

"Yes, her."

He shrugged. "And?"

"We had coffee at Cat's. She said that there was somebody who wanted to speak to me about something."

Jamie said nothing.

"Do you remember reading about the theft of a painting from a house in Stirlingshire? A painting by Poussin?"

Jamie said that he had a vague recollection of it. "It was quite valuable, wasn't it?"

"Yes. Not as valuable as that da Vinci that was stolen from Drumlanrig Castle—the one they eventually found in the safe of a Glasgow firm of lawyers. But it was still worth a few million."

Jamie began to lift himself out of his deck-chair. The flimsy contraption started to wobble and then, with a sudden loud ripping sound, the canvas gave way. This had the effect of making him fall, causing the restraining bar on the chair to slip from its home and the whole chair to fold in upon itself.

Jamie gave a howl of pain. His left hand had been unfortunately placed and had become trapped in the collapsing frame.

"Jamie!" She struggled to get out of her chair. There was another ripping sound, but the canvas held and Isabel was on her feet. Jamie had extricated himself from the chair mechanism and was nursing his hand.

"Painful," he said.

"Are you all right?"

He nodded. "I knew that would happen."

They both laughed. "Why does anyone sit in dangerous chairs?" Isabel asked.

"Why does anybody do anything dangerous?"

Jamie asked, examining his hand for signs of damage.

"I don't know," said Isabel. "Boredom, perhaps. Danger gives a bit of spice to our lives."

He turned to her, resuming the conversation that had been interrupted by the failure of the deckchair. "You were saying, this person—whoever it is—wants to speak to you. It's going to be about the theft of the Poussin, isn't it?"

She looked down at the ground. "Yes."

He sighed. "You've done something like this before. That artist you traced. When we went to Jura. Remember?"

"Yes. But this is different."

He reached out to take her hand. "Do you think it's a good idea? Do you really think so?"

She began to lead him back to the house. "Yes, I know. I know what you mean. It's vaguely ridiculous that here am I, the editor of a philosophical review of all things, and I keep getting involved in the messes that people get themselves into."

Jamie agreed. "Yes, it is ridiculous. And yet it seems to go on happening."

Isabel sighed. "I don't exactly advertise."

"Well, you know my views," said Jamie. "I don't think it's a terribly good idea."

"No, it may not be a good idea, but some of the things we have to do are not particularly good ideas—but we have to do them anyway."

"You don't have to do this. Nobody says you have to do this."

"No. But this poor man, this Munrowe man—apparently he's pretty cut up about it. And all he wants to do is talk. I can't really refuse to talk to him."

They made their way into the house. Isabel slipped an arm around his shoulder and asked him if he was cross with her.

He hesitated. "No, I'm not cross. If anything, I suppose I should be proud of you—which I am. I'm very proud of you." He paused. "But please be careful over this one. This isn't just some minor issue you're helping with—this is really serious."

Isabel sought to reassure him. "I'm only going to be speaking to him. That's all."

It was as if he had not heard. "And the point about serious matters like this is that people get hurt."

"I shall be very careful. I promise you."

They went inside. She bathed Jamie's hand, as the clash with the deckchair had broken the skin slightly. She patted it dry with a clean towel and then kissed it. He looked at the clock; Charlie would have to be fetched in half an hour or so. He put his arms about Isabel and embraced her, pulling her to him. Her hands were on his shoulder blades. It was warm in the house and the sound of a mower drifted in from over the road through an open window, bringing with it the smell of cut grass.

CHAPTER FOUR

THE ARRANGEMENT, made by Martha Drummond, and relayed to Isabel later that afternoon in a telephone call from Martha, was that Duncan Munrowe would come, as Isabel had suggested, to the German bakery in Bruntsfield at one o'clock the following day. Isabel's housekeeper Grace had been on holiday but would be back in the morning and would be able to collect Charlie from nursery school in place of Jamie, who was recording in Glasgow.

Grace had been in Stranraer, where she had a cousin who was married to a farmer. Each year she went to visit this cousin for a week, and inevitably came back sleep-deprived and vaguely grumpy as a result. "He snores something terrible," she explained to Isabel. "I'm short of a week's sleep. He goes to bed at ten every night—regular as clockwork. By ten-fifteen the snoring starts, and it goes on all night. You hear it throughout the house and it makes the walls shake. I'm not exaggerating—all night. Snoring and snorting."

"Poor man," said Isabel.

"Poor man? Poor us. My cousin hardly sleeps, she says, and no sooner do I drop off than I'm woken up by the sound of his snoring down the corridor."

"It sounds as if he might have sleep apnoea," suggested Isabel. "My father had it. You stop breathing every so often and wake up. People who have sleep apnoea are usually chronically sleep-deprived." She thought of the cumbersome mask her father had sometimes used to deal with the problem. "He could be helped."

"Not him," said Grace. "He's stubborn. He doesn't think there's anything wrong."

This discussion of sleep led to the matter of Charlie's afternoon nap. In Grace's absence, Charlie had taken to resisting this period of rest, and yet he was clearly tired.

"His mind seems very active," said Isabel. "He wants to keep going."

She paused, remembering her conversation with Jamie about Charlie's mathematical ability. "He seems to be very keen on counting things at the moment," she went on. "Have you noticed that?"

Grace did not seem surprised. "Yes, of course I have. I've been teaching him, you see."

Isabel frowned. "Teaching him mathematics?"

Grace nodded. "Yes. I'd noticed that he was quite good at counting and so I've been giving him lessons. I've taught him how to divide things, and some basic multiplication. I found a book in the library that tells you how to do this. It's by a Korean woman who's had two of her children win prizes in the Maths Olympiad. She explains how it's done."

Isabel was not sure what to say. So that was how Charlie had been able to come up with what seemed to be naturally brilliant answers: he had been taught. For a few moments she was silent. She trusted Grace with so much of Charlie's life, and she was not sure why she should feel concerned about her teaching him mathematics. At the back of her mind was a feeling that one had to be careful with method when it came to mathematics: she seemed to remember being told that if you developed the wrong way of doing mathematics when you were young, you could be lumbered with it for the rest of your life. It was the same with many activities—from typing to playing the violin: it was sometimes far harder to unlearn bad habits than to learn them in the first place. But the issue would have to be handled delicately; Grace was touchy and could take offence at the slightest reproach, even if unintended.

"I suppose he must have natural ability," said Isabel mildly.

Grace looked thoughtful. "Probably no more than any other child of his age. It's the teaching, I think. The book is really good. It says any child can be really good at calculating if you follow their method."

Isabel looked doubtful. "Surely not every single child. Genes must play some sort of role," she said. "Mathematical ability and musicality often go together. Jamie's a musician, after all, and maybe Charlie gets it from him."

Grace shook her head. "It's the book, I think."

Isabel decided not to argue. This was not the time to voice her reservations—especially when Grace was feeling sleep-deprived as a result of the snoring Ayrshire farmer. "Oh, well," she said.

"Yes," said Grace. "I'm going to teach him to count money next. There's a chapter on that in the book. It's called 'The Baby Accountant.'"

Isabel bit her lip. She was grateful to Grace for all she did for Charlie, but did she really want him to be a baby accountant? Charlie should develop at his own pace, she thought. He should get every help, naturally, but Isabel was definite that she did not want to be a pushy parent who made her child jump through all sorts of hoops. Surely Grace did not want that for Charlie either. Surely not.

"MISS DALHOUSIE?"

He was already sitting at a table when Isabel arrived at Falko's Konditorei, the German bakery and coffee shop along the street from Cat's delicatessen. There were only a few other people in the café, but even had there been a much larger crowd Isabel would have had no difficulty in picking out Duncan Munrowe. It was largely a matter of dress—a jacket in a quiet browny-green; a dark-blue tie, discreetly checked; brown brogues: the uniform of the moneyed countryman—nothing ostentatious, nothing loud. And that was just the clothing; the physiognomy, too, revealed his origins: regular features, chiselled, showing a certain intelligence, even if not the face of an intellectual or aesthete. It was a handsome face, she thought, and the man's overall bearing was impressive.

"Isabel, please."

"Of course. And I'm Duncan: Duncan Munrowe."

They shook hands. The handshake, too, conformed to type.

Duncan Munrowe thanked her for agreeing to see him. "It's an awful cheek on my part," he said. "We haven't met, and here I am inviting you to listen to my problems."

Isabel laughed. "I don't mind." And she decided that she did not; her immediate impression of him was positive. This man, she decided, was exactly what he purported to be: a country gentleman, for want of a better term; nothing more, nor less, than that. He was at the opposite end of the spectrum from . . . She hesitated: Who **was** at the other end of the spectrum? It came to her: Professor Lettuce and Christopher Dove. Scheming philosophers. Waspish backbiters.

"Well, you're very kind," Duncan said. "But I must admit I feel a trifle embarrassed."

She assured him that this was unnecessary. As she did so, she considered his voice. There was a hint of a Scottish burr, but only a hint. That would have been taken out of the Munrowe voice two or three generations ago through being educated at schools that modelled themselves on the English public-school system, even if they were in Scotland. Or they would have been sent off to the South, to Harrow or Eton, or the like, where the conditioning of the English upper class would have been all-encompassing and where young Scots became indistinguishable in voice and outlook from their English contemporaries. That practice was changing, but there were still many people who lived in its shadow.

They placed their order with the waitress. Isabel glanced about her; it was not crowded, and the nearest table, from which their conversation might easily be heard, was empty.

"I suppose it would help," Duncan began, "if I told you a little bit about our collection. I've heard, by the way, that you're interested in art."

"Oh?" She wondered how he knew this. It would be Martha, of course, who had seen her mother's painting and had perhaps noticed some of the other pictures. And Martha would probably have overstated Isabel's knowledge of the subject, which was, by her own admission, modest.

"Yes," he said. "Guy's mentioned you—I know him too. I've bought the odd thing from his gallery, but I must admit I haven't really added very much to the family collection."

That explained it. Isabel regularly discussed art with Guy Peploe who ran the Scottish Gallery in Dundas Street.

"As you may know," Duncan continued,

"quite a bit of our collection is in the Scottish National Gallery on the Mound. Which is where it should be, in my view. Private collectors are just custodians, I think. They look after works of art but they don't really own them. Not in any absolute sense."

It was an admirable sentiment, and Isabel found herself warming all the more to Duncan. This was not one of those well-heeled people who are smug about their possessions. "Do you think that many others share your view? Other collectors, that is."

Duncan shrugged. "Some do, as you'll see if you look at any of the big collections. Look at the Burrell in Glasgow—Burrell gave everything he had to the city—the whole shooting match. And there are lots of other examples. The Met in New York is full of collections that have been given or bequeathed. The Wallace Collection in London. That odd place outside Philadelphia that used to let you look at it only when there was a full moon or whatever. The name escapes me, but he handed over the lot, didn't he? Or sort of handed it over."

"The Barnes," said Isabel.

"That's it. He gave the lot, didn't he?"

"Yes. And will you?" asked Isabel.

For a moment a shadow passed over his face,

and she realised that her question, which had just slipped out, was intrusive, even rude. You did not ask people just how charitable they intended to be.

"I'm sorry. I shouldn't have asked you. It's none of my business."

He smiled. "Not at all. It's a reasonable question, and I'd raised the subject anyway. No, I'm not going to give everything away. I'm going to pass some on to the next generation."

"Fair enough."

"But the more important things will go to the Scottish National Gallery." He stopped, and looked at her, lowering his voice. His tone, now, bore a note of apology. "The Poussin, for example."

"The one that was stolen?"

"Yes, although I suppose that's very much in doubt now." He paused again. "And that makes me feel extremely regretful. After all, I promised it to them."

Isabel felt that he hardly needed to reproach himself over that, and told him as much. He listened attentively, but she could see that her words did not persuade him. It was something to do with honour, she thought; this man was out of his time, barely at home in an age as casual as ours. There were people like that.

"Tell me about the painting," she said. "I looked it up but one can never really tell from a photograph."

He responded enthusiastically to her comment. "I couldn't agree more about photographs. You don't get any sense of the presence of the painting—the atmosphere it creates just by being there in the room. For that, you have to see it in the flesh, so to speak."

He sat back in his chair. The waitress had arrived with their order—an open sandwich for Isabel and a slice of quiche and a salad for Duncan.

He seemed suddenly to have remembered something. "Have you noticed something about Caravaggio?"

She was not sure how to answer. One could hardly be unaware of Caravaggio, but to notice something . . . His use of light?

"It's just this business about seeing a painting in a room, in front of you. Caravaggio is so powerful he sterilises any other paintings on the wall in the same room. It just doesn't work. He overpowers them."

"Poussin doesn't?"

"The opposite. Poussin is a tremendously courteous painter. He doesn't shout at you. Far from it."

They began their lunch. She saw that he ate delicately, and slowly, which surprised her. She had imagined that he would have a hearty appetite; country people usually did. But then she remembered that Duncan Munrowe was very far from being a typical country landowner.

"The Poussin we have lost," he went on, "is a late one. Like many of his paintings of that period it has what the experts call a 'cool palette.' In other words, it's not very bright. Those lovely, rather faded colours."

"Like **A Dance to the Music of Time**?"

He nodded. "Yes. Or that other one—you know, the one where the giant is carrying the man on his shoulders, the one in the Louvre?"

Isabel did know it. "One of my absolute favourites," she said. "The man standing on the giant's shoulders is just so utterly extraordinary. But it's not in the Louvre—it's in New York, in the Met."

He blushed. "Of course. I forget what's where. For me, the Louvre's . . ."

Isabel knew what she thought of when she thought of the Louvre. There was a certain inevitability to it. "The **Mona Lisa**?"

He shook his head. "No. I'm afraid that painting does very little for me—I suppose because it's become so well known. And the room it's in is always full to the brim with parties of teenagers on their Paris trip. You can hardly breathe."

"So you search out Poussin?" she prompted.

"Yes," said Duncan. "And also that wonderful Ghirlandaio—the one in which the young boy is looking up in wonderment at his grandfather with the very bulbous nose. Youth and old age. It's such a lovely painting and the look in the old man's eyes is just extraordinary. How do you capture a look of such fondness? How do you get that in paint? Yet he does. It's a magnificent painting."

"Which is what great painting is about," said Isabel. "Capturing those profound human emotions."

Duncan agreed. "That's right. And it makes one ask if we have any great artists among us at present. Who are they? Who's doing that sort of thing now?"

"David Hockney can," said Isabel. "Look at the emotion in those paintings of young men, and some of the portraits too."

"And Lucian Freud?"

"Yes, him too."

He looked thoughtful. "But great painters seem to be thin on the ground, do you think?"

"Perhaps." She steered the conversation back to the Poussin. "So, what happened?"

"The theft?"

"Yes."

He put down his knife and fork. "You may know that we open the garden—and the house—to the public on a couple of days each summer. It's a great way of sharing. We've always done it at Munrowe House."

"And that's when it was stolen?"

"So it seems. We were quite busy—there were almost two hundred people who came and had a look round. Maybe more."

She asked whether they were free to wander around the house as well. Was nothing done about watching them?

He looked at her ruefully. "Of course we had arrangements. There were five or six volunteers—friends of ours, or people who work on the estate next door. We tried to make sure that there was somebody in each of the rooms that was open to the public. There were six of those—the main drawing room, the dining room, the library and so on. But the system didn't work, I'm afraid, and there were spells in between shifts when there was nobody in a room."

Isabel was curious as to how a painting could have been carried out in broad daylight, with people milling around.

"I'm afraid that was very simple," said Duncan.

"The Poussin was in the drawing room, and that room has a French window that opens on to the garden. But the bit of the garden in question is secluded, and there's a sort of hedged corridor that goes round to the back of the house. It would have been very easy to take the painting out by that route and then bundle it into a car parked near the kitchen. Very simple, I'm afraid. We didn't check beforehand to see whether that door was locked—and it wasn't."

He sighed. "The insurance people hit the roof when they came round. I pointed out to them that if it had been as obvious as all that, then why had they not raised it with me when their man came round last year to look at the alarm system? They wanted to check that we had proper alarms and they had a good walk round the house. They said things seemed fine then."

"And how did they respond to that?"

"Silence. They answer the questions they want to answer and ignore the others. They've been very tight-lipped about this." He paused. "I'm afraid I've been seriously distressed by these people. Seriously . . ." His voice faltered.

Isabel reached across to touch him gently on the forearm. He looked down at her hand, surprised, but did not draw back. She left her hand where it rested for only a moment or two, but it was enough to establish a connection of sympathy.

"It's obviously been pretty upsetting for you," she said. "The loss of the painting in itself must be bad enough, but to have it compounded by a row over insurance must make it all so much worse."

He gave her an appreciative look. "Yes, I'm afraid you're right. I should perhaps have been a bit more robust about it all, but I'm afraid I just found the whole thing . . . well, a bit tawdry. I feel dirtied by it. It's odd, I know, but that's the way I feel."

"But that's the way that anybody who's been burgled feels," Isabel said. "It's a violation. Your space has been invaded. It's a shock. And then along come insurance people who make you feel guilty about it, although you're the victim. It's entirely understandable."

They were silent for a while. Then Duncan said, "That's why I asked to speak to you. I wanted to have somebody on my side, if I could put it that way. Lawyers are all very well, and I could have asked Douglas Connel—he's very helpful, but he's doing a lot of other things for me at present and I felt it would be burdening him unduly."

"I know Douglas," said Isabel. "I'm sure he wouldn't mind."

"Maybe not. But I also thought that for this it might be better to have somebody who isn't a lawyer." He looked at her cautiously. "And there's a reason for that."

Isabel waited for him to explain. He picked up a paper napkin and folded it carefully, and then refolded it.

"We've had an approach, or rather, the insurance people have had an approach. It's tentative at the moment, but it looks as if something might be happening."

"An approach from the thieves?"

"Possibly."

"And are they going to talk to them?"

"I imagine so. The insurance company wants to avoid paying the claim if at all possible. If they can get the painting back from the thieves for less than the claim, then that suits them just fine."

"I see."

"Remember those Turners that were stolen in Germany?"

Isabel remembered it, but only vaguely.

"They got them back through negotiation with the thieves," Duncan said. "In our case, though, there's something unusual going on."

She waited. The waitress had come to clear their plates.

"They want to talk to me," he said quietly. "They've made the initial approach to the insurance company, but they seem to have gone off them for some reason. Maybe it's something the insurers said. Perhaps they rather scared the thieves off. Anyway, they're now talking directly to me."

She asked what the insurance company thought of that. They were surprised, he said, and unsure what lay behind it. They felt it might be unwise for him to talk directly to the thieves and they were also at pains to stress that Duncan had no power to negotiate in relation to the return of the painting. That was their affair as insurers and the thieves would have to go to them for that. After a while, though, they had changed their tune when it came to initial talks, especially after the thieves had gone quiet for a few weeks. Duncan could talk directly to anybody, as long as he kept them informed and did not try to commit them to any payment.

"So what would you like me to do?" Isabel asked.

Duncan stared at her uncertainly.

"I'm perfectly happy to help," she prompted. "You needn't feel awkward about asking."

"I have to meet them," he said. "They've told me they're going to be in touch about a meeting. I don't yet know where it's going to be."

"How did they contact you?"

"Initially by letter. Anonymous, naturally. Printed on a plain sheet of paper and postmarked Glasgow. It told me nothing."

"You showed it to the insurance people?"

He nodded. "They photographed it. I'm not sure if they showed it to the police. The police have been informed, of course, but seem to be taking a bit of a back seat at present. It seems the insurance company doesn't think it helps to involve them too closely at this stage, as far as I can tell."

"You said—'initially.' Have they been in touch again?"

He shifted in his seat uneasily. "They telephoned me. At three in the morning."

She waited for him to continue.

"They asked me if I had received their letter. That's how I knew it was the same people. The insurance people say that you get all sorts of cranks phoning up pretending to be the thieves, trying to get in on things. At least we know this is the same group."

It occurred to Isabel that they might still be impostors who had nothing to do with the theft. How could he tell?

"The letter had a photograph with it. It was a close-up of a section of the painting under strong light. It couldn't have been taken when it was in our possession, on the wall—the lighting was quite different."

Their coffee had arrived. Duncan took a sip, looking at Isabel over the rim of his cup. "They said they'd phone to make the arrangements quite soon. They said it wouldn't be them I would be meeting—it would be somebody acting for them. I thought I might tell them that I'll be accompanied by a friend. I'll stress that you have nothing to do with the insurance company."

He waited expectantly. "All right?"

Isabel nodded. "All right."

He looked relieved. "Thank you. And I'm sorry that this has all been about me and I haven't asked you anything about yourself. I know that you edit a journal—Martha told me that—and I know that you have a reputation as being somebody who sorts out people's difficulties. But apart from that?"

"I live in Merchiston," Isabel said. "Just round the corner from here. I run the journal from the house. And I'm married to a musician. He plays the bassoon."

Duncan listened politely. "I see."

"And I have a three-and-three-quarter-year-old

son called Charlie. And that, I suppose, is it. And you? Do you have family?"

"I have two children by my first wife," said Duncan. "My daughter is thirty and I have a son of twenty-seven. Both live in Edinburgh—my daughter lives in Nelson Street. I'm going down there immediately after this. We see each other regularly."

"And your wife?" Isabel asked.

"Frederika. Freddie for short. I remarried about ten years ago. I had lost my first wife to cancer a few years earlier. The children were still at school. Alex—that's Alexandra—was just about to leave and Patrick had a couple more years to go. It was very difficult for him. Had he been a little older, he would have coped better, I think."

Had his words been written, the last sentence would have been underlined in red, thought Isabel.

"It's always difficult," said Isabel. "I lost my mother at quite an early age. I was twelve."

"Yes, it's not easy. Alex says that her memories sometimes get jumbled up—even though she was almost eighteen when her mother died."

"They will," said Isabel. "I remember my mother, but the memories are sometimes fuzzy, like a film that's not quite in focus. I remind myself by looking at photographs and by thinking about her."

Isabel thought for a moment: **If she could only walk in through that door**. **If she could only do that . . .**

They were both silent. Then Duncan glanced at his watch before looking out of the window, as if expecting somebody. His appointment in Nelson Street, Isabel imagined; his daughter opening the door to him, a kiss on the cheek, the exchange of small talk, a cup of tea—how precious. She noticed the watch, which was thin, and made of rose gold. It was discreet, understated. It was exactly right for him.

"Alex has been very upset by the whole business," he said. "She was particularly attached to that painting—she always has been. I keep off the subject because it's just too painful for her."

Isabel thought this quite understandable. She was reminded of a picture of her own that she could not bear to lose—a drawing by James Cowie of a boy, one of his Hospitalfield portraits. Cowie drew the young people whom he taught; they were delicate portraits, entirely natural, catching what the language of James VI's time referred to as "man's innocency." **Innocency**:

what a wonderful word, and different, in some indefinable way, from **innocence.** The difference, she thought, lay in the poetry.

"And I must confess it's painful for me too," Duncan suddenly added. "I suppose I'm mourning that picture. Or that's what it feels like."

He reached for the raincoat he had draped over a chair. "I'll tell Martha about our meeting," he said. "She'll be pleased."

Isabel inclined her head. "Good."

Duncan rose to his feet. "Dear Martha."

Isabel was not sure what to say. So she said, "Of course."

It was the best thing to come out with in any circumstances in which one was at a loss for anything more. "Of course" fitted most occasions, as it meant that whatever the other person had said was perfectly understandable, and indeed correct; which is what most of us want to hear.

"Although she can occasionally go on a bit," he added.

Isabel noticed that there were the traces of a smile about his lips.

"Of course," she said. "But we all can, can't we?"

"Of course," he said.

They went to the counter, where he paid the

bill. "I'll be in touch, if I may, when we hear from . . . from these people."

"Please do."

"And we'd very much like you to come out to the house. Come and have dinner and stay the night. You and your husband. And little . . ."

"Charlie."

"Yes, Charlie too. Would you like to do that?"

She said she would. She was intrigued. But it was more than that. She had taken a liking to this man—to the subtle and sensitive mind that she had detected beneath the unlikely exterior. And she felt sympathy for him. He had lost a painting that he loved and that he had been, generously, intending to give to the nation. The thieves, then, had not just stolen from a private individual, they had stolen from the whole nation. If she could help to deal with that—even if she had no real idea what she could possibly do—then she would do it.

They said goodbye on the pavement outside. He turned and walked back into Bruntsfield, on his way to visit his daughter in Nelson Street. Isabel watched him go and reflected on how a casual observer, driving past, perhaps, and seeing him in the street, might come to entirely the wrong conclusion: might see a rather formal, even slightly military figure, might take him to be exactly what in one sense he was—a country gentleman—and would not imagine for a moment that this was a man who knew, and cared about, art; who could mourn the loss of a picture. But then we can misjudge one another so easily, she thought; so easily.

CHAPTER FIVE

THE FOLLOWING DAY, which was a Saturday, Jamie was playing in a concert in St. Cecilia's Hall and Isabel had a ticket. Grace had agreed to look after Charlie and arrived early so that she could do his dinner and give him his bath too. Isabel would have preferred to do that herself, but she knew how much Grace enjoyed her time with Charlie and so she did not begrudge it.

"And perhaps give him a quick mathematics lesson," she said.

She spoke jokingly, but Grace was immediately defensive.

"I only do that when he's fresh and in a mood to absorb things," she said reproachfully. "The end of the day is no time for that sort of thing."

Isabel made a conciliatory gesture. "Absolutely not." She thought of something else to say. "Could you put some of that oil in his bath? His skin seemed a little dry the other day."

Grace looked sideways at Isabel. "But I always do. You have to be careful about that."

If she always did it, then the implication was that Isabel was at fault. "I am careful," she said, meeting Grace's gaze.

They heard Charlie playing in the morning room with Jamie, and Grace went through to greet them. Isabel retreated into her study. **You have to be careful**. Of course she was careful about dry skin—as if she did not know about it. It was too much—did Grace think that she knew more about looking after children than Isabel did? It was ridiculous. She looked up at the ceiling. No, it was not really ridiculous: what was ridiculous was her own attitude to Grace's entirely understandable lack of tact. All that Grace wanted to show her was that she knew what she was doing, and the reason why she felt she had to do this was because she thought that she—Isabel—would not think that she knew . . . Isabel laughed, and the tension, the resentment, disappeared.

"What are you laughing at?"

It was Jamie, who had followed her into her study and was standing behind her. Isabel crossed the room to close the door behind him—Grace had acute hearing.

"It's something Grace said," she explained. "She reminded me that you have to be careful about children getting dry skin."

"Charlie's skin isn't dry."

"No, but sometimes it can get a bit on the dry side. If you don't use that baby oil stuff."

"But I always do."

She smiled. "Not you too! I didn't say that you didn't use it. I'm not accusing you."

"But Grace is? Grace is accusing you of letting his skin get dry?"

Isabel laughed again. "No, this is becoming absurd. She just wanted me to know that she knew about it. I got all huffy and came in here thinking what a cheek she had and then realised that I had no reason to think that. And shouldn't. So I stopped. And that's when you came in."

Jamie shrugged. "An argument about nothing."

Isabel agreed, but pointed out that a great deal of life was all about small things like that: arguments about baby oil, about eggs, about who's put something in the wrong place. She had not yet mentioned the Korean mathematics book, but now she did.

"I meant to tell you. She's giving him mathematics lessons."

Jamie's face fell. "You mean . . ."

"Yes, she's taught him how to divide."

"But I thought it was his natural ability . . ."

Isabel smiled. "It is. No amount of tuition would enable an untalented three-year-old to divide. No, he's obviously got ability."

Jamie sat down. He looks cross, thought Isabel. First, the dry-skin affair, and now mathematics.

"She should have asked us," Jamie said eventually. "I mean, things like that—educational matters—are parental affairs, wouldn't you say? I wouldn't try to teach some other person's child how to do mental arithmetic. Would you?"

Isabel sat on the arm of his chair. It was the most comfortable chair in the house and it occupied pride of place in her study, where it had always been. Jamie liked it and would sometimes sit reading in it while Isabel worked; she liked having him there, but his presence did not help her to work. Isabel had always found it difficult to concentrate with other people in the room; they distracted her, as she found herself wondering what they were thinking. It would be fascinating to have some sort of printout of the thoughts of other people—a stream-of-consciousness report. It would read, she suspected, like a badly constructed novel, by an author who had no sense of the flow of narrative. **Look at her. Where did she get that? I had something like that back when I was living in that flat. Who lives there now? Did I turn the iron off? I'm feeling a bit hot. What did the weather forecast say? Bill hasn't telephoned. He said he would.** And so on, for page after page.

She addressed his question. "It's different with Grace. She has a lot of responsibility for Charlie. She's not quite family, but she's close enough. And that makes her an important part of his life."

He looked up at her. "I suppose so. But still . . ."

"Yes," she said. "But still."

"I'd like to see the book."

She suggested he ask her.

He got up out of the chair. "We still need to think about all that. We need to ask ourselves whether we really want him to have lessons at this point. I'm not sure that I want to turn him into a performing monkey."

Neither did Isabel.

"And there's another thing," said Jamie. "You have to be careful how you teach things. Music teachers are very careful about teaching very young children. You can get it all wrong and then they grow up with bad habits. Or you can ruin their lips—you don't let small children play brass, for example."

"We need to talk to her," she said. "Both of us. But not now."

"When?"

She sighed. "After the weekend." She wanted to enjoy the concert and did not want to go out after a row with Grace. But there was more to it: she also wanted to make it easy for Grace; she did not believe in painting people into a corner and making them lose face. So she would have to work out a method of doing it that would mean that Grace would believe it was her decision. It would not be easy, and Isabel had to admit that she had no idea how she could possibly do this.

THEY WALKED to St. Cecilia's Hall. The weather had held and the evening air was balmy. In the Meadows, the large slice of park that separated Edinburgh's Old Town from the Victorian suburbs to the south, spontaneous games had sprung up: rounders played by a mixture of parents and eight-year-olds; a small game of cricket with only five or six fielders and a tennis ball. Isabel looked up at the branches of the trees that formed a canopy above the footpath they were following. The trees were in full leaf, but sky still showed through gaps in the foliage, a fading blue with drifting lace-like clouds. It made her dizzy to look at clouds when they were moving, as these were, and Isabel reached for Jamie's arm so that they might stop for a moment.

"Look at those clouds," she said. "They're very high. Cirrus, I think."

Jamie looked up too. "I don't know the names. Does it help if you know the names?"

She shrugged. "In the same way as it helps to know the names of trees. Or flowers. People tend to know about trees and flowers, but not about clouds. Strange, isn't it?"

"Maybe it's because they're always there," said Jamie. "We take for granted things that are always there."

As they continued on their way, Isabel felt a deep sense of contentment. There were other cities where, on an equally fine evening, much the same scenes as these would be played out. There were cities of equal or similar beauty: Venice, Vienna, St. Petersburg. But this place, this city, this particular sky was **hers**, the place where the accident of birth had placed her. And she knew it so well; knew each turn of its winding streets; each cliff-face of ascending stone; each sweep of skyline.

As they made their way down Forest Road, and passed Sandy Bell's Bar, she remembered how, some years ago, she had been there with that man who had had the heart transplant. And before that, she had been there to listen to the music, and had heard Hamish Henderson sing "Freedom Come All Ye" and his heartbreaking "Banks of Sicily"; and a young Irishman launch into "Sam Hall." He had had such expressive eyes, and had sung as if he meant every word—"My name it is Sam Hall, and I **curse** you, one and all."

And in Candlemaker Row she remembered how she had walked down there not all that long ago with Jamie after a concert in Greyfriars Church, and they had talked about the Covenanters, or she had thought about them—she could not quite remember which. She slipped her hand into his.

"Nervous?"

He shook his head. "I like what we're playing tonight. And it's not very demanding for me—the benefits of being down on the bass line."

When they arrived, Jamie went into the green room with his fellow musicians, leaving Isabel to choose a seat in the upstairs room. The concert was part of a series organised by the Early Scottish Music Society, and there was to be a drinks reception afterwards, for which preparations were already being made. Jamie had suggested that they stay for this, as it was an opportunity for the performers, who otherwise would not have time to socialise, to get to know one another. Isabel was happy to agree; she had friends who had season tickets to these concerts and they might be there.

The concert began. A couple of pieces were familiar to Isabel—the rest were new, but there were full programme notes that explained who the composers were and put their music in context. She did not go out at the interval, but remained where she was, reading the notes for the second half. Jamie caught her eye and smiled; she returned the smile. She felt so proud of him.

At the end of the concert, the audience went downstairs, where most stayed for the reception. A group of young women in black skirts and white tops circulated among the guests, offering glasses of wine and small, rather greasy snacks. Isabel took a sausage on a stick and nibbled at it: it was not at all warm and seemed to be packed with cold fat. She steeled herself to swallow it. The Scottish diet was famously unhealthy, and it seemed that the same applied to Scottish canapés.

There was no sign of her friends, and she found herself in conversation with a couple she had not met before. Looking for something to talk about, she asked them where they lived. Their eyes lit up: they had recently moved to a new house and were full of the details. "It has a large conservatory," the woman said. "With a vine—an established vine."

"And there's a terrific garden," said the husband.

"Yes, terrific," agreed his wife. "The people before us were demon gardeners. Demons."

Isabel sipped at her wine, discreetly eyeing the prospects for escape. Jamie was on the other side of the room, with the musicians. They were enjoying themselves, and a peal of laughter sounded across the room to make the point. She pointed to him. "My husband."

The woman looked across the room. "On the right?"

Isabel shook her head. "On the left. And I must have a word with him, if you'll excuse me."

Isabel could tell that the woman was interested. The musician on the right was a short man with a thickset neck, much older than Jamie. She has assumed, thought Isabel, that that is the sort of husband I should have. And now she had seen Jamie and was thinking: How did **she** get **him**? People are transparent, Isabel thought; so often we can tell exactly what they're thinking although they may not have said a thing. And I am equally transparent: this woman knows that I'm not really interested in our conversation and that I don't really have to have a word with Jamie; not an urgent word; not anything that couldn't wait until they've finished telling me about their garden.

The woman's interest in Jamie changed now to offence that Isabel wanted to get away from her. "Please," she said. "Don't let us hold you up."

Isabel blushed, and moved away. She did not like to give offence, but sometimes it was difficult not to do so. Sometimes the ordinary contingencies of social life meant that offence was inevitable: the turning down of an invitation that one could not accept because one had another engagement—that could give offence, no matter how genuine the excuse: **she doesn't want to come; she says that she's got something else on . . . that's what she says.** Or at a cocktail party—those occasions that Isabel sometimes called "trials by cocktail"—you had to move on; you couldn't stay and talk to the same person for hours; and yet how to detach yourself? What formula could one use for getting away? Could you simply say, "I've enjoyed our chat," and walk away? That was somewhat abrupt. "I must fill up my glass." "But it's quite full already." "Oh, is it? I hadn't noticed." Perhaps one might try: "I need some fresh air. I must get to a window." "Oh, so do I! I'll come with you." As a last resort, a quick glance at one's watch, and then, "I really have to go. What a pity." "Oh, so do—" "No. Actually, I'll stay—you go. Goodbye."

Isabel moved towards the other side of the room. She sensed that the woman was watching her; she felt her eyes upon her, and thought she should be seen to be walking in that direction. Then she hesitated: Why? Why should she worry about what somebody whom she had just met, and whom she would probably never meet again, should think about her? She had done nothing wrong; she had been perfectly polite when they had been going on about their garden. She had done nothing for which she should reproach herself.

She stopped. There was a young man standing in front of her. He had just finished talking to a woman in a purple dress, a large woman who was a regular attendee at Edinburgh concerts and who was considered vividly eccentric by many; an enthusiastic exponent of a wide range of subjects, on which she entertained strong and unconventional opinions. The young man looked bemused, which often happened when people spoke to that particular woman for the first time. She was now making off towards her husband, who was standing near the door; a rather insignificant-looking man who had the appearance of being permanently overwhelmed; shell-shocked, perhaps, after years of marriage to that woman. The Scots expression **hauden doon**—held down—was made for people like him, thought Isabel.

Isabel caught the young man's eye. She had the feeling he wanted to speak to her.

"Enjoyed the concert?" she asked.

He looked at her gratefully; in a room full of people talking, we do not wish to be by ourselves. "Yes. A lot. I love early music and we don't get enough of it, I think."

"I like it too."

He transferred his glass from right hand to left to be able to shake hands. "I'm Patrick Munrowe."

It took a moment for the name to register. But then, in an instant, she saw the resemblance. Of course he was Patrick Munrowe; there was

Duncan's forehead, and the same eyes; the same presence.

The coincidence struck her sharply. "Your father's Duncan Munrowe?"

He nodded, somewhat surprised. She looked at him appraisingly. He was slightly taller than his father with the same good looks, but had an air of vulnerability about him; the air that some men have of being slightly lost.

"I had lunch with him yesterday, you see."

He looked thoughtful. "Here? In Edinburgh?"

"Yes, he was in town."

"I see. I didn't know."

There was nothing in his tone to suggest that he was aggrieved to hear that his father had been in Edinburgh and had not told him, and yet Duncan had made a point of saying that he always saw his daughter when he came to town. If the daughter, then why not the son?

"I think it was a pretty brief visit," she said hurriedly. "It was business."

He started to enquire. "You're a . . . ?" He did not finish the sentence.

"It was about the loss of the painting."

"So you're with the insurance company?"

"No." She was not sure how to proceed, being uncertain as to whether the approach from Duncan was meant to be confidential. She had already given it away, if it was. "No. I've got nothing to do with that side of it. I was asked by Martha Drummond to speak to him about it."

The mention of Martha's name had an immediate effect: he looked incredulous. "Her?"

"Yes. I believe that she's a friend of your father's."

"I suppose so. It's just that, well, frankly, I find that woman rather difficult to take. Sorry."

"She may not be everybody's cup of tea."

He took a sip of his wine. "Has he asked you to help him?"

Isabel felt that she could hardly decline to talk about it now. "He has. I'm not sure what I can do—if anything. But I think your father needed a sounding board, so to speak."

He nodded. "Fair enough. He was very upset by it, you know."

"I know."

"And it wasn't because of the money side of it. Pop is very unworldly. He's one of the least materialistic people I know."

Isabel said that she had formed the impression that it was the painting that counted rather than its monetary value.

"Dead right," said Patrick. "With him, it's a question of . . . well, there's no other word for it but **honour.** It's a question of honour that he promised the painting to the Scottish National Gallery. That's what's really hurt him—the possibility that the painting might never be recovered or could be damaged."

"I can understand that."

He looked at her with interest. "May I ask what you do? Are you a psychologist?"

"No. I'm a philosopher."

He seemed impressed. "There aren't many people who can answer that question that way. That's what you actually do—philosophy?"

She explained about the **Review** and about the sort of articles she published. And then she turned the question back on him. "And you?"

His reply was delivered in a tone of self-deprecation. "Nothing nearly as interesting, I'm afraid. I work for a company that advises on investment in pharmaceutical companies. I've been doing it for the grand total of six years so far."

She wondered about his age. Duncan had told her, but she had forgotten. Twenty-something—twenty-seven? So he must have gone straight from university into the job. And that left another forty years to do it. Forty years of working on drug companies. Forty years.

"I'm not sure that I'd say that was uninteresting. Drugs don't strike me as boring. And isn't what you do a form of intelligence gathering?"

He smiled. "I suppose you could look at it that way. We look at pharmaceutical companies with a view to putting the investors' money in them. I suppose that's intelligence gathering. I look at smaller companies—the ones who think they might just invent the cure for something big."

"And do they?"

"Sometimes, but very rarely. I've recently been looking at one that is trying to find an Alzheimer's drug. There have been one or two possibilities, but at the end of the day they've fizzled out. Then somebody comes up with something that makes everybody's efforts look a bit expensive. Such as eating oily fish. Apparently that stops your brain shrinking and protects you against Alzheimer's. But there's no profit in that."

Isabel laughed. "Sardines? A tin of sardines a day?"

"Exactly. And if you're worried about strokes, then . . ."

They were interrupted by Jamie, who had left

the group of musicians. He took Isabel's hand and squeezed it lightly.

"Lovely concert," said Isabel. And to Patrick, "This is Jamie."

Patrick smiled at Jamie. "Yes," he said. "You played the bassoon, didn't you?"

"I did."

"I played a curtal once," said Patrick. "At school. We had a music teacher who loved old instruments. He arranged for us to play sackbuts and sordunes and whatever."

Isabel asked what the curtal was.

"The precursor of the bassoon," Jamie told her.

"And the racket," prompted Patrick. "Don't forget the racket."

"That's another early instrument," said Jamie. "It looks like a little pot. You blow down a crook into the little pot and a deep sound comes out. It's a sort of bassoon for people who were waiting for the bassoon to be invented."

Patrick laughed. She saw that his eyes had lit up during this conversation. "Imagine people wanting to play instruments that haven't yet been invented. One might say, 'I really want to play the saxophone, but Adolf Sax hasn't invented it yet.' "

Isabel smiled. She liked a conversation that went in odd directions; she liked the idea of playfulness in speech. People could be so depressingly literal.

Jamie now turned to her. "I think perhaps we should go home. Grace doesn't want to stay over tonight, she wants to get home."

Isabel explained to Patrick, "Grace is our babysitter."

She saw Patrick's eyes move quickly to Jamie and then back to her. It was quick, but she noticed. There was a look of disappointment on his face; it was unmistakable.

"I must be on my way too," Patrick said quietly.

Isabel felt a sudden sympathy for him. "Where do you live?"

"I live in the New Town," he said. "St. Bernard's Crescent."

"I like it there," said Isabel.

"Yes," he said flatly. "So . . ."

"Well, I'm sure we'll meet again," said Isabel. "Your father has invited me to the house."

"You'll like it there too."

He smiled and began to turn away. Isabel took Jamie's arm and led him through the crowd, towards the door. Outside, in the darkness, she looked up at the towering stone buildings that lined the narrow thoroughfare of the Cowgate. A soft rain was falling, a spitting.

"Your bassoon?" she asked. "You've left your bassoon behind."

"They're looking after all our instruments. They have a van that will bring everything back tomorrow."

They began to make their way back towards the Grassmarket, undecided as to whether to walk home or catch a taxi.

"That was Patrick Munrowe," said Isabel. "His father is the man whose painting was stolen."

Jamie seemed distracted by something. "That second piece we played," he said. "I'm not sure it was a success. The flute—"

"What did you think of him?" pressed Isabel.

"Of Patrick?"

"Yes."

"I was interested to hear that he had played the curtal. He knew what he was talking about."

"And?"

"Well, I don't know."

"Gay?" asked Isabel.

"Maybe," said Jamie. "Did you think so?"

"Yes," she said. "He was very disappointed

when we mentioned Grace and getting back for the babysitter. Did you notice it?"

Jamie had not. "That second piece," he said. "We sounded much better at rehearsal."

"It was because he hadn't realised that you and I were together. That was why."

Jamie was silent. Isabel's deduction embarrassed him. "You mean . . . Well, how can you tell? And anyway, what does it matter?"

"Oh, it doesn't matter at all. But I think there's an issue between him and his father. It may have nothing to do with that, or it may. I can't tell."

"Gaydar can be misleading, you know," said Jamie. "It needs to be calibrated."

"Like sympathy," said Isabel. "And all our emotions and feelings. Shame. Anger. Love. Pain. Calibration is required if we are to use them sensitively."

"How do you calibrate pain?" asked Jamie.

"By cutting out the background pain of the world," answered Isabel. "By cutting all that out, not registering it, and responding only to those painful things that we can do something about. Because otherwise . . ."

Jamie had seen a taxi approaching; the thin band of yellow light above the vehicle's windscreen weaving its way towards them. He stepped out into the road and raised an arm.

"Because otherwise what?"

"Because otherwise we couldn't get on with our day-to-day lives. The pain of the world would burden us too much."

"True," said Jamie.

CHAPTER SIX

THERE WAS an unspoken understanding between Isabel and her niece Cat that when Cat went away on holiday or was otherwise unable to get in to the delicatessen, then Isabel would take over, even with very little notice. It would have been more sensible for Eddie to do this, but Eddie, for all his willingness to embark on a long tour of North America with his uncle—and uncle's girlfriend—and to follow this with a spell working at a ski resort in Alberta, still lacked the confidence to be left in sole charge of the delicatessen. Isabel wondered whether this might be changed by his having reached the milestone of his twenty-first birthday and having met his new girlfriend Diane—or the Huntress, as she had unfortunately become lodged in Isabel's mind, though not a reference to any man-hunting on her part (Eddie was not the most obvious prey for a dedicated man-hunter), but to the occupation of the Greek goddess of that name. Eddie was still unwilling to accept full responsibility and had shown signs of alarm when Cat telephoned the following Monday morning to inform him that she had come down with a norovirus and would be off work for at least three days, possibly more. Cat had reassured him that Isabel would help out and that he would not be left to manage by himself; she had then phoned Isabel and broken the news to her.

"I hate asking you," she said. "But I really can't go in. I don't want to go into details—"

"Then don't," said Isabel quickly.

"But I'm bringing up the most amazing amount of fluid," Cat persisted. "I have no idea where it's all coming from. And the diarrhoea, I'm not exaggerating, I promise you—"

"I'll be there," Isabel interjected. "How many days?"

When Cat warned her that it could be the whole week, Isabel's heart sank. There were spells in her life—often as long as a month—when the affairs of the **Review of Applied Ethics** could safely be put to one side, or benignly neglected as Isabel put it, but this was not one of them. The proofs of the next issue had arrived, and an entire article was being withdrawn on the grounds that the author had placed it elsewhere without telling Isabel. He had been keen, she believed, to have a back-up home for it if another possibility of publication—in a rather more prestigious journal—came to nothing. The prestigious journal had accepted the paper and the author had either forgotten to inform Isabel timeously or had become too embarrassed to do so, eventually leaving it to a secretary in his department to let her know what was happening. Isabel had mentally composed a stinging rebuke, and had gone so far as to type it out as an email, but had eventually decided not to send it. The delete button, that saviour of how many relationships, had again done its work: the swingeing censure had been replaced by a mild, rather sad reproach: **It would have been helpful to know about this before I sent everything off to the printer; but no matter, I'm very pleased that you've found such a good home for your very fine piece. And their circulation is admittedly so much larger than ours, and looks as if it will remain so, no matter how hard we try.** The "no matter how hard we try" was later removed; reproach should not too quickly become self-pity.

All this, though, meant that she had to find an article to take its place, contact the author and have all the editing done within the next three days. That was feasible, even if she were to be busy in the delicatessen, but it would mean that she would have to work in the evenings as well as all day—something she did not particularly enjoy. She was, after all, a mother with an affectionate and demanding three-and-three-quarter-year-old to look after. She wanted to spend as much time with Charlie as she could, and now she would be unable to get away from the delicatessen until six-thirty every evening, by which time the bath would be over and the bedtime story would be about to begin.

But she could not let Cat down, and, after a quick consultation with Grace, who had just come in at the door, and a rushed telephone conversation with Jamie, who was on his way down to the Academy to start one of his teaching days, she finished her breakfast quickly and started out of the house.

Eddie greeted her warmly. He always arrived at the delicatessen early and he had coped perfectly well with the rush of people who called in on their way to work. That rush had now abated, and there were only one or two customers browsing the shelves when Isabel arrived.

"It's been all go," said Eddie, wiping his hands on his apron. "I've taken over two hundred and fifty pounds in . . ." He looked up at the clock above the refrigerated display. "In forty minutes. How about that?"

"Very good," said Isabel, reaching for a fresh apron from the hook on the wall. "You spoke to Cat, I take it?"

"I did," said Eddie. "She's got projectile vomiting, you know."

Isabel looked away. Any sort of vomiting was bad enough, but projectile vomiting . . .

"I've never had projectile vomiting," Eddie went on. "I was really sick for a day or two on the trip, though. We were in a place in Idaho and I was really hungry. We'd booked into a motel just outside town, and my uncle and his girlfriend had gone to a bar. I stayed in the motel. Then I found that I got really hungry, and so I went to this hot-dog place and ordered a really big hot dog. You should have seen it, Isabel, it was humungous. And it tasted really good."

Isabel busied herself with sweeping excess grounds off the work surface around the coffee machine. "But it wasn't?"

"No," said Eddie. "I think it had **E. coli** in it. Or something like that. I was seriously sick. Not projectile vomiting, but I felt really bad. The man in the motel said it was **E. coli.** He said that there was a lot of **E. coli** about and some of those hot-dog places make their hot dogs out of dead horse meat. Yuck. That's what he told me. He said the horses die, and if they go like that, rather than being sent to the slaughterhouse, they shouldn't be eaten. But apparently the mafia have a racket in horse meat, and they sell it to these hot-dog places and pretend that it comes from cows."

"Well, you survived," said Isabel. "And I'm sure Cat will too. So let's get things organised."

Eddie worked calmly and efficiently, and yet Isabel suspected that if she were not there, he would be jittery and anxious. "Could you manage by yourself, do you think?" she asked him during a lull at the counter.

He looked at her with alarm. "Why?"

"I just wondered."

"Do you have to do something else?" His voice was taut with anxiety.

"It's all right, Eddie," she said calmly. "I'll stay. I'm not going anywhere."

He visibly relaxed. "Good," he said. "I know I should be able to handle things by myself, but I get this tight feeling—right here . . ." He pointed to his chest. "And it makes it hard for me to do anything. I know it's stupid, really stupid. But . . ."

She put a hand on his shoulder. "Eddie, you're doing just fine. You're fine."

He looked down for a moment, and then raised his eyes to meet hers. Something passed between them—a moment of understanding, she thought. He had never told her what had happened to him—she had an idea—but now it seemed to her that he had somehow acknowledged that she knew, and that fact made it much easier for him. He was getting better, she was sure of it; time's healing effect—the old saw, the folk wisdom—was absolutely true. It was something to do with memory: things forgotten lost their power.

She changed the subject. "How's Diane?"

Eddie smiled. "You could meet her," he said. "She's around today. I could phone her and ask her to drop in." He looked at Isabel enquiringly. "That's if you want to. Only if you want to."

"Of course I want to meet her, Eddie. Phone her. Tell her to come after lunch some time, when we're not so busy."

He reached for his mobile phone and made the call.

"She can come," he said. "She wants to meet you too."

"Good."

Eddie looked anxious. "I hope you like her, Isabel."

"I will."

He hesitated. "She's older than me, Isabel."

Isabel paused. "Much older?" she asked, trying to keep her tone natural. What if Diane were fifty?

"A bit," said Eddie. "Twenty-six."

Inwardly, Isabel breathed a sigh of relief. "Well, that's nothing, Eddie. I'm older than Jamie. It's nothing to worry about."

Eddie looked shifty. "There's something else," he said.

"Yes."

"I may have told her that I'm a bit older than I really am." He began to mumble. "I told her I'm twenty-four."

Isabel frowned. "That's a bit stupid, Eddie. What on earth possessed you to do that?"

The censure was unplanned; and she herself was surprised by its forcefulness. Almost immediately, she repented. Isabel was sensitive about telling other people what to do in a moralistic sense—that was most definitely **not** the role of the moral philosopher. Philosophy was there to guide people to the right and the good—not to wag a disapproving finger at them.

She tried to make up for her mistake. "I'm sorry, Eddie. I shouldn't have said it was stupid. It's just that . . ." She saw his face crumple. "It's just that it's best to be honest in a relationship. And I'm sure that you yourself want to be honest, don't you?"

"Of course."

She reached out to take his hand. He resisted for a moment, and then allowed her. "All of us are dishonest in some respects—from time to time. Hands up all those who've never been dishonest about something. See, my hand didn't go up."

He smiled weakly. "You don't lie to people. I know you don't."

"I try not to. But sometimes I'm tempted to. Lying can be so much easier."

"Easier?"

"Yes, in the short term. But any advantage it confers doesn't usually last very long."

He thought about this for a moment. "What shall I do?"

Isabel squeezed his hand. "That's for you to decide."

"I should tell her?"

"You could."

He nodded. "I will."

Isabel smiled at him encouragingly. "I suspect that you'll find she won't mind. If she loves you . . ." She was not sure whether she should have said that.

Eddie looked at her. "How can I know that? How can I know that she loves me?"

Isabel let go of his hand. "That sort of thing is usually obvious. If she wants to live with you, then I'd have thought that she probably does."

Eddie bit his lip. "I could ask her, I suppose."

"You could."

He hesitated for a moment before continuing. "How do you know that Jamie loves you?"

"He married me," said Isabel. "He stood in the Canongate Kirk and made a declaration to that effect. In public."

"That's what I want to do," said Eddie. "I want to stand up in front of a whole lot of people and tell Diane that I love her. And I want to do that soon."

"I understand," said Isabel. "That's how one feels when one is in love. But perhaps you shouldn't do anything too sudden."

"Why not?"

She did not want to pour cold water on his enthusiasm. "Because one of the things about falling in love is that you can fall out of it again. So you have to be sure."

He was adamant. "I am. I am sure."

• • •

LUNCHTIME WAS particularly busy that day. Both Eddie and Isabel were kept at it solidly from twelve-thirty until shortly after two, when the shop suddenly emptied.

"You go and sit down," said Eddie. "Diane will be here in ten minutes."

Isabel went to one of the tables and flopped down on a seat. One of the customers had left a newspaper behind, a copy of the **Financial Times,** and she paged through this idly as she waited for Eddie to bring the restorative cup of tea he had promised her. She was not particularly interested in the doings of the markets, but the paper had good arts coverage too, and she found herself absorbed in a review of a recent staging in London of a new opera on the life of a Colombian drug baron. Opera could be as recondite, as obscure, as it liked, she mused, because people expected it. And the plot really did not matter too much either way—Philip Glass's **Einstein on the Beach** had no plot at all, as far as Isabel could ascertain, and there were operas with plots so complex that lengthy explanations were required before one could work out what was going on. And a silly plot—of which there were numerous examples—was not necessarily a drawback. Isabel had always considered that **Così fan tutte** was all about nothing very much, and yet it was one of the most beautiful of Mozart's operas.

She read the critic's review. "Why are we fascinated by the life of large-scale wrongdoers?" he asked. "Why do we find the tawdry doings of the wicked anything but banal?"

Isabel stopped reading for a moment. The tawdry doings of the wicked: it was a beguilingly succinct dismissal of evil. And it was quite right, she thought, to deny any possible romance to wrongful deeds. Most major criminals, in or out of uniform, in or out of political office, in or out of the corporate boardroom, were simple bullies, prepared to use force to achieve their goals—and a Colombian drug lord would be a bully par excellence. Should we even bother to look at the life of a bully? What was there to say about it?

"This man," the critic continued, "is vile. He has used murder to progress through the criminal **cursus honorum**. He has profited from the endless misery of the illicit drug trade. He has grown rich on death. And yet here is a sophisticated London audience, a group of middle-class music-lovers, thrilling to the biography of this foul creature. And when he dies, as he does in the final scene, the music that accompanies his death is every bit as tragic as that which sees Mimi out in **La bohème**! Can that be right, or is there something here that needs to be considered by a social psychologist?"

Isabel looked up. Eddie was leading a young woman to her table. She thought: **the Huntress**, and then corrected herself. Not the Huntress; not the Huntress. Diane, plain and simple; Diane.

"This is Diane."

Isabel folded the paper and stood up to greet her visitor.

Eddie, who was clearly nervous, announced that he would bring two cups of tea. "Diane doesn't drink very much coffee, do you, Diane?"

"No," said Diane. "I don't."

"Too much coffee is bad for you," said Eddie.

"Everything in moderation," continued Isabel.

"In what?" asked Eddie nervously.

They were still standing, and Isabel gestured for Diane to sit down. "In moderation," she said to Eddie.

He nodded and went off behind the counter. Isabel noticed that Diane's eyes followed him. Yes, she thought, she loves him. I've seen the answer Eddie wanted.

"I'm really pleased that I'm getting the chance to meet you," said Isabel. "I'm very fond of Eddie."

She discreetly studied Diane as she spoke. Twenty-six was about right, she thought. And she's rather attractive in a slightly bony sort of way. Too thin? One had to be aware of that because so many people were anorexic now. Eddie himself was thin, though, and he definitely did not have an eating disorder, whatever other problems he might have. He ate rather a lot, in fact; he was always nibbling on the shavings from blocks of Parmesan or on scraps of ham or salami.

"He's very fond of you too," said Diane.

They were both silent for a moment. "What do you do?" asked Isabel.

"I'm a nurse," said Diane. "But now I'm studying to be a physiotherapist. I've got two years to go."

"They'll go very quickly," said Isabel.

"I think so," said Diane.

There was a further silence.

"Eddie tells me that you and he are planning to share," said Isabel. **To share** sounded better than **to live together,** she felt. It was not suggestive of anything beyond simple cohabitation, and sounded less prying as a result.

Diane said that this was their plan. "But . . ." Her voice trailed off.

Isabel waited.

"But I don't really see how we can."

"Why?"

"Money," she said simply. "We can't afford it. A flat costs at least eight hundred a month for a one-bedroom place. Usually more. Often a thousand."

"It's expensive," agreed Isabel. She was out of touch; she had thought three or four hundred was about right.

"And there's something else," Diane went on. "My parents are dead against it."

Isabel raised an eyebrow. "But you're twenty . . ."

"Twenty-six," supplied Diane. "Yes. And Eddie's . . ."

Isabel held her breath.

"Twenty-one," said Diane.

Isabel stared at her. She was taken aback, but now she made up her mind very quickly: this was her chance to defuse the situation for Eddie. "Eddie sometimes likes to think he's twenty-four," she said. "I suppose it's because he'd like to be twenty-four and sometimes we—"

"Sometimes we make things up," said Diane. She explained. "I know somebody who was in his year at school. That's how I realised." She shrugged. "I understand. I really do. I remember wanting to be older than I was. I really did. So, don't worry."

"He wants to tell you, you know," whispered Isabel. "Make it easy for him."

"I will," said Diane. "Of course I will."

Isabel felt a surge of affection rise within her. She liked this young woman. She was just right for Eddie. She loved him, and she was straightforward and sensible. She was exactly what Eddie needed.

"Your parents?" prompted Isabel.

Diane looked apologetic. "I live with them at the moment," she said. "They live here in Edinburgh, in Murrayfield. They've got this large house, you see, and it's much cheaper for me to stay there than to rent a flat, or even a room in a flat, while I'm a student."

"Naturally," said Isabel. "And lots of people do that, don't they?"

Diane confirmed this. "But it's a bit more complicated in my case," she said. "They give me money. I've taken out a large student loan, but it's never enough, even if you're careful. So they give me money each month."

"Many parents do that. And the child can pay it back later on."

Diane nodded. "But the complication is this: they don't like Eddie. They just don't."

"Have they seen much of him?"

"They've met him twice. It wasn't a success."

Isabel sighed. "Eddie might not come across all that well on a first or second meeting. He's shy. He becomes anxious."

Diane said that she knew that, but the problem with her parents was deeper-rooted. "They think he's not good enough for me. It's as simple as that. And . . ."

Isabel waited for her to continue.

"And they think that it's not going to last. They think that I'll grow out of him; that I'll realise we don't have very much in common; that I'll decide Eddie doesn't quite fit in." She paused. "They're snobs, you see."

Isabel was not sure what to say. It certainly sounded to her as though Diane's parents were behaving snobbishly, and yet she could hardly admit that she agreed with her and her parents really were snobs. One may speak disparagingly of one's own parents, but one did not like to hear others expressing the same sentiments.

"They've said that if I go and live with Eddie, then I won't get any more money. They spelled that out."

Isabel waited a few moments before saying anything. Then she said, "I'm very sorry to hear it."

"No," said Diane. "But you see the problem now?"

"I do," said Isabel.

"So we can't live together," said Diane. "It's just not on. Eddie thinks it is, and I'd love him to be right. But he isn't. It's just not possible. I'm too much in debt as it is. End of story."

CHAPTER SEVEN

❖

CAT'S RECOVERY WAS QUICKER than expected. On the following day she telephoned the delicatessen to tell Isabel that she was now up and about and that it looked as if the vomiting had stopped. She felt well enough to come in to work but thought it wiser to remain off for a further day in case she was still infectious. Isabel encouraged her in this. "The last thing you want is to pass these things on," she said. "One wouldn't wish projectile vomiting on anyone."

After Isabel had rung off, Eddie, who had overheard Isabel's side of the conversation, called out to her, "What did you say about projectile vomiting? Is she still doing it?"

"Why the big interest in it?" asked Isabel. Vomiting was vomiting, she thought, projectile or otherwise.

Eddie defended himself. "Well, it is pretty interesting, isn't it? I wonder how far she was projecting? Two or three feet, do you think?"

Isabel assumed an expression of disgust. "Really, Eddie, I don't share your fascination with the subject."

"Well, you mentioned it first," he said. "You were talking to her about it. You raised the subject."

"I just said that it's not something you would want to pass on to others. That's all. And it isn't, is it?"

"Of course not." He looked thoughtful. "I suppose with projectile vomiting you could really pass it on, couldn't you. If you hit anybody, even if they were standing a couple of feet away, thinking they were safe . . ."

"Eddie! You're disgusting."

"I was just thinking aloud."

"Well, please don't. You can keep those sorts of thoughts to yourself."

He was silent for a few moments. Isabel had noticed that Eddie's mood was very changeable that morning; perhaps he was anxious about Diane. She eyed him carefully. Now, something had come over him; maybe something triggered by this odd discussion. She had seen him do this before—slip into a sombre mood—although she thought that it happened much less frequently these days.

He lowered his voice; there was a customer within earshot, browsing the shelves. "What if you thought that you might . . . might have something because of something that happened . . . What should you do?"

Isabel looked at him with concern, causing him to glance away sharply.

"I'm not quite sure what you mean," she said carefully. "Do you mean, what if you think you've got some sort of infection: Should you go to a doctor? Is that what you're asking me?"

He hesitated. He was fiddling with the strings of his blue-striped butcher's apron. The strings were frayed and he was tugging at them nervously. She noticed again his less than clean fingernails. He was just a boy; just a boy with the unwashed hands that boys have. And suddenly, with no warning at all, he had become a frightened boy.

He spoke slowly, stumbling over the phrases. "Yes. That's right. Except it may not be your fault that you might have something that . . . something that you wouldn't want to have. And then you suddenly think, maybe I shouldn't take the risk of passing it on to anybody. Say, a heavy cold, or something like that. Something like what Cat's had. That stuff. Or even . . . or even something worse than that. But it wasn't your fault, you see."

She waited, but he seemed to have finished what he wanted to say.

"Something worse?" Isabel asked quietly.

Eddie nodded mutely. He had been standing on the other side of the counter, and Isabel now crossed over to him. Taking his hand, she led him through the door into Cat's office. He did not resist. His hand, she thought, felt so soft. Over by the shelves, the customer turned and looked briefly in their direction, but then turned away.

"Eddie, I think I know what you're talking about. I think I do—but I'm not sure."

"I . . ."

"No, listen to me, Eddie. You don't have to tell me. I don't want you to feel that you must. There are things that happen to people that are very cruel, and people don't have to talk about them if they don't want to. You know that, don't you?"

His gaze was fixed on the floor, his head bowed. But he nodded—almost imperceptibly.

"So all I'm going to say to you is this: I know that something bad happened to you, and I'm so, so sorry, Eddie. And if you think that because of this thing that happened you may need to have a check-up, then that's exactly the right thing to do. I'm sure that you'll be all right because it must have been quite some time ago, mustn't it, and you seem fine, don't you? But you can set your mind at rest."

He said nothing. He was weeping.

Isabel put her arm around his shoulder. She drew him to her. His frame was shaking with sobs. "Do you want me to go with you? I can go with you to the doctor."

He reached in his pocket for a handkerchief that was not there. Isabel took a tissue from the box on Cat's desk and handed it to him.

"Yes, please."

Isabel put her hand against his cheek. She reached for another tissue and dabbed at his tears.

"Dear Eddie," she whispered. "You've been very brave. And you're not alone, you know. You've got me, Cat, Diane. You've got all of us. Your friends."

"I feel stupid," he said. "And I feel dirty too."

She was shocked by his words. "Eddie, every one of us, every single one feels stupid about something. And maybe dirty too. And often it's not a big thing and it's not our fault either. All right, Eddie? All right?"

"I still feel stupid."

Isabel felt a rush of sympathy for the young man. "I know somebody who can help," she said. "They help people who have these worries. It's a charity. I've supported them in the past. You can talk to them and they'll arrange everything for you. And I'll come too, if you like."

His voice was small. "Please."

There was a knocking sound from outside. The customer who had been browsing was now standing at the counter knocking peremptorily on the glass, demanding service.

"I'm tempted to make her wait," said Isabel under her breath. "Impatient woman."

Eddie gave a wry smile. "She's a real cow, that woman. She comes in quite regularly. She thinks she owns the place."

Isabel touched him lightly on the shoulder. "Everything fine now?"

He nodded.

WHEN ISABEL RETURNED HOME that evening, exhausted by what had turned into a busy early evening in the delicatessen, Jamie had already bathed Charlie and dressed him in his pyjamas. The small boy, beaming with pleasure at the return of his mother, launched himself into Isabel's arms, burying his face in her hair.

"Clever Mummy," he said.

She looked at him with delight. "How very kind, Charlie. But I'm not all that clever, darling. Just average."

Jamie smiled. "Yes, you are. Not average, I mean. Yes, you're clever."

Isabel ruffled Charlie's hair. "**You're** the clever one, I think. You're the one who can tell me what two and three make."

"Five," said Charlie immediately.

Isabel looked at Jamie, who made an "I told you so" gesture.

"That's absolutely right," she said. "Two and three do indeed make five."

"Olive," said Charlie. That had been his first word, and he still referred to it frequently.

"Olive?"

"More olives," said Charlie. "More olives now."

Isabel looked at Jamie. "Have you been giving him olives?" she asked. She had been trying to cut down on the number of olives Charlie ate because there was too much salt in the brine in which they were stored. She did not think that too much salt would do him any good.

Jamie shook his head. "No," he said. "Grace . . ."

"Grace!" shouted Charlie. "Grace got olives."

Isabel sighed. It would be another thing they would have to discuss with Grace: olives and mathematics—both, in their way, problematic.

Jamie looked at his watch. He had a rehearsal that evening and would have to leave shortly if he were to be on time.

"Oh," he said, "that man you were talking about—Duncan Munrowe—called this afternoon. He said could you phone him back this evening. He asked me not to forget to pass on the message. He asked me twice. I got the message . . . about the message."

He handed her a slip of paper on which a telephone number had been pencilled.

"Did he say anything else?" asked Isabel.

Jamie thought for a moment. "He said something about there having been a development." He looked at her almost reproachfully. "Yes, that's what he said. He said there had been a development."

Isabel waited until Jamie had gone off to his rehearsal and she had settled Charlie before she telephoned Duncan Munrowe. Charlie was clingy—he often was when she had spent an entire day out of the house—and she allowed him a small extension on his day, sitting on the edge of his bed, his tiny hand now moving, now restful in hers, as she told him a story of her own making. She had turned out the light, but in spite of the curtains the room was not completely dark. At midsummer, in Scotland, the night is never truly dark, and Charlie's bedtime came well before sunset. Even later, approaching midnight, the sky only dims, fades into something between the clarity of day and the opacity of night, a long-drawn-out crepuscule.

A week or two earlier she had started to tell Charlie a story that had immediately thrilled him and that he had insisted on hearing again. It had become a serial, the episodic life of a man made out of mud, who loved the rain but at the same time had to avoid it—for obvious reasons. "He'd melt, you see," she said. And Charlie had nodded wisely; he knew that from sand-play at the nursery.

"Some of his friends had melted," said Isabel. "And he missed them."

She did not know why she had said that; it was the wrong note to introduce into a bedtime story; an adult note of loss that would only sadden a child. And yet every child had to confront the notion of loss at some time, and perhaps this moment came earlier than we liked to imagine.

"He could make his friends again," she added. "He could find some mud and make his friends again."

"No," said Charlie. "Friends all gone."

But now the man made out of mud was happy, as he had discovered a pond where mud ducks lived and he was throwing bread made out of mud to these mud ducks. Not a sophisticated story line, thought Isabel, but Charlie was rapt; this was social realism to him because he knew a real pond where there were real ducks to which he threw bread with his father.

The story over, and Charlie on the verge of sleep, Isabel leaned forward and planted a kiss on his brow. She felt a wisp of his hair against her lips; it was so fine, and smelled of soap and the fresh linen of his pillow, and something else that she could only label love, or happiness, or something like that. Then she crept out of the room and made her way into her study where she had placed Jamie's note on her desk.

She dialled the number. It took a long time for the telephone to be answered, but Isabel was prepared for this; people who lived in the country often seemed to take much longer to answer than those in towns. Their houses were bigger. She had never seen Munrowe House but she could imagine that it had lengthy corridors and inconveniently placed telephones. She imagined a bell ringing in one of those corridors, and Duncan looking up from what he was doing and trudging off to answer it.

"Munrowe House," he announced politely.

It sounded quite appropriate to Isabel, but she could not help but wonder: At what point should one give the name of one's house on the telephone? It would sound ridiculous to answer 36 Oak Avenue, or Flat 28, or something of that sort.

"Munrowe House," Duncan repeated.

She thought: **The house speaks**, and smiled. "It's Isabel Dalhousie."

He thanked her for calling back. "I didn't want to burden your . . ."

"Husband. It was my husband."

"Yes, I didn't want to burden your husband with the details, but the other side has been in touch again."

She found the expression rather strange. "The other side" was how lawyers spoke in litigation. Or spies, she imagined. But the thieves really were the other side, she thought. Criminals of any sort put themselves on the other side from the rest of us who were not criminals, or were only occasionally criminal. Isabel had received a parking ticket recently and had reflected on the fact that she was required to pay a fine. Did that make her a criminal, even if only briefly and in a very attenuated way? Surely not. Yet it was still an offence that she had committed—the wording of the penalty notice made that quite clear.

"What did they say?" she asked.

"They want a meeting. They've given me a time."

"I see."

She could hear Duncan's breathing at the other end of the line. She could sense his anxiety.

"Have you spoken to the insurance people?"

He said that he had. "They wanted to come but I told them that the other side said that they wanted to see only me." He paused. "And I'm going to interpret that as meaning you and me. They'll just have to accept that."

She wanted to repeat what she had said before—that she did not see what she could possibly bring to such a meeting, but she had agreed to be there and she would not renege on it.

"They haven't given me much warning," Duncan went on. "They want to meet tomorrow. Do you think you could possibly make it?"

Cat would be back and Isabel would not be needed at the delicatessen. But there were those journal proofs, which even now stared reproachfully at her from their position at the top of her in-tray. She sighed, and failed, through sheer tiredness, to mask the sound.

"I know it's no notice at all," said Duncan apologetically. "It's not my idea . . ."

Isabel reassured him. "No, don't apologise. I'll be all right. Where is the meeting going to be?"

She was not prepared for his answer.

"Here. At the house."

He detected her surprise. "I know," he said. "It sounds very brazen, but I gather this is not the thieves themselves we'll be meeting, but a lawyer acting for them, or for an intermediary."

"Their lawyer!"

Duncan explained that the insurers had told him at the outset that anybody who did get in touch would probably not be the original thief, or even the people in possession of the painting. "They said that it could be lawyers," he said. "And they were right."

"Do lawyers write anonymous letters? You said the original letter was anonymous." She imagined an anonymous letter from a firm of lawyers. It would be signed **Anon** or **From a Friend,** as anonymous letters tended to be, but it would then say: **For and on behalf of Messrs . . .** and give the name of a firm.

"No, it's not anonymous," said Duncan. "It's

not from the person who wrote the original letter. This one is on headed notepaper."

"Let me get this straight," Isabel said. "This is a lawyer acting for somebody who isn't the thief but who knows the thief? Is that right?"

"Yes."

"So we're two links away from the thief? There's the thief, then there's a second person, and then there's the lawyer, who's acting on behalf of the second person."

Duncan was patient. "Yes, that's more or less it. The insurers said that this is the way it often happens. The second person—the intermediary—goes to a lawyer and says, 'I hear there's a reward for the return of such a painting. Well, I know where it is and will you arrange for me to get the reward if I tell you where the painting is?' That's one of the ways it can happen. There are, of course, others."

She asked about these other ways.

"If there's no reward, the intermediary can just ask for money from the owner—which means ultimately from the insurer, as the insurer may already have paid up. Or he can go straight to the insurer and ask for money for the safe return of the painting."

Isabel thought about this. "That sounds like paying ransom," she said.

Duncan agreed. "And nobody likes to do that."

"Well, we can talk further about it," said Isabel. "Shall I come up a bit before the meeting?"

"Yes. Could you make it before ten in the morning?"

She thought of her car. She had not used it for weeks and she hoped that it would start. Jamie had been pressing her to get a new one, but she was attached to her green Swedish car and was unwilling to replace it. Swedish cars were under threat and might disappear—overtaken by a torrent of anodyne cars from somewhere on the other side of the world, produced in great numbers in factories run and staffed by robots; those strange, impersonal factories in which there appeared to be no people, just machines with extended mechanical arms that moved according to some pre-programmed choreography. She did not want that. She wanted a car with idiosyncratic lines; a car that looked at home on winding Scottish roads, that could complement a backdrop of granite and heather. As long as it started. That was important too.

She paused. Was there anything wrong in wanting to have things about you that were made in places you knew, or liked? Was it a form of nationalism—a jingoistic position that was prepared to expect other people to import one's goods but not to buy theirs? For a long time—since the Industrial Revolution really—the West had expected the East to buy the things we made, but now the tables had been turned and they were making things more quickly and cheaply than we were. Was it unfair, then, to turn round and decline their goods in favour of our own? Or could one prefer one's own goods because they were made by people for whom one had, by virtue of shared citizenship, some form of responsibility? **Charity begins at home**. Was that a narrow, selfish adage or was it simply an inescapable, bedrock fact of life in human society? Does the one in need on your doorstep have a greater claim than the one in need in a distant country—if the level of need in each case is exactly the same? It was an old, old problem—the sort of thing that students of philosophy discussed over endless cups of coffee in their first year of study, little imagining that they would still be pondering the very same question twenty years later. And twenty years later, were the answers any clearer? Isabel thought they probably were not. But then one thing you did learn with the passage of time was not to ask too many questions. That was the difference, she decided, between being twenty and being forty. That, and other things, of course.

CHAPTER EIGHT

THE CAR STARTED UNCOMPLAININGLY, only protesting slightly as it moved the first few inches of the forty-mile journey to Munrowe House. It was the brakes, Isabel realised: two weeks without movement in the damp climate of Scotland meant that tiny filaments of rust would have built up between the brake pads and brake drum, the beginning of a slow bonding that could turn into a more permanent embrace if the car was unused for six months—or so her mechanic, the obliging Mr. Cooper at the small garage on the canal, had told her. "Cars are like people," he had said. "We rust up if we don't exercise; well, so do they." He had gone on to warn her of the consequences of fluids being left in an engine that was idle for months on end; of how they would eventually eat away at the pipes in which they were trapped, making irreparable holes in cooling systems, causing radiators to fall from their mounts. All of that could happen so easily, he said, and he had then fixed her with a baleful stare, as might a doctor who knew that his advice on diet or exercise would go unheeded.

Each time the car started after a spell of disuse, Isabel vowed to treat it better in the future and to give it the weekly ten-mile run that Mr. Cooper recommended; but knew that she would not, and that one day his predictions would come true. For now, though, the Swedish car sounded contented enough, and smelled just right too: that odd odour it had—a mixture of old leather, rubber and machine; a mustiness that would be dispelled by the winding down of a window and the resulting rush of morning air.

It was shortly after eight o'clock when she left the house, which meant that she would have an hour for the journey and an hour to talk to Duncan before the arrival at ten of the lawyer—the thief's lawyer, as she thought of him. That took some getting used to—the notion that those who flouted the law could use the law, even through an intermediary, to pursue their objectives. But lawyers did precisely that; that was the whole reason for their existence: they put forward a point of view even if that position was manifestly unworthy or perverse. Lawyers stood up in criminal courts everywhere, every day, and argued on behalf of defendants who had hurt others in all those ways in which others can be hurt. She understood that well enough: everybody had this right and at least some of those accused were innocent. Yet this was something different: here a lawyer seemed to be assisting somebody to benefit from a crime rather than defending somebody who had already committed the crime. It somehow **felt** different . . .

The traffic was light. Isabel drove out by way of Colinton, past the Victorian military barracks at Redford, and then on to the road that skirted the city and the lower slopes of the Pentland Hills. The sky was empty to the south, over the soft folds of the Pentlands, but to the north there was a bank of cirro-cumulus, a mackerel sky, or **Schaefchenwolken**—"sheep cloud"—as she remembered her father calling it. For some reason he had used German when talking about clouds and sea conditions; an odd habit that she had accepted as just being one of the things he did. "The weather," he had once said to her, smiling, "is German. I don't know why; it just is. Sorry."

And there were those **Schaefchenwolken**, high above Fife and stretching out over the

North Sea. That meant a depression was on the way, and rain might arrive in a few hours, even if for the moment the weather was fine. Isabel sat back in her seat and relaxed her grip on the wheel, allowing her mind to wander. There was a lot to think about: the conversation that she knew she would have to have with Grace about mathematics; the anxieties that poor Eddie had revealed the day before and that would require what was bound to be an emotionally trying trip to the doctor. She reflected on this and decided that Eddie had no reason to worry: they must have talked to him about it when whatever had happened happened. And then it occurred to her that he might not have reported it. That was always possible; people were too ashamed, they suffered in silence. And if that were the case, then Eddie would have received no help, no support at all. Did Cat know? Was she aware of what he might have been going through all these years?

And then there was Cat herself to worry about. There had been no word of a boyfriend for some time now, which might be good news, or might just as likely be bad. If there were no boyfriend, then it could be a sign that Cat was taking a romantic sabbatical—a nice notion, that, thought Isabel. "I'm sorry, I can't get emotionally involved with you—I'm on sabbatical from that sort of thing." It would be like a strict diet: no chocolates, no lovers. And people might speak with the same enthusiasm about the benefits: "Do you know, I've felt so much better, so much lighter, since I gave up men. I have so much more energy, and my clothes seem to fit me again."

On the other hand, Cat's silence on this topic might mean that there was an unsuitable man in the background, concealed lest Isabel slip into disapproving-relative mode. That had happened before, when Isabel had only found out about a boyfriend of Cat's by accident. That awful tightrope walker, for example: Cat had initially not been open about him—understandably so. If I were going out with a diminutive tightrope walker who wore elevator shoes, then I might be reticent too . . . Isabel stopped herself. It was wrong to write him off because he was very short—that had no bearing on merit. Gandhi had been very short, as had Beethoven. But Bruno, as the tightrope walker was called, was unlike Gandhi or Beethoven: he had no merits at all—at least as far as she could make out; he was domineering and, she suspected, violent too. She shuddered. What would have happened if Cat had married him and she, Isabel, had had to welcome him into the family? She would have done her best, but surely her true feelings would have shown and Cat, sensing this, would have challenged her. "You don't like him, do you, Isabel? You don't like him because he's a tightrope walker." "Listen, Cat, that's got nothing to do with it. It's him; it's what he is within himself that's the problem."

By the time Isabel drew level with Stirling, the mackerel sky had drifted away. She glanced at the shape of Stirling Castle against its backdrop of green hills, with the Wallace Monument rising spikily behind it. Isabel smiled. Scottish rugby crowds still sang about William Wallace, seven hundred years after he had defeated the English army of cruel Edward, "and sent him packing," as the song had it, "tae think again." Well, he had, she supposed, but why did we still need to sing about it? She automatically answered her own question: **Because we may not have very much else, apart from our past**. It was not the answer she had expected to arrive at, and she thought it was probably wrong, and defeatist. We did have a great deal else. We had this land that was unfolding before her now as she turned off towards Doune; these fields and these soft hills and this sky and this light and these rivers that were pure and fresh, and this music that could send shivers of pleasure up the spine and make one so proud of Scotland and of belonging. We had all that.

DUNCAN MUNROWE CAME OUT of his front door to greet her. "Your car," he said, "is lovely."

"It doesn't always start."

He smiled, and touched the roof of the car as if to confirm that it was real. "The best cars don't," he said. "I'd never want a car that had so little personality that it always started."

This brief exchange confirmed what she had felt over that lunch in Edinburgh. Her host was slightly eccentric. Out of touch with the modern world. His own man.

She looked up at the front of the house. It was fairly modest in its proportions—a comfortable country house of the sort that in the very early eighteenth century, when she suspected it was built, would have housed a minor country gentleman—one who did not actually have to farm, but had the farming done for him. And it still housed exactly such a man, she thought, as she glanced discreetly at Duncan and took in his outfit: the moleskin trousers, the waistcoat, the Harris tweed jacket. One would not drive a tractor or unload bales of hay in those clothes. One might watch other people do it instead. And that, she thought, was a good enough definition of the **rentier** class as any. And of me too, she found herself thinking, guiltily. The land and gas company in Louisiana that enabled her to live as she did was based on the physical work of others—people whom she did not know. Her maternal great-grandfather had been responsible for that, and the trickle-down effect had seen to the rest. He would never have imagined that she, his descendant, living in twenty-first-century Scotland, and editing a philosophical review, of all things, would be reaping the benefits of the financial plotting and scheming at which family history held him to have been such a master. At least it was not plantation money—or slave money, to give it the name that more accurately reflected its origins. They had not been involved in that, as far as Isabel knew, for had they been, she could never have accepted the legacy, even generations later. Or at least she hoped she would not have accepted it, although there was plenty of slave money in Britain. There had been the great plantations in the West Indies, and the descendants of the people who benefited from those—the sugar families and others—must still be there, still enjoying, although attenuated by the years that had passed, their sticky, suffering-based fortunes. She hoped she would never have accepted it, or its equivalent, although honesty required one to remind oneself that when there were bills to be paid, an offer of money was harder to reject than when there were no such bills. Other people's money, we tell ourselves, is always less deserved than our own.

At school she had known a girl who came from a family that had done very well out of coal mining two generations earlier. They had been good people, and charitably inclined, but Isabel had once said to this girl, with all the thoughtlessness of her sixteen years, "Think of all the miners who got sick and died." And the girl had stared at her mutely, and turned white, and then cried. Something had been said by the girl's father to Isabel's father—they knew one another through membership of a golf club—and Isabel's father, who never spoke harshly, had said to her, "Don't blame other people for things that happened before they were born. And don't blame them for things that seemed right at the time, even if we come to see that they aren't right any more. And finally, remember that our people—that's your mother's people and my people—were probably not angels, because **nobody** was an angel in those days, except those people at the bottom of everything, who had no alternative." He had held her gaze, and she had shrivelled inside with embarrassment and guilt. It had been so easy to strike a position of moral superiority—it always is—but she had not intended to hurt her friend. Her father had paused for a moment, and judged the lesson to have been learned. "Remember that, darling, and say sorry for what you said. That's all you have to do."

Was Duncan speaking to her? She had been thinking about unearned money and her father and coal mining, and as often happened when she was thinking, time became slightly distorted and seemed to pass without her realising it.

"Sorry, what was that?"

"Nothing," he said. "I didn't say anything."

She looked again at the front of the house. "Early eighteenth century?"

He smiled. "Very close. 1698. There's a date carved into one of the lintels on the other side." He gestured towards the door. "Do come in. I'll show you round, if you like. My wife, I'm afraid, is in London. We have a small flat down there, and she likes going to the opera."

"So do I," said Isabel. "If I lived in London, I'd live at the ENO and Covent Garden. Or New York. Imagine living in Manhattan and being able to walk—to walk!—to the Met."

"I'm told you're half American," he said.

They were entering the hall—a comfortable, simply furnished room from which a stone staircase ascended at the far end.

"Yes," said Isabel. "On my mother's side." And then she wondered: Who told him? Did Martha know about her mother? Possibly. Or had he been asking people about her? She looked up at the ceiling, which had a surprisingly elaborate cornice: plaster thistles, twined about one another, were interspersed with roses. It was in good condition, and although it was predominantly white, here and there were traces of other colours: the thistles green in their foliage and receptacles, with faded purple just to be made out on some of the flower heads. The roses, though, were untouched, and were the white of the surrounding plaster, which was significant.

"Roses," she said.

Duncan followed her glance. "Yes. Roses." He paused and said, "Long before our time. My grandfather bought this place in the nineteen twenties. The roses, we think, date back to the early seventeen hundreds. And, yes, they are—"

"Jacobite."

He nodded. "The family who lived here then were fairly strongly of that persuasion." He looked up at the cornice. "The Jacobite white rose. We believe that one of them helped Prince Charlie on his way to Edinburgh. Fed his troops or something like that. Probably gave him money."

"And suffered the consequences when Charlie came unstuck?"

He looked down again. There was sympathy in his eyes. "They lost the place, but stayed alive. Others were less lucky."

She reflected on how human sympathy could be felt for ancient misfortune. The Jacobite uprising—that lost cause that almost succeeded—had been in 1745; over two hundred and fifty years separated us from them, and Duncan felt sympathy for those amongst the ranks of the losers who had occupied his house. One could feel sorry for any suffering, Isabel supposed, even if it was a long time ago, but surely there were limits—a point at which hearing of suffering no longer engaged our emotions. The Christians facing the lions in Rome? The victims of the Assyrians who enjoyed massacring the inhabitants of besieged towns? The distance in time was too great; suffering, to move us, must be warmer than that.

Suddenly she said, "It helps if you know the name."

He looked at her in puzzlement. "I'm sorry . . . I'm not quite with you."

She explained. "I was thinking about suffering

and the passage of time. We can feel more sympathy for the victims whose names we know."

He looked at her with interest. "Yes, I suppose that's right."

"Aberdeen man lost at sea," she muttered.

"What? Aberdeen . . ."

"It's how an Aberdeen newspaper was said to have reported the sinking of the **Titanic**. I suspect it's apocryphal, but it makes the point, doesn't it?"

He laughed. "Local papers always see the world in that way. That's what they're about." He gestured for her to follow him and led the way into a room off the back of the hall. "The library," he said. "Rather a lot of unread books."

Her eyes went to the shelves that stretched up to within a few inches of the ceiling. All four walls were covered; piles of books stood here and there, teetering, vulnerable, she judged, to the slightest footfall. "But who doesn't have a lot of unread books? It's nice, though, just to know that they're there."

He picked up a book that had been placed on the edge of a nearby shelf. "I suspect you've read much more than I have. Scott. You know, I've only read one of his novels? Just one. **Rob Roy**."

"Scott was very prolix. You can't read everything. I've never got beyond the beginning of Proust. I love him, but I can't seem to get beyond about page three."

They were comfortable in each other's company, and this confession seemed to accentuate the ease of their relationship. The confession itself was not entirely true; Isabel had read more Proust than that, but other people undoubtedly found it reassuring to think that one had only read a few pages. Certainly those who claimed to have read Proust in his entirety got scant sympathy from others. And yet, she suddenly wondered, should you actually lie about how much Proust you've read? Some politicians, she reminded herself, did that—or the equivalent—when they claimed to be down-to-earth, no-nonsense types, just like the voters, when all the time they were secretly delighting in Proust . . .

"We should take a look at some of the paintings," Duncan said. "That's more to the point."

Isabel put Proust out of her mind and followed Duncan into a large drawing room. In some respects it was typical of drawing rooms in such houses, furnished with armchairs and sofas in good but faded fabric, a sofa table with a silver tray on which stood a couple of decanters, a fireplace—Robert Adam or a follower, she thought—and this was where the similarity with a hundred such rooms in Scottish country houses ended: the paintings. One wall was completely covered, floor to ceiling, hung with large works which even as she entered and saw them side on, Isabel could more or less identify: a small Renoir of a woman, ruddy-cheeked as all of his women, in a hat; a de Hooch interior, with a Dutch girl and light slanting in from a window—almost a Vermeer, but not quite; what looked like a Bonnard—and must have been, Isabel decided.

She caught her breath. "I hadn't expected . . ."

"We're very lucky," he said.

Isabel moved into the middle of the room to get a better view of the paintings. "There's everything you'd want," she said.

"That's what people tell me," said Duncan. "And that's where the Poussin was. Over there." He directed Isabel's attention to the wall above the fireplace.

If she had expected a glaring hole, she was disappointed. An ornate candlestick, in candelabra style with crystal drops, had been placed at either end of the mantelpiece and had made up for any visual emptiness that the removal of the Poussin might have caused. She could just discern, though, a rectangular shape—a section of wallpaper that had been protected from fading by the picture that had once hung there.

"I can see where it was," she said quietly. "It must break your heart."

He looked at her in gratitude—as if she were the first person to acknowledge his loss. Others must have said something, she thought; he must have been comforted. Unless there were those around him who **wanted** him to lose his Poussin . . . A jealous neighbour, one with no paintings of his own, might have smarted at the thought of the great works nearby. Farmers could be envious of each other, she had heard; could resent another's better crops, better animals. **Thou shalt not covet thy neighbour's ox, nor ass.** The Commandment was unambiguous, and also mentioned wives and houses. **Nor his Poussin, if he hath one . . .**

Duncan was saying something about one of the other paintings. ". . . it's thought to be the first of a number of paintings that Lotto did for . . ." Yes, how interesting. Of course. And what better way of dealing with sheer envy than stealing the thing of which you feel so envious. **It's mine now, it's mine!** A secret pleasure, and not enough for some, no doubt, but there were many for whom covert satisfaction would be quite enough and sweeter, too, than any public triumph.

"There are others upstairs. Rather more, I'm afraid." He looked at his watch. "I should show you the letter."

Isabel dragged herself away from the paintings. "I'd like to see it."

"We can look at it in the kitchen," he said. "I have coffee brewing, if you'd like a cup."

They left the hall to follow a short corridor into a kitchen dominated by a large cooking range and a scrubbed pine table. Three cups were neatly lined up on the table, alongside a jug of milk and a bowl of sugar lumps.

Duncan handed her a piece of paper as she sat down. "This is it," he said.

"Thank you."

He remained silent as she turned her attention to the paper. It was a printed letter, headed with the name of a firm of solicitors in Perth. Isabel thought it looked slightly crudely printed—thanks to modern printers, anybody could make a letterhead these days, and put anything they chose on it. At the foot of the letter were two names—the names of the partners, both women.

It did not take long for Isabel to read. The letter was signed by a Heather Darnt, one of the partners listed. It established that the firm was acting for a client who was aware of the whereabouts of the painting. **We stress that our client is not the party responsible for the theft**. Why not say **the thief**? thought Isabel.

Our client is keen to facilitate the return of this painting, the letter went on. **He does this in the hope that he can in this way prevent damage being done to an important piece of artistic heritage. That is his only motivation.**

That, and money? Isabel asked herself.

CHAPTER NINE

❖

ISABEL LOOKED AT HER WATCH. She had imagined that they would have plenty of opportunity to talk before the lawyer arrived, but the time seemed to have disappeared. There was a lot she wanted to discuss with Duncan, but now there was only half an hour before they would be joined by the lawyer. There would be discussion of the recovery of the painting: proposals, no doubt, and figures. She was struck by the naked effrontery of it—an effrontery that was there, she supposed, in all deliberate crime. By his acts, the criminal effectively said to the victim: **You don't matter**. And that, Isabel thought, was the most fundamentally wrong of all attitudes, whether it lay behind acts of great cruelty or the mundane crime of bag-snatching. **You don't matter**. How could anybody look another person in the eye and say that? Quite easily, it seemed—there were enough instances of it, every day, every moment of every day, in just about every context of human life.

When Isabel had read the letter, Duncan suggested that they move through to the drawing room, taking their coffee with them. Once there, they seated themselves on a settee, Duncan at one end, Isabel at the other. Isabel noticed how comfortable the settee was, with its plumped-up feather cushions. Penury was a matter of hard chairs and mean cushions; prosperity—old money—was a matter of feathers: an absurd reductionist view of it, but at times quite strikingly true.

"They could have taken anything else," Duncan remarked. "They could have taken any of the others and I wouldn't have felt it." He pointed to the wall behind them. "That Gimignani behind us," he said, "I wouldn't have blinked an eyelid if they'd carted that off. Or the Ramsays or the Raeburns. You can replace those—not with exactly the same painting, but something that does pretty much the same job."

"They knew its value," said Isabel.

He nodded miserably. "I know," he said. "But somehow it made it personal. As if they wanted to hurt me."

"I doubt that," said Isabel. "If they wanted to hurt you, they could have done something really unpleasant. Set fire to something perhaps. There are plenty of ways of hurting somebody in such a manner that you can get away with it."

"I suppose so."

She watched him. He belonged to a sector of society that did not like to show its feelings. Displays of emotion, in their view, were vulgar—showy. And yet there was no doubt in her mind now as to how he was feeling.

"I assume that the existence of the painting was well enough known," said Isabel.

Duncan thought for a moment. "If you did your research," he said. "It's in some of the books on Poussin—not in others. Under the photograph it usually just says **Private Collection**, but there's a literature on this. If you trace the painting's progress through the salerooms, you can find out when it was bought by my grandfather. And you'll see his name down as the purchaser. Those were more trusting days."

Isabel was interested in his mention of the literature. "People have written about it?"

"Yes. There was a small literature on it before Blunt made his attribution. Prior to that, it was thought to be by a seventeenth-century Veronese painter. Then Blunt looked at it and gave it the nod. His word counted for more than anything else at the time."

"Anthony Blunt?"

Duncan smiled. "The very same. Better known as a spy than as the authority on Poussin, I suspect." He paused, and glanced quickly at his watch. He was anxious—she could see that.

"When did he see it?"

"In the mid-seventies. A guest recognised it—a distant cousin of my father's who happened to be an art historian. He had been at the Courtauld during Blunt's reign there, and he knew him well enough to phone him up and tell him about it. He said that he was sure enough to encourage Blunt to come up to look at it—my father was unwilling to let it leave the house. He was very attached to that painting."

"So Blunt came up?"

"Yes, he did. He was very grand, apparently. Very tall and with a certain haughty detachment. He could look right through you, my father said. I remember his saying that Blunt's look was like ice."

Isabel had read something to that effect. And yet Blunt was human; others had spoken of his generosity, his kindness, his warmth. "Perhaps he wanted to keep people at a distance. Shyness sometimes has the same effect, and then we reach the conclusion that somebody is cold, when in fact they're just reserved."

Duncan agreed. "Yes, people are very quick to dismiss others they've never met. Blunt kept his distance, I imagine, and I don't see what's wrong with that. I can't understand why people expect everyone to open up immediately to everyone they meet." He looked at her, as if assessing whether they could speak at this greater level of intimacy. "Reticence can be a virtue, don't you think?"

Isabel was not sure. "Keeping yourself to yourself? Possibly . . ."

Duncan continued. "Not wearing your heart on your sleeve. Not displaying your private life for all to see."

"As on those television programmes? Where people expose their relationship problems to the public gaze?"

He nodded. "Exactly. We live in an age where the assumption is made that you can—perhaps should—talk about every aspect of your life, even to complete strangers."

"Some would simply call that honesty," Isabel suggested. And she thought of a line from Auden where he talked about being **honest like children**. It was from the Freud poem; Auden said that Freud taught us the benefit of such honesty. Children were honest—often disarmingly so—but could an adult be the same?

Duncan shifted slightly further down the settee, away from her—as if distancing himself—putting into practice the reticence to which he had just referred. "Sorry," he said. "I'm not being rude—or unduly reticent. It's just that the sun was getting in my eyes."

A beam of morning sun, warm and discrete, a shaft of yellow, was coming in through a window on the side of the room; it was this that he had shifted to avoid. **A yellow knife,** thought Isabel; **a yellow knife through the air of the room.**

"Yes, we have to be honest," he said. "But honesty is not incompatible with a certain reserve, or reticence—call it what you will. Call it privacy, perhaps. It makes sense, I should have thought, to talk about a sense of privacy. People have every right to some degree of privacy and perhaps that's what reserved people feel. They value their privacy."

Isabel had nothing against that. She, too, believed that there were areas of our lives that we were entitled to guard against the eyes of others. People may have nothing to hide in their living rooms, but they were entitled to curtains that would keep others from looking in.

"What you say is interesting," she said. "And I think I agree with you—for the most part."

He smiled. "Good. I imagined that we might agree on quite a number of subjects."

That, she realised, was a statement of friendship. "So did I," she said.

She gazed thoughtfully at the place where the Poussin had been. Sir Anthony Blunt had been gay.

She dropped the question into the conversation without really considering it; it seemed to be the next place for their discussion to go. "Do you think that people need to state their sexuality? Do they need to tell people?"

He did not answer immediately, and she glanced at him. He had folded his arms across his chest, a gesture that Isabel always interpreted as protective. Had she unthinkingly presumed too much by asking the question? Had she strayed into the very territory of the private they had been discussing?

His tone now was distant. "No," he said. "It's their own business. What does it matter to the rest of us if somebody is . . . that way? I don't see it as any business of mine, frankly."

She noted his use of the term **that way**. It was old-fashioned, but she felt that it also disclosed a certain distaste. Not to use an accepted term raised the distinct possibility that one did not like that expression, or did not share the assumptions that went with it. **Gay** was a word that gay people themselves had endorsed and was different, therefore, from the mean-spirited language that others had used in the past.

The topic was obviously not one he wanted to discuss, and so she moved away from it, not wishing to intrude further.

"So you say Blunt accepted the painting?" she asked.

Duncan seemed relieved that they had come back to art. "Yes. I was in my late teens then and not all that interested in the paintings. I knew what they were, but I had yet to develop much knowledge of art. That came a bit later."

"Were you here when Blunt came?"

"No, I was away at boarding school. I heard about it from my father."

"You heard about the icy look?"

"Yes, although I wouldn't want to make too much of that—as I've said. I was more interested in the fact that he came up after he had been revealed as a Soviet spy. I'd read about all that in the newspapers, of course. They had a field day, as you can imagine."

"Indeed they did," said Isabel. "After all, who could invent a better story for them? Soviet agents. The rarefied world of art connoisseurship. The fact that he was some sort of cousin of the Queen's. There was something for everybody in it." She had been about to add sex to the list, but stopped herself in time.

"They loved it. They bayed for his blood, but, as you know, he had been given immunity by the government in return for spilling the beans. They couldn't prosecute him or no government immunity would be worth the paper it's written on in the future."

Isabel agreed. **Pacta sunt servanda**—agreements should be honoured. It was one of the most basic of the rules we needed to function as a society. **Keep your promises**.

"He was a broken man afterwards," said Duncan. "I read a biography a few years ago that described it rather well. He continued to live in London but was careful about going out. He went to the cinema in Notting Hill once and was recognised. The audience slow-handclapped him until he left. Can you imagine it?"

Isabel was busy doing just that. She saw the cinema and Blunt coming in—that tall, aesthetically distinguished figure who must have found it very difficult to appear anonymous. She saw him sitting down in his seat, perhaps with a friend or two—some people, at least, stuck by him—some of his old friends and students from the Courtauld who either forgave him or thought there was nothing to forgive. She saw another member of the audience a few rows forward turn his neck and stare and then whisper to those around him. And then she saw more heads craning to see whether it really was him, and then, perhaps more as a joke than anything else, or an act of bravado, a man somewhere started to clap slowly. And then the psychology of the crowd took over, and people felt the bravery of the group. The slow-handclapping swelled—a crowd will always pick up a stone—and Blunt, at first confused, begins to realise it is him they want to leave. Me? A glance exchanged with his companions, and then a retreat that not even a proud and unrepentant man—if he really was like that—could find anything but humiliating. **Their bad manners**, a companion whispers, but Blunt, too shocked, is unable to speak.

"He never apologised," said Isabel. "Or did he?"

"He said that he regretted it," said Duncan. "That's not the same thing as saying sorry."

"But perhaps he didn't feel sorry," said Isabel. "He was recruited in the nineteen thirties, wasn't he? A lot of people believed then that communism—and the Soviet Union—were the only forces really standing up to fascism. So maybe he felt that what he did was right."

Duncan did not disagree. “Yes, it was ideological—to begin with. Then when Stalin came along it was too late. Blunt wanted out, but it was difficult.”

“So he thought he had done the right thing?”

“Undoubtedly.”

Isabel gave this some thought. “But he was wrong, wasn’t he? And the whole point of his offence was that he betrayed his country.”

Duncan’s smile was challenging. “Is that always wrong?”

She thought that if he were expecting a simple answer, she was not going to give him one. “That depends on what one’s country is up to, doesn’t it? We don’t think that people who betray their own country when it happens to be a tyranny are doing wrong, do we? Russians who betrayed the Soviet Union were welcomed here with open arms, I seem to remember.”

“So no real betrayal?” he said. “Because they were acting in the real interests of their country anyway—those interests being obscured by the tyranny in power?”

“Something like that. There’s a difference between loyalty to a government and loyalty to a country.”

He pressed further. “Which would cover Blunt? And Philby? And Maclean and Burgess?”

"We didn't have a tyranny in power. That's the difference."

She could see that he was not prepared to make that distinction. "I'm not happy about that," he said. "Let's say that there was a coup in this country—in Britain—and we had an unelected government. We could still owe a duty of loyalty to our fellow citizens not to betray the state of which we were all members."

Isabel looked up at the ceiling. There was a crack in the plaster, stretching from one side to the other, a zigzag, a San Andreas fault. "Tribal feeling?"

She had not intended to sound flippant, and she was not ready for the look of sheer anger that passed across his face. "I'm sorry," she said. "I didn't mean to make light of it."

He clearly felt guilty for showing his anger. According to the code by which he lived, a gentleman did not do that. That's what he was thinking, she decided; that's why he was reproaching himself.

He made a reassuring gesture. "I know that." He paused. "You know, it's very stimulating for me to have this conversation. Living out here, I don't get enough of that sort of thing. My neighbours . . ." He sighed. "They don't talk about these things—their interests are mostly horses and cattle. I couldn't discuss loyalty with them—not at all: they'd find it too awkward."

"That's understandable," said Isabel. "Most people don't question themselves about such matters."

"Maybe they should," Duncan mused. "Maybe we're all too used to spending our time in a state of . . ." He frowned as he tried to find the right term. "In a state of deadened acceptance rather than . . ." Again he struggled. "Engagement. Yes, that's it—engagement."

"Maybe."

He brushed some imaginary lint off his trousers; we clean things that are already clean. His shoes, Isabel noticed, were highly polished—so highly so that they caught the light from the window, as a mirror might. Why, she wondered, would one spend so much time—and it must have taken a lot of time to get that shine—in buffing leather? People dressed for certain things, of course, for a special meeting or task—what had Michael Longley written about Emily Dickinson? She dressed each morning with care for the act of poetry . . .

They were interrupted by a car drawing up outside the house, the sound of crunching gravel drifting in from outside; it was like a wave breaking on the shore, thought Isabel—it had the same quality. Duncan rose to his feet quickly.

"We can finish our conversation later," he said. "We've touched on things that we need to talk about a bit more."

She said that she agreed. Loyalty, Anthony Blunt, Poussin, living with passion rather than with dull acceptance—there was a lot to be said about all of these subjects. Whole books had been written on them; whole libraries—or sections of libraries in the case of two of them. And nobody ever claimed to reach a definitive conclusion, nor felt they had put the matter to bed. "You could talk about these things for ever, don't you think . . . ," she began, but was cut off. Duncan was moving towards the door, distracted to the point of ignoring her; he suddenly appeared rude, which was most unusual for him, she thought, but he did not mean it. He's afraid . . . That explained it. He was afraid of this lawyer and what she represented, or rather the person she represented, the thief, he who had come into this room and taken the beloved painting, disregarding the consequences of his action, the distress caused by the act of misappropriation. She returned to her earlier thoughts on the shocking attitude of the criminal towards his victim—it was the moral primal scene, to borrow the language of Freudians: the realisation that people could treat others as if they did not matter. And yet they did—they behaved exactly like that—all the time, and with conviction. Whole nations said it to other whole nations. **You do not matter. You do not count.**

CHAPTER TEN

❖

ISABEL WAS NOT PREPARED. After Duncan had left the room to meet the lawyer, she had risen from the settee to stretch her legs. Moving to one of the windows, she was looking out of it, over a box hedge and lawn to trees beyond: sycamores, with some birch. The branches of the birch, silver and green, swayed against the sky, brushing it, but only just, as the breeze was a slight one. She thought of Poussin and his skies; that blue, that bright blue that was none the less cold, framed, as it so often was in his paintings, by clouds. He had understood clouds—appreciated them, and now . . .

"We can talk in here."

She turned round. Duncan was showing a woman into the room, and he was looking in Isabel's direction. The first thing that Isabel noticed was that Heather Darnt, a woman she judged to be in her early forties, was wearing jeans. The denim was dark, but it was definitely denim, and it was tight, disappearing into high black boots. Above the jeans was a white cotton formal shirt and an inappropriately large Orthodox cross necklace. But when Isabel's eyes went to the face, she saw a spreading port-wine birthmark across the lawyer's left temple. It was not small, but no attempt had been made to conceal it—indeed, as she approached to shake hands, Isabel saw that her choice of lipstick, liberally applied, was in an exactly matching shade of port wine.

They shook hands. Isabel found, to her surprise, that she was trembling. She tried to smile, but it was hard; she did not feel like smiling.

"Miss Darnt has driven over from Perth," said Duncan.

It was insignificant information, but it was something to say. "Oh yes," said Isabel. "Perth . . . that's where you practise?"

It was small talk, and she felt foolish making it, but she was distracted by everything: by the jeans—unexpected of a lawyer making a business call; by the birthmark to which one could not be indifferent; by the Orthodox cross; by the fact that this woman was acting for figures from the shadowy world of art theft.

Duncan gestured for them to sit down.

"Yes," said the lawyer, in answer to Isabel's question, "I practise in Perth."

Isabel wanted to say: **And do you always do this sort of thing?** Instead, she said, "I've been told about the theft." She found herself emphasising the word **theft**, as if to shame the other woman.

Her eyes drifted up to the birthmark. She found it hard to look away, but when she did, and glanced at Duncan, sitting at the other end of the sofa from Heather Darnt, she saw that he was staring at it too.

The lawyer had brought a small bag with her, a cross between a briefcase and a handbag, and she now leaned forward to extract a manila file from this. As she did so, she said, "These are present from birth. They result from dilated capillaries."

Isabel drew in her breath inadvertently. "I'm sorry." She felt ashamed and embarrassed. Duncan, she noticed, was blushing.

The lawyer did not look at either of them, but concentrated on the file before her. "It's all right. No harm done."

Isabel persisted. "It was very rude of me."

Heather Darnt looked up at her, and Isabel

felt her eyes again move helplessly to the birthmark. Now the lawyer looked amused. "You don't have to apologise. I'm used to it."

"The painting . . . ," began Duncan, in an obvious attempt to move the conversation on.

"Yes," said the lawyer. "The Poussin."

She pronounced it **Powsinn**, and Isabel noticed a flicker of amusement cross Duncan's face. And so did the lawyer.

"Clearly, I mispronounce it," she said calmly. "I very evidently don't have your advantages."

Isabel winced. "We all know what we're referring to. It doesn't matter how one pronounces it."

The lawyer looked at her with amusement. "Sometimes pronunciation matters a lot."

Isabel looked away. There were some encounters that started off on the wrong foot and never recovered. This was one of them.

"The painting," said Duncan. And then, correcting himself, "My painting."

Heather Darnt busied herself with removing a paper clip from the top of a sheet of paper, and then slipping it back into position. Isabel watched her: She's the nervous one, she thought. I have no cause to be anxious, nor does Duncan; but **she** does.

"Where is the painting?" Isabel asked suddenly. "Have you seen it?"

The lawyer did not look at her as she answered. "I believe that the painting is in Scotland. I don't know exactly where in Scotland, but it's still here." She paused. "Have I seen it? The answer to that is no."

"So how do you know that it's in the country? How do you know that it hasn't been destroyed?"

The lawyer seemed to weigh these questions carefully. When she answered, she spoke slowly and guardedly. "I have taken what has been said to me on trust."

Duncan's expression changed. He now looked angry, thought Isabel. "On trust from thieves?"

Heather Darnt continued to move the papers in her hands, folding one and tucking it behind another. "It can be seen," she said. "We can make arrangements for you to see it. The insurance company, I think, will want that to happen. It's standard practice when there's a reward."

Isabel looked enquiringly at Duncan. They had not discussed a possible reward. "Who's offering a reward?" she asked. "Are you?"

"No, certainly not me," he answered. "The insurance company."

Heather Darnt seemed surprised that Isabel was unaware of this. "It's very common," she said. "That's how paintings are recovered. By means of the reward."

Isabel wanted to make sure she understood. "And these people you're acting for," she asked, "they're after the reward?"

The lawyer answered the question with a nod.

Isabel asked another question. "Who are they? The thieves themselves?"

The lawyer shook her head. "No. They're people who are in touch with the people holding the painting."

Isabel considered this. "What exactly does 'in touch' mean?"

Heather Darnt gave her a look that was on the verge of pitying. "What it usually means. In touch. Speaking to one another."

"Seeing one another face-to-face?"

The lawyer shrugged. "Maybe. Maybe not. I can't speak for them."

But that, thought Isabel, is exactly what a lawyer does, and if I were to be as sarcastic—and as rude—as you are being, that is what I might point out to you.

She was blunt. "May I ask who's paying you?" And quickly answered her own question. "I imagine it's these people who know the thieves—the thieves' friends."

The lawyer said nothing. An eye twitched slightly, but otherwise she remained impassive.

"But the money really comes from the ransom, doesn't it?" Isabel continued. "A slice of that ransom comes to you through the intermediary." She paused. "You profit from the theft."

Duncan looked at Isabel nervously. He was about to say something when the lawyer spoke.

"Any lawyer who does anything profits from the needs of another—or from misfortune." She spoke slowly and quietly, as if explaining a simple truth to a young person who was having difficulty grasping it. "How do you think criminal lawyers are paid? Where do their fees come from?"

Duncan interrupted. "I don't think this is a particularly constructive line of discussion," he said. He gave Isabel a warning glance. "I'd like to talk about how we are to see the painting. How is that going to be arranged?"

The lawyer turned her attention from Isabel to Duncan. It was a deliberate—and very obvious—piece of body language. Isabel was now facing a half-turned-away shoulder and would have had to address that if she had had anything more to say.

"We will arrange a place," said Heather Darnt. "We'll give you a time when you'll get a telephone call telling you where to go. It'll be somewhere in Edinburgh."

We, thought Isabel.

"And you'll bring the painting to . . ."

"Not me. Them. They'll bring the painting."

Duncan glanced at Isabel, then looked back at the lawyer.

"Of course," went on the lawyer, "if there is any question of the authorities being present, then they—the current holders of the painting—will be aware of that and the whole discussion will be off. They have indicated that if there is any involvement of anybody other than yourself and the insurance company, then the painting will be destroyed. It will be safer for them to do that than to risk . . . other consequences."

Duncan gasped. "They'll destroy a Poussin . . . just like that? For nothing?"

The lawyer spread her hands in a gesture of resignation. "These people are not aesthetes, Mr. Munrowe. They are—"

"Art thieves," interjected Isabel.

The lawyer began to turn back to face Isabel, but clearly thought better of it. "The world is as it is," she said quietly, addressing her response to Duncan but evidently intending it for Isabel.

"People may think that we live in a world where moral boundaries are very clearly delineated, but lawyers know otherwise. Nothing is that straightforward, is it? For the most part, great concentrations of wealth are in the hands they are in because somebody, a few generations back, was rapacious." She paused. "I don't wish to be rude, Mr. Munrowe, but I'd like to point out that the fact that there are certain very well-off families in Scotland—people living in big houses in the country and all the rest—merely reflects the successful thefts of the past. The Highland Clearances made some people very rich indeed. That was based on burning people out of their homes—yes, burning them. Or profiting from the back-breaking labour of men down the pits or in the steel works. The big Glasgow shipowners—who built the ships? Who was blinded by the flying rivets? Who died at thirty-eight, forty? Not the shipowners."

Isabel lowered her eyes. All of this was true, but she was not sure that it justified the stealing of a Poussin that was destined for the National Gallery of Scotland.

Duncan could not conceal his embarrassment. "You clearly feel very strongly," he said. "And I understand your argument."

"Do you?" said Heather Darnt sarcastically. "Do you indeed? Well, that's good."

Duncan rose to his feet. "I think we've covered everything," he said decisively. "Although I imagine the insurance company will have something to say about its conditions. They'll want to satisfy themselves that the painting is undamaged, and so on. But that, I suppose, can be sorted out later—after I've met with these . . . these people." He paused, looking down at Heather Darnt with an expression that revealed his distaste. "Will you let me know when I'm to be in Edinburgh to expect—and act on—that telephone call?"

The lawyer stood up. She did not look at Isabel. "I'll phone you later today and tell you what day it will be. Expect a call from me at about four this afternoon—maybe a little later."

Now she turned to Isabel. "It was good to meet you," she said.

Isabel tried to raise a smile. The niceties had to be maintained, even in extremis—sometimes they were all that stood between us and the collapse of civil discourse. "Yes," she said. "I enjoyed our meeting."

How easy it was to lie, she thought, not only about Proust, but about other, more important things. It was the simplest thing in the world to utter words that bore no relation to one's true feelings or intent. That was something that was well known to tyrants and their spokesmen. They could stand there and say "The people are on our side" in the face of all the evidence to the contrary. And they did say that, even as the mob reached their palace gates; even as their henchmen defected and forswore the cause; even as the bombs rained down on their last redoubts. **The people are on our side.**

Heather Darnt was trying a similar tactic. She was asserting the rightfulness of what she was doing, whereas it was, for all her attempted justification, manifestly wrong; perhaps she had succeeded in convincing herself—people did that, repeated an excuse or a rationale until they believed it. But surely she should have refused to act for a client who was obviously in league with the thieves; surely she, or any other reputable lawyer, should have refused to have anything to do with the negotiation of a ransom. And as Isabel thought this, it occurred to her that the insurance company should do the same and refuse to pay ransom. If they paid, then the principle would be established that you could demand a ransom with impunity—and expect to be paid it. Their solution was to call it a reward, but what, Isabel wondered, was the distinction?

Heather Darnt was shown out to her car and drove off down the drive. When Duncan came back in, he looked slightly apologetic. "What an unpleasant woman," he began, and then checked himself. "I'm sorry, I shouldn't really—"

Isabel cut him short. "Shouldn't? Why not? You're absolutely right: she **is** unpleasant. And . . ."

He looked at her expectantly.

"And, frankly, I don't see the distinction between her and the thieves. She's obviously in pretty deeply with them. Of course, there's all those references to clients and intermediaries and so on, but do you know what I think?"

He was watching her closely. "Tell me."

She had not formulated this until a few moments ago, but now it seemed to her to be so obvious: "She's one of them—one of the thieves."

As she spoke, Isabel found herself thinking of the power of words. A single word, a phrase, a sentence or two could have such extraordinary power; could end a world, break a heart or, as in this case, consign another to moral purdah.

"I think you may be right," he said. "I did not like her."

Isabel shrugged. "But that, I suppose, is neither here nor there. If we want the painting back, then I suppose we do what we have to do: pay the ransom."

"Well, it's the insurance company that will be paying. But, yes, that's what it amounts to." He paused, as if engaged in the process of weighing choices. "What should our priority be? Money, or a beautiful painting?"

Isabel thought: **This is why I'm here; this is why he wants to involve me.** It was all very well being the editor of a journal of applied ethics; you could deliberate to your heart's content on the rightness or wrongness of actions, but none of it was real; not until somebody actually came up to you, as Duncan now was doing, and said: "Tell me what to do."

"It amounts to paying ransom," she said quietly, almost to herself. "No matter how you dress it up."

"I know," he said. "And surely that's wrong."

She made a gesture of hopelessness. "Put yourself in the position of a person who has to pay ransom to get a relative back from a kidnapper. Think of those people—and there are quite a few of them right now—who have relatives being held by pirates in Somalia." It sounded ridiculous to be talking about pirates in the twenty-first century, but that was exactly what they were. There were still pirates in the world, just as there were still slaves. We imagined that our world had gone beyond all that, but it had not.

"Oh, I'd pay," said Duncan. "Who wouldn't?"

"Governments," answered Isabel. "Governments won't negotiate with terrorists, will they?"

Duncan said that he understood why they took that position. "If they did," he said, "then it would just get worse and worse."

Isabel nodded. "And art thieves? If we negotiate with them? If we pay the ransom they demand, then they'll simply be encouraged."

He was silent for a while. "Maybe I shouldn't," he said.

She had not intended him to reach this conclusion quite so quickly. And she was not entirely sure that this was the position at which she would herself arrive.

"I wouldn't necessarily reach that conclusion," she said.

He looked at her with interest. "But you implied . . ."

"I was voicing a general doubt," she said. "Individual situations may differ. Everything depends . . ." She looked at her hands. **I am not being helpful**, she said to herself. **He wants guidance, and I am giving him doubt**.

"You should save the Poussin," she said

decisively. "If that's what you want, then there's no reason why you shouldn't participate in the business of arranging the ransom. Artistic value trumps the general social interest in this case, I think."

He seemed relieved. "I hoped that you'd say that."

She smiled at him. "I can see what that painting means to you. I understand."

"I'm glad you do. Sometimes I wonder if it's just me—whether I've become excessively attached to it, but then, when I think it through, I come to the conclusion that great art really is as important as we say it is. It's nothing to do with material value—money just complicates the matter. It's what art stands for."

She inclined her head. "Of course."

The decision made, they were both relieved to be able to allow their conversation to become more general, more relaxed. Duncan wanted to talk about Poussin, and Isabel sensed that this was helpful for him.

"There's something that particularly interests me about Poussin," he said. "He was a landscape painter as much as he was a figurative painter, you know."

She did know that. "Yes. I saw that exhibition **Poussin and Nature** a few years back. He had a lot to say about the natural world."

"Exactly," said Duncan. "He may paint something dramatic, something fairly intense in human terms, and yet there it is, shown in a natural setting."

"And a calm one at that," said Isabel.

"Yes. Classical landscapes always have that air of peacefulness about them. Do you know the Poussin in the National Gallery in London? The one of the man killed by a snake?"

She remembered being in a room full of Poussins in the National Gallery, but it had been a long time ago.

"It's a very powerful painting," Duncan continued. "That poor man lying on the ground with the snake coiled around him. And the man who has discovered him running up the path to report the matter—too late."

Suddenly she recalled it. "There's a boat, isn't there? Men fishing somewhere nearby."

"Yes. Poussin makes the point, doesn't he? Normal life goes on in spite of tragedies occurring all around it."

She smiled in recognition. Auden had said exactly that. "About suffering, they were never wrong, / The Old Masters: how well they understood / Its human position . . ."

"That's vaguely familiar," he said.

"It's Auden's poem about Brueghel's **Fall of**

Icarus," she said. "You may know the painting—there's a ploughman tilling a field in the foreground and a ship sailing out of the bay below. Icarus can be seen falling into the water—his legs disappearing—but everybody gets on with their business in spite of the tragedy. The ship has somewhere to sail, the man has his field to plough. If they notice, they don't pay much attention."

Duncan was silent for a moment. "I suppose that's true. I suppose that even as we sit here talking, somebody, somewhere in the world, is facing imminent execution—about to be shot or given a lethal injection—something brutal, some piece of licensed awfulness like that. And we sit here and talk about art and its meaning and think of a dinner that awaits us this evening, or a conversation with friends, or anything, really."

Isabel looked at him, and he held her gaze for a few moments before looking down. It was as if he had unwittingly shown to her something of himself that he would rather not have revealed—for all his earlier talk of an appropriate reticence. She felt an urge to reach out and touch him, to reassure him that he could be honest with her, that there was no need for him to shelter behind the identity that he otherwise presented to the world—that of the countryman, the gentleman farmer. But she did not: there were limits to the intimacy that had suddenly grown up between them, and she knew that if she infringed these limits, he might retreat again. So she was silent, and looked at her watch. He nodded. "I understand," he said. "You must get back to Edinburgh."

"Will you let me know when they get in touch?" she said.

"I will." He hesitated before continuing. "I take it that you're happy to come and see the painting?"

"I want to do that," she said.

"I'm glad. I'll feel less exposed with you there."

He saw her to her car.

"I'll say it again, that really is a very good car. I love Swedish cars," he said. "In fact, I love everything Swedish."

She knew what he meant. There were many in Scotland who felt that their country had somehow been misplaced—that it should have been closer to Scandinavia.

"Perhaps one day," she said.

He laughed. "Scotland will become more Swedish?"

She made a gesture of mock despair. That

would never happen. We would have to change everything, she mused—ourselves, the way we thought, our attitudes and our clothes.

JAMIE COOKED DINNER that evening using a recipe for a vegetable paella that he had read in the **Scotsman** weekend magazine, cut out and then stuffed into a pocket of his jacket. He was an enthusiastic cook but a sporadic one, and would often only announce to Isabel in the late afternoon that he would cook that evening—if she wanted him to. By then she would have made her plans for their meal, but would readily shelve them in order to have the evening off. There would be Charlie's supper to prepare, but that was simplicity itself: his tastes ran to macaroni cheese, spaghetti and a curious mixture of cauliflower and olives that he had named **cauliolives** and always devoured with gusto. Oddly, for a child, he seemed to have little interest in sweet things, apart from ice cream: macaroons, irresistible to other children, would be left untouched, and marzipan, if ever he encountered it, spat out in disgust.

While Jamie cooked, Isabel read Charlie his bedtime story. He had discovered A. A. Milne—or that writer had been discovered for him—and loved to hear the poems in **Now We Are Six,** especially the lines about King John, who was not a good man—who was not spoken to for days and days and days, but was miraculously given the present he so yearned for. "Good boys get presents," said Charlie, looking up at his mother with a mixture of challenge and hope.

"They do, Charlie," said Isabel. "And give them too."

He had nodded wisely; he understood, she suspected, about reciprocity—or at least had some glimpse of what it meant, but probably only in the crudest, most elementary terms. Plenty of people gave gifts to get gifts back, and Charlie at present was among them. That would change, of course—unless he remained one of those who never grew into altruism. And they existed. Her mother's cousin, Mimi McKnight in Dallas, had told her once about one of the Mobile aunts, an ancient Southern lady, all powder and eau de cologne, who had been famous for being incapable of giving anybody anything at all, not even on important birthdays, when a homemade card was all that she would rise to. On her death, a sealed will was discovered in a drawer, stating that there was nothing to leave and therefore there would be no legacies. It was not true; she was comfortably off, but could not bring herself to acknowledge that fact, nor the claims that any of her family might have on her.

"What lies behind an attitude like that?" Isabel had asked.

Mimi had thought for a moment and then said, "Ask Dr. Freud."

"Fear?" suggested Isabel. "Fear of having nothing left?"

"Possibly," said Mimi. "Or a stony heart."

Now, with the last of the Milne recited—for a second time—she switched out Charlie's light and kissed him goodnight. He was drowsy and already half asleep, but he puckered his lips slightly as she planted the kiss on his forehead. She could have wept; she could have wept for the love of him, as any mother might while watching over her child. There was no human emotion stronger than this, she felt; biology dictated it and the heart willingly became party to the bond. That was what Renaissance artists meant when they painted those beautiful, entrancing madonnas: their work was commissioned by religious piety, but the spirit that moved the artist was nothing to do with that but everything to do with maternal tenderness and love, with what she felt now . . .

Jamie had laid the table in the kitchen and

poured Isabel a glass of New Zealand white wine; the chilled glass was covered in a mist of condensation, small rivulets beginning to move down towards the stem. She took the glass in her hand and held it up to the evening light from the window. Outside, viewed through the wine, Scotland was blurred and made golden-yellow. Up above, there were clouds, and beyond them was a slice of blue that made her think again of Poussin and of his skies; it was the same shade of blue that the artist had habitually used in his paintings, a blue that spoke of the cold that was there in any real sky, at that altitude.

Jamie was busying himself with the chopping of parsley.

"I'm using curly parsley rather than the flat-leaf sort," he said. "Do you think it matters?"

"That's fine," said Isabel. "Flat-leaf parsley has a stronger flavour. Curly will probably go more easily with the other things you're using."

Jamie finished chopping the parsley and moved on to garlic. "Double quantities," he said, smiling at Isabel. "To protect us against any vampires that may be lurking around Edinburgh." He held up a half-chopped bulb of garlic and then crossed the room towards her, holding it out in front of him for her to sniff.

She took the hand in which he held the garlic. She steadied it and then sniffed at the half-sliced bulb. It bled—the garlic bled—a clear liquid.

"Lovely," she said. "Sinful."

He stood before her. She looked into his eyes.

"I love it," he said. "It goes with everything, doesn't it?"

"Except kisses," she said.

He lowered his hand. "No? So one should kiss people **before** eating garlic?"

"If that's what one wants to do," she said. And I do, she thought. I want to kiss you. I want to kiss you.

He leaned forward and kissed her on the lips. Then again. And once more.

"I have to cook," he said, drawing back.

"Yes, indeed." She took a sip of her wine. "I had an uncomfortable meeting today," she said.

"Oh? Tell me about it."

She answered his invitation with a question. "Do you know that feeling when you meet somebody who's ill-disposed to you—right from the beginning, before you've even had the chance to offend them?"

Jamie had encountered that. "Yes, I know it. There's a conductor who hates me. I could tell straightaway. The moment he lifted his baton at the first rehearsal, he hated me."

"Why?"

He shrugged. "Maybe he doesn't like bassoons," he said.

Isabel thought: No, it was not that. It would have been something quite different; something to do with the way that Jamie looked, something to do with who he was. Envy? Jamie was young, and older people can hate the young just because they are young and because they are going to have the world for a long time yet.

Jamie tipped a pile of chopped vegetables into a large cast-iron frying pan and moved it on to the plate of the cooker. The oil in the pan sizzled. "Who was this person anyway?" he asked.

"She's a lawyer from Perth," said Isabel. "A woman called Heather Darnt."

"Never heard of her," said Jamie. "But I don't like her either."

Isabel smiled. "Thanks for the solidarity. She's horrible." She realised that to describe somebody as horrible sounded very childish. She had a friend—someone she had known at school—who used expressions like that, who spoke the same way as she did when they were both fifteen. People could be **horrible,** or **horrid,** or, by contrast, **fab,** or **cool**. These adjectives were interspersed with Scots terms, words that were vividly expressive, as Scots can so often be. The overall effect was one of decisive partisanship.

"Or maybe not exactly horrible," she continued. "Just rude. Cold. Rather sinister."

Jamie nodded. "The sort of person you can picture commanding a firing squad? There are more people like that than you imagine."

"I know."

"And so what did she say?"

Isabel told him about their conversation and the promise that the painting would be available for inspection. He listened intently, stirring the vegetables in the frying pan as Isabel spoke. When she had finished, he turned and fixed her with a stare.

"You're not going to go?" he asked. "You aren't going to go and meet these people, are you?"

"Duncan wants me to," Isabel replied. "And I've agreed."

For a moment Jamie said nothing, and turned back to his cooking. "I know I can never persuade you not to do things," he said over his shoulder. "So I won't try. But just be careful with this one."

"It'll be in full public view, I imagine," said Isabel. "They won't want to give us an actual address to go to."

"Why not?"

"Because we could pass that on to the authorities, and they could turn up and recover the painting."

"So how will you do it?"

She did not know the answer to that. "I imagine that it will be in a bar or a café, or somewhere like that. We'll be told to meet them somewhere at the last moment."

Jamie looked doubtful. "Why somewhere public? But won't it look very odd if you start examining a painting in the middle of a bar?"

"I imagine they won't want somewhere private because they'll want to be able to melt away into a crowd, or into the traffic perhaps. So it's likely to be somewhere public, but where . . ." She looked at him helplessly. "I don't know exactly. In fact, I don't know at all. I'm not very good at these things."

He smiled at her. "I could say, then, that perhaps you shouldn't take them on. But I won't say that. I really won't."

"What will you say instead?"

He hesitated for a moment. "That I'm really happy that you're the way you are. That I'm glad that you're not somebody who can ignore the troubles of others. That you're the most perfect woman I've ever met in my life and that I love you more than the . . . more than the Atlantic Ocean."

She put down her glass. "What you've said is more than enough for any woman," she said. "To be loved more than the Atlantic Ocean . . ."

"It's true," said Jamie. "I know it sounds odd . . ."

The Atlantic stood for so much—for breadth and openness and empty, watery wastes—and was not the most obvious metaphor for love; but she knew why he should have thought of the sea in trying to say what he wanted to say: Burns had talked of the duration of his love, which would last, he said, **Till a' the seas gang dry,** and so she said, "I understand. It doesn't sound odd at all—not to me."

CHAPTER ELEVEN

IT WAS ALEX MUNROWE, Duncan's daughter, who contacted Isabel with the suggestion that they meet, rather than the other way round. Isabel had thought of getting in touch with her: having met Patrick, the son, her curiosity about the family had been aroused. Duncan had said very little about his daughter, other than to mention that she lived in Nelson Street and to let drop the information that he saw her regularly when he came down to Edinburgh. There was nothing unusual about that, even if it suggested that Duncan might have a preference for the company of his daughter. He would not be the only father to feel that way; many fathers had closer relations with their daughters than with their sons. The evolutionary biologists might have something to say about that, thought Isabel, and if they did not, then the Freudians certainly would. But in this case it was no real concern of hers; she had not been asked to involve herself in the internal dynamics of the Munrowe family, and it was only curiosity that drove her to speculate about Alex.

The telephone call came on the day following Isabel's trip to Munrowe House and her uncomfortable meeting with Heather Darnt. After introducing herself, Alex apologised for telephoning Isabel at home. **But there's nowhere else to telephone me,** she thought.

"My father gave me your number," Alex continued. "He said you wouldn't mind my getting in touch."

Isabel assured her that she did not mind in the least. "In fact, I was hoping to meet you at some point. Your father told me all about you." She said that without thinking; Duncan had mentioned her, but had hardly said very much at all.

There was a silence at the other end of the line and Isabel wondered whether she had inadvertently given offence. But she had not. Alex confessed that she had been finishing off a piece of toast and had been licking butter off her fingers. "I know that sounds rude," she said. "But I have to go out shortly and there are two calls I have to make."

"It's not rude at all," said Isabel. "There may be some occasions when you certainly shouldn't phone somebody, but while eating toast is not one of them."

There was a further silence before Alex cleared her throat; a crumb had gone down the wrong way, Isabel decided.

"My father is very grateful to you. So am I."

Isabel felt embarrassed. "I've done nothing."

"You're being a support for him," said Alex. "Martha Drummond said you would be, and she was right."

"Well," said Isabel, "I'm sorry that he's had this happen to him."

"It's awful," agreed Alex. "Of all the pictures they could have taken, to take that one . . . It's just so cruel."

"Yes," said Isabel. "It is." She waited for Alex to reveal why she had called.

"Could we meet?" asked Alex. "So that I can put a face to the name."

Isabel agreed, and a time was agreed for later that day; she was going over to that side of town, and she could drop in at about four in the afternoon, if that suited Alex.

It did. "Sponge cake? Sandwiches? Coffee? Tea?"

"Sandwiches, if you're making them," said Isabel.

"Cucumber?"

Isabel laughed. "You guessed."

"Nobody dislikes cucumber sandwiches. Or nobody I've met."

Isabel suddenly wondered: Are there cultures where the cucumber, for some reason, was spurned? People had such strange ideas about food: apples had, in some places, once been regarded as sinful—Eve's fault—and potatoes had been seen as encouraging laziness. Cucumbers, surely, had escaped censure, and, rather, had attracted admiration, even though it was not always complimentary to be described as being "as cool as a cucumber." The French might describe a lover as a **little cabbage,** but not, she thought, as a **little cucumber**. Certainly not. She smiled.

"Are you still there?"

"Yes," said Isabel. "Sorry. I was thinking." She did not say that she was thinking about cucumbers.

Alex gave her address, and they rang off. Grace had just arrived and Isabel could hear her in the kitchen emptying the bin in a way that told her that something had incurred her housekeeper's displeasure. When things were knocked together or banged, it was a clear sign that some incident, probably something in the newspaper, had served to irritate Grace.

Isabel left her study and entered the kitchen. Grace had just tipped the contents of the bin underneath the sink into a large black plastic sack. She looked up as Isabel entered.

"Have you seen the **Scotsman** today?" Grace asked.

I was right, thought Isabel.

"There's an article about a wee boy in Fife who's a real expert in physics. He's just nine and he's outstripping the seventeen-year-olds. They won't let him go to physics classes at the secondary school."

Isabel was not prepared for this. She had been putting off a discussion about Charlie and mathematics, but this report seemed to be leading in that direction.

"Who's preventing him going there?" she asked.

"The education committee." Grace spat the words out with maximum distaste. "Those councillors. What have they ever done? That's what I ask? They've all made a career of being politicians and they've never done anything in their lives. And then when a boy of real talent comes along, they say things like, 'Our resources must be fairly shared—we can't encourage one child at the expense of another.' Can you believe it? That's what they said."

Isabel moved towards the kettle. A cup of coffee could often calm Grace down, and she decided that this was an occasion for just such a tactic.

But Grace continued. "It's the same with Charlie, isn't it?"

Isabel was noncommittal. "I'm not sure—"

Grace cut her short. "Yes, it is." She looked reproachfully at Isabel. "He's doing very well, you know."

Isabel frowned. "We're very grateful to you, Grace. We're very grateful to you for everything you do. But in this particular instance, I think that there may be a case for speaking to an expert . . ." And here she looked at Grace before going on, "I freely admit I'm out of my depth here. I don't know how to teach mathematics—how to get the right approach. We could ask an expert—maybe somebody at one of the schools, at Watson's perhaps." She paused. "Don't you think that's a good idea?"

"We already have an expert," said Grace. "The

book I've been using to help Charlie is written by a world expert. She's in California."

"The fact that somebody is in California doesn't necessarily mean that she's . . ." Isabel searched for the right word. "Reliable. In fact, California is the sort of place where all sorts of fads take hold. It's famous for that. It's a big place for fads."

Grace came back immediately. "Not this book. The book I've been using is definitely not faddish. It's been proved."

Isabel sighed. "I think we need to talk about it," she said mildly. "If children learn mathematics the wrong way, they can develop bad habits. Then you can't get them to do it the right way ever again."

Grace narrowed her eyes. "I'm not making any mistakes," she said. She turned away. "And if you don't trust me with Charlie, then quite honestly I don't really see how I can continue to work here. I'm sorry, but what other conclusion can I reach?"

Isabel gasped. "Oh, Grace, I didn't mean to upset you. I really didn't. Of course I trust you with Charlie. We both do."

"Then why did you say that?"

Isabel spoke softly. "I didn't say what you

think I said. All that I said was that mathematics is the sort of thing that perhaps an expert . . ."

"An expert? That is, anybody but me. That's what that means, doesn't it?"

Isabel shook her head. "No, not at all. I'm not an expert either. Nor is Jamie."

"And you haven't even read the book," said Grace. "You've accused me of making all sorts of mistakes and you haven't even read the book." She turned away and began to undo the strings of her apron, which dropped to the floor as she loosened it. She did not bend down to pick it up, but patted her hair as if to compose herself for her next move. "I'm sorry that it's ending in this way," she said.

"Look," said Isabel. "I'm really sorry if I've offended you. I didn't mean to. You must know that, Grace. It's just that neither Jamie nor I want to push Charlie too much. We want him to have time to be a little boy. There'll be time for mathematics later on."

Grace was not listening. "I was merely doing what needed to be done," she said. "No more than that."

"Well, then, let's talk about it. Let's sit down and work it out."

Grace moved away. "No. It's too late for that. I'm going now," she said.

"Grace—"

The kitchen door slammed. Isabel sat down and put her head in her hands. Grace had resigned twice before, and on both occasions had been persuaded to return. In neither of the previous cases did Isabel feel it had been her fault—and she was right: she was an infinitely considerate employer. She imagined that once again Grace would be prevailed upon to change her mind, but it would involve prolonged explanations and assurances. And neither of the previous resignations had been so firm and so reproachful, which did not bode well for a rapid resolution. Jamie would have to be involved, Isabel decided. Grace normally ate out of his hand, and he had been responsible for bringing the last resignation to an end. He would be an ambassador, sent on a mission of reconciliation and peace-keeping, the bearer of a diplomatic note and a peace-offering.

That was what Grace would expect, and it was what she would get, although for a brief moment Isabel allowed herself to speculate on what would happen if she were simply to accept Grace's resignation. Would Grace then apologise and ask for her job back, or would she stand on her dignity? It was inconceivable that Grace should go. She had been there for ever, it seemed, and the house would not be the same without her. Isabel owned the house, it was true, but that did not make her feel that she, alone, had the right to be there. The right to be in a place came in different forms: the legal title was one such form, but only one, and could sometimes be considerably weaker than moral rights of another form altogether. Those with legal title often misunderstood that; they thought that a piece of paper—a legal device—spoke more eloquently than any human link, any claim of long presence or association. But they were wrong, even if they had the crude mechanisms of enforcement on their side.

No, Jamie would be sent on his peace mission and, with any luck, Grace would soon be back at work as normal. Charlie might ask where she was, but Isabel was prepared for that. She had resolved never to lie to her young son, and she would not start now. So if he asked where she was, Isabel thought that she might simply say that Grace was reviewing her position. She had no idea how that would sound to a three-year-old, perhaps rather as if Grace had gone off to watch a film. Then she realised that this was meretricious. She would say to Charlie that Grace had gone home because she was cross. She hoped that she would not be cross the next morning, but she could not be sure. That would be both truthful and comprehensible, and Charlie, she was sure, would accept it. Children understood that adults could become angry—curiously so, and for no apparent reason, just as the weather could change and a smiling day might suddenly frown.

The contretemps with Grace left her feeling slightly raw, despite Jamie's later assurances that she could likely be persuaded to withdraw her resignation. "And she won't make a fuss about the mathematics," he said. "You'll see—she'll have picked up your concerns about that and won't make a fuss."

Isabel hoped that he was right, but as she made her way down to her meeting with Alex Munrowe, she decided that if Grace was determined to persevere with her mathematics teaching, then they would simply have to have another talk. She did not relish the prospect of specifically overruling Grace on the matter, but she had her duty as a mother to consider. And it was not unreasonable, she thought, to insist on something when it came to the education of her son; surely Grace would understand that and would see it from Isabel's point of view. That was what she hoped, but there remained a nagging doubt. Grace could be stubborn, and it was just possible that this question of mathematics was going to be a battlefield that neither of them wanted but neither felt she could avoid.

ALEX'S FLAT in Nelson Street was on the second floor of a four-storey tenement, built in the early years of the nineteenth century when the Edinburgh New Town spread confidently down the hill towards the Firth of Forth. Nelson Street was a short street by the standards of its neighbours, a brief, sloping link between two sets of elegant private gardens. Unlike most New Town streets, which ran in a straight line or, at most, followed a leisurely curve, Nelson Street had a zigzag where it was interrupted at a right angle by another street; Alex lived in the **zag,** just before it opened out on to the broad square of Drummond Place. Her flat was served by a common stair that ascended from behind a classical panelled door. This staircase, chilly in spite of its being summer, still retained its original heavy mahogany handrail and ornate ironwork banisters: craftsmanship that had been built to last, and had done just that. The stone stairs themselves were worn by centuries of feet, creating in the middle of each step a small curved indentation—not enough to make the stairs hazardous but deep enough to remind the visitor that he or she was not the first to walk that way.

The door off the landing had two names on it, each separately engraved on a small brass plate. Isabel noticed that the screws holding these plates were countersunk so as not to protrude even by the smallest fraction of an inch above the surface; it was an odd detail for her to notice, and not, she decided, one loaded with meaning—except that, perhaps, it was because we were so used to cheapness in our surroundings, to sloppiness, that craftsmanlike standards stood out and reminded us of what had once been taken for granted.

She tugged at another brass fitting—a lever with a small model of a human fist at the end—and heard the tinkling of a bell somewhere inside the flat. After a few seconds there came the sound of footsteps and then the turning of the latch. The door opened to a woman who looked about thirty, attractive in spite of an unusually high forehead—or because of it—and possessed of the same reserved look that she had noticed in Duncan Munrowe.

They shook hands, and Isabel followed Alex into a drawing room at the end of a short corridor.

"We can sit in here," said Alex. "Facing west, we get a bit of afternoon light. In the morning, the kitchen gets it—it's on the other side."

"My orientation too," said Isabel.

"Martha Drummond says you live near her. It's rather nice up there, isn't it?"

Isabel nodded. "Do you know Martha well?"

Alex hesitated. "I do. Yes, quite well."

There was something in her tone that suggested that Martha might have been a heart-sink friend for Alex, much as she was for Isabel.

"There's a Stirlingshire connection," Alex went on. "Martha's father was a close friend of my grandfather's. The two families go back a long time—generations before that, they knew one another too. You know how Scotland is."

Isabel smiled. Of course she knew how Scotland was.

Alex gestured to a sofa. "Please . . ."

Isabel sat down and looked about her. The room was a typical drawing room of the sort that was to be found in virtually all the flats in that part of Edinburgh. Being Georgian, the proportions were almost perfect—if not actually perfect—with the length of each wall being more or less 1.6180339887 times the height of the ceiling: the golden section.

Isabel had always thought that it was a tragedy that the Victorians had abandoned this ratio and favoured high ceilings. The result had been rooms that were rather like cubes; rooms that we could not feel fully comfortable in because we were intuitively predisposed to relate warmly to **phi** (1.61 etc.). She imagined, for a moment, going into a room one liked and exclaiming, "**Phi!**" People might say, "Don't you mean **phew**?" and one would reply, "No, **phi**!" She smiled at the thought.

Alex was staring at her. "What's the joke?"

Isabel shook her head. "Just a ridiculous notion about the golden section." She could not retell it, but said instead, "I do love these Georgian rooms."

Alex looked about her, as if noticing the decor for the first time.

"The curtains came from my father's house," she said. "He sent us off to university with curtains. I thought it rather odd at the time. Most of the other students arrived with stereos and laptops and so on. My brother and I arrived with curtains."

Isabel laughed. "Well, I went off for my first year at Cambridge with one of those machines that makes tea for you while you're still lying in bed. I remember that people laughed at me, but they saw the point in due course and one or two of them actually asked me where I had got it."

Her eyes wandered from the curtains to the mantelpiece, which was of old pine, with an elaborate moulded frieze along its length. This frieze was dominated by the figure of a woman leaning on an upright anchor; around her feet, and off to each side, were shells stacked in profusion, with crabs and twists of rope. A pair of delicately painted Chinese ginger jars, **famille rose,** stood on the mantelshelf, and on the wall above was a large painting in an elaborate gilded frame.

Isabel drew in her breath. "That's not another Poussin, is it?"

"Yes," said Alex, and then, almost immediately, and smiling in response to Isabel's look of astonishment, she qualified her answer. "And no. Gaspard Poussin, or Gaspard Dughet to give him his original name. He was Poussin's brother-in-law—and his pupil. He changed his name to Poussin after he married Poussin's sister."

Isabel got up from the sofa and examined the painting more closely.

Alex joined her. Isabel noticed that she had been eating garlic.

"It's a beautiful painting," Isabel said.

"I'm glad you like it," said Alex. "He painted

just like his master when it came to the overall composition. You see that hill village there? Very typical of Poussin. And that lake in the foreground—again, you see a lot of that in Poussin—Nicolas Poussin, that is. And those trees: those aren't bad at all—they could be the real thing, I suppose. Except this painting is not immensely valuable. It was in the house, upstairs; my father gave it to me as a house-warming present when I bought this place."

Isabel leaned forward to peer more closely at a figure that the artist had placed under a tree. "A shepherd?"

"Probably. Dughet liked shepherds. But I suppose if you looked at any stretch of countryside in the seventeenth century, it would have been well peopled by shepherds. Not today, of course."

"And beside the lake? Over there?"

"That's somebody sleeping. I don't think there's anything untoward going on. If that were Nicolas, then he might have had that figure constricted by a snake. He was fascinated by snakes. You know that—"

"Painting in the National Gallery in London? **Man Killed by a Snake**. Yes. Your father talked to me about it."

"Did he? Well, he taught me all about it

when I was ten. He took me all the way to London to visit the National Gallery and stand in front of the Poussins. And the Rembrandts. I remember wanting to go outside and feed the pigeons in Trafalgar Square, but I couldn't do that for hours because we had a whole list of paintings to see."

Isabel laughed. "It could have put you off for life."

"Yes, but it didn't. I think it had the opposite effect, actually. It made me love art. I just love it."

Duncan had not told Isabel what his daughter did, and Isabel had not found out. Alex was seeing her on a weekday at four in the afternoon—this suggested that she did not have to observe regular office hours. She said that she had bought the flat, and so she must have had some money, presumably money from somewhere in the family. But what about the other person who lived here? She recalled the other name on the brass plate: A husband? A live-in boyfriend? Did she support him, or did he support her? She glanced at Alex's left hand; there was a small diamond ring on the fourth finger that caught the light, now, as Isabel looked—a tiny spark of white fire.

Alex had noticed the direction of Isabel's gaze and interpreted it accurately, but if she resented the curiosity, she did not show it. "I live with my fiancé," she said. "He's called Iain. Iain Douglas. He's a doctor—an orthopaedic surgeon."

Isabel looked away, feeling embarrassed at having been caught in the act of curiosity. But of course people thought about these things—we summed up others all the time; it was getting caught at it that was difficult. She remembered once having been in a queue for tickets at the Festival Theatre, and she had seen a fashionably dressed woman standing nearby looking at her cardigan with what seemed to be unambiguous pity. Their eyes had met, and the other woman had looked away guiltily, pretending to interest herself in a poster for a forthcoming performance of **Macbeth** in Turkish. Isabel had wanted to go up to her and say, "Yes, I know, it's a bit shabby, but honestly, don't worry, I've got better clothes at home." She felt that they might then have coffee together, drawn to one another by this sudden moment of fellow feeling and sympathy. And she might have said to the woman that she should not worry about how she—or others—dressed, and that there was liberation on offer for those who were trapped by fashion. But that would be going too far, and could be hurtful, even if it were true. While the full truth should sometimes be told, it should not **always** be told.

She returned to the sofa while Alex, saying that she was going to fetch the tea, left the room. On her own, Isabel could not help but look at the spines of the books on the bookshelf that took up half a wall. The lower shelves were filled with books too large to be housed further up: most of them, she noticed, on art. There was a large book on Vermeer and a three-volume set on Vuillard. **Netherlandish Art 1660 to 1700: From van Eyck to Dürer**. Her gaze moved upwards. **The Making of Classical Edinburgh. The Island of Jura. Cabinetmaking for Pleasure and Profit . . .**

Alex had re-entered the room, carrying a tray on which there was a teapot, a small jug and two cups.

"Most of those are mine," she said. "Iain has very little time for reading these days."

Isabel blushed. It was the second exposure of her curiosity. But again she thought: One's **entitled** to look at the books on a person's shelves. That's what bookshelves are for: display.

"Did you study art?" she asked, as Alex put the tray down on a table behind the sofa.

"Yes. History of Art at St. Andrews."

"And do anything with it?"

Alex gave her a look that struck Isabel as being slightly defensive. "What can you do with a degree like that? Become a curator, I suppose, if you're lucky enough to get one of the tiny handful of jobs going. Work in a commercial gallery carrying paintings up and down stairs?"

Isabel knew what she meant. It was the same with a degree in philosophy. A tiny number of those who studied philosophy managed to earn their living teaching or writing about the subject, or even thinking about it; the rest had to turn to something else. She had been extremely lucky in that respect, and, even then, that she was still running the **Review of Applied Ethics** was entirely owing to the fact that she had been in a position to buy it. Had she not been able to do that, the **Review** would be in the hands of Professor Lettuce by now, ably assisted by his partner-in-crime, Professor Christopher Dove.

It was pure privilege that determined where so many of us ended up in life, Isabel reflected; it was nothing to do with merit, it was privilege. Or, putting it another way, it was a matter of accident, or luck. To be born in circumstances where one had enough to eat was the first resounding piece of luck, and good luck could be piled upon you from that point onwards. To be given a good education, not to be struck down by debilitating illness, not to have, like Heather Darnt, a disfiguring birthmark that must, with all the courage in the world, make one's teenage years an agony of embarrassment and exclusion—all of that was pure luck and nothing to do with desert. That was so, unless one believed in karma or some other notion of the acquisition of merit in a previous life. There were plenty of people who believed that—millions upon millions of adherents of Hinduism did—and it was not luck in their eyes. In such a view, Professor Lettuce had something to worry about; he may have got sufficiently far in the cycle of reincarnation as to be a professor of philosophy, but he was certainly going no further in the next life. He would be descending rather than ascending, Isabel thought, and was surely in danger of coming back as a toad or some other lowly creature. Or perhaps bad professors came back as research assistants, stuck on the lowest rung of the academic ladder and obliged to endure the humiliations of that uncertain and unrewarding position. Or as a lettuce, if it was possible to come back as a vegetable . . .

Alex was looking at her.

"I'm sorry," said Isabel. "I have a tendency to drift off a bit."

"I asked you what you thought of that woman."

"Which woman?"

"The lawyer."

Isabel did not hesitate. "I'm afraid I didn't like her. I think she's in league with the thieves."

She was aware of the fact that she should not have said that; it was a direct imputation of criminality, and she had no evidence to substantiate the allegation.

Alex laughed. "Oh, come now! She's a lawyer. Lawyers represent people—even thieves—but that doesn't mean they're in league with them."

Isabel looked sheepish. "Yes, you're right. I shouldn't have said that."

Alex had now poured Isabel a cup of tea and was handing it to her. Isabel noticed that there were no cucumber sandwiches on the tray. She felt a momentary disappointment; sandwiches had definitely been mentioned on the telephone. Indeed, there had been an undertaking to serve cucumber sandwiches and, once again, **pacta sunt servanda . . .** She was never sure about the positioning of the **sunt**: she was inclined to put it at the end, as in **Carthago delenda est!**, which Cato was said to have proclaimed; but it was also possible to leave the **sunt** out altogether and say, more succinctly and equally gerundively, **pacta servanda**. Could one say, she wondered, **cucumis ministranda est**—cucumber must be served?

Alex sat down. "So what's going to happen?" she asked.

"I gather that the insurance company has offered a reward. That's what usually happens."

Alex nodded. "I heard that." She paused. "And that'll be paid to the lawyer?"

"Yes. And she will pass it on once the painting has been recovered."

"So she acts as the holder, so to speak?"

Isabel said that she would. "I suppose they just have to trust her not to disappear with the money. Lawyers tend not to disappear."

Alex raised an eyebrow. "There must be crooked lawyers. Every profession has its rotten apples." She took a sip of her tea. Her eyes were on Isabel, who felt that she had to say something; the silence that had descended was slightly uncomfortable.

"With your interest in art," Isabel began, "you must have been particularly upset by all this."

"Absolutely," said Alex. "I was. I loved that painting, you know. I adored it. So the really important thing is to get it back."

"Especially since it's going to go to the nation eventually," said Isabel. "That makes it even more important."

Alex was about to say something, but seemed to check herself. She looked at Isabel's cup and offered her more tea. "Tell me," she said as she began to pour. "Tell me: Have you got any idea who's behind this?"

Isabel sighed. "None at all. You see, I know absolutely nothing about the world of art theft."

Alex digested this silently. Then she said, "But Martha said that you were somebody with a reputation for sorting out extremely difficult situations. She said that you had helped people find out all sorts of things."

Isabel shook her head. "Would that that were true. I suppose I've been able to help a few people who have found themselves in a bit of a mess, but nothing more than that. I have no qualifications for any of it."

"Perhaps being a philosopher is the best qualification of all," suggested Alex.

"For what? For tracking down art thieves? Surely not."

Alex persisted. "For understanding things that are difficult to understand."

"To an extent," said Isabel. "But not this sort of thing."

"So you have no idea?" asked Alex, again.

"No," said Isabel. "Sorry."

Alex shifted in her seat. She leaned back, closed her eyes and then opened them again, to fix Isabel with a playful but still serious stare. "So what if I were to suggest to you that it's my brother?" she asked.

CHAPTER TWELVE

❖

HOW EXACTLY DID SHE put it?" asked Jamie.

They were sitting at the kitchen table, their evening meal over, the dishes stacked in the dishwasher, their two wine glasses, which Isabel preferred to wash by hand, now rinsed and standing inverted on the drying rack. It was half past nine, and at fifty-five degrees and fifty-six minutes' latitude, where Edinburgh lay, the sky still had plenty of light in it; Isabel loved these white nights of summer.

"How did she put it? Well, at first I thought it was a joke—but then I realised that it wasn't quite that."

"Not quite?"

"No. I think that she . . . well, she sort of meant it. I know that sounds pretty vague, but that's how I felt."

Jamie looked puzzled. "I'm not sure what 'sort of meaning' something amounts to."

"It means that you mean it, but aren't really sure." Isabel paused; she was not sure Alex had meant it when she suggested that her brother might be behind the theft of the painting. Perhaps she had intended to raise it as a possibility—something that she thought might be true but for which she had no evidence. And, as it happened, Alex had initially not taken the matter further, but had merely shrugged and raised an eyebrow when Isabel had asked her why she thought her brother might have stolen the painting. After a while, though, she had said, "He's greedy, my brother."

"Any more greedy than the rest of us?" asked Isabel.

Alex laughed. "If you mean more than me, yes, much more. He likes money. He likes the way it smells. He likes the power it gives you." She warmed to her theme. "He works in the pharmaceutical industry, you know. Oh, he likes to portray it as all being very high-minded, but it's all about money and profits—just like any other industry."

Isabel found herself defending Patrick. "Don't most people enjoy such things? Maybe those of us who feel ourselves free from all that—and I assume you, like me, are one—would have to admit that we're still susceptible."

Alex had looked at her slightly askance. "Not many. My brother, you see, needs money because of his habits. They're expensive—some of them very expensive. And I suspect that he'd do anything for money."

Isabel had expected her to continue on this theme, but she steered the conversation in another direction. About twenty minutes later, when Alex brought the visit to an end, Isabel felt that she had learned very little about the other woman, who had seemed more interested in finding out about her than revealing anything about herself. She had elicited at least some information, though: she had discovered that Alex was engaged; that she was interested in art; and that she had what seemed like an unusually strong dislike of her brother. Isabel already knew that there was a close relationship between Alex and her father, and she could imagine why this should be: Alex's manner, her air of slight reserve, something that might easily be mistaken for shyness, mirrored that of Duncan Munrowe; he would see himself in her, no doubt, more so, perhaps, than he might in his son—if what Alex had said about Patrick's venality were true.

"It sounds to me," Jamie said, "as if this is a classic case of sibling jealousy. And if it is, then I wouldn't pay any attention to what they say about each other." He leaned back in his chair. "Why would he steal one of his father's paintings? Presumably he'll get his share of everything when he and his sister eventually inherit. Why steal now?"

"He may need the money now rather than later. She mentioned expensive habits."

Jamie shook his head. "Again, we don't know whether that's true or not. Other people's habits are expensive—our own, never." He paused. "And anyway, what are you going to do with the information, even if you decide to take it seriously? Are you going to tell the father that his son's a thief? You want to be supportive towards him—I don't think that telling him that will be all that helpful, frankly."

She agreed. "You're right. It's probably best for me to put it out of my mind."

"Good."

She hesitated. "Although it's difficult, isn't it, to forget something you've been told? Mud sticks. We used to say that as children."

Jamie smiled. "Yes. It does." He looked at her affectionately. "What else did you say?"

"As a child?"

"Yes."

She looked out of the window. A branch from the tree that grew outside the kitchen moved against the sky, gently, almost imperceptibly. The things that we said as children stayed with us, like certain religious beliefs which we might have grown out of even if the faith that underlay them might still be there. One might stop believing in angels, for instance, and yet feel their presence, or think one does; one might stop believing in hell and still feel nagging concern over the possibility of punishment. As a child she had picked up the superstitious belief that one should never store shoes above one's head—to do so resulted in headaches that could last for two weeks or more. Even now, her shoes were stored only at foot level.

"Isabel?"

She gave a start. "What did we say? Well, we said something about where you put your shoes."

"I didn't," said Jamie. "But I did say something about frogs giving you warts."

"But of course they do," said Isabel. She smiled; there is a particular delight in discovering that those whom one loves share similar memories of childhood. "You should never pick up a frog. And then there was something about bread."

"Oh yes?"

"We said that if you cut bread crooked, you've told a lie."

He laughed. "But I always do. You've seen my toast."

"There must be exceptions," said Isabel. "Every rule has its exceptions."

Jamie remembered something. "And what about getting a cut in the skin between one's thumb and forefinger—in that bit of webbed skin? What about that?"

"Oh, that," said Isabel. "Everybody knows the consequences of that: lockjaw."

"Yes," said Jamie. "And you died, just as you were likely to die of blood poisoning if somebody stabbed you with the nib of a pen."

"We ignore these things at our peril," said Isabel gravely.

Jamie thought of Charlie. He cast his eyes up at the ceiling; it was how they referred to their child when they were in the kitchen and he was in his room directly above. "Do you think he'll pick these things up?"

"I'm sure he will," said Isabel. "But I hope that he doesn't have the fears we had—the real fears. Remember your boyhood. You must have been frightened of some things."

He had been. He had been frightened that his father would die; he had been frightened that a boy called James MacArthur would punch him and break his nose, as he had threatened to do on a number of occasions; he had been frightened that somebody would come into his room at night when he was asleep and put a pillow over his head—a fear that came from hearing of what the wicked uncle did to the Princes in the Tower. Much later, as a teenager, he had been frightened that he would never find a girlfriend, and that he would die without ever discovering sex.

"All of those things?" said Isabel sympathetically.

"Yes. And what about you?"

She thought. "As a very small girl I was frightened that the cat we had would be run over. I was frightened that my pants would fall off in gym."

Jamie let out a hoot of laughter. "What a terrific fear! That your pants will fall off!"

"It was very real," said Isabel. "And it happened to a girl in my class. Toffee Macleod. Her pants fell off. I wouldn't be surprised if she never fully recovered."

"Toffee Macleod? What a name. What happened to her?"

"She went to Australia and married a pilot. That's as much as I know."

"Nobody in Australia would have known," said Jamie. "She left her shame behind in Scotland."

Isabel was about to say something more about Toffee—to tell the story of how she was the first girl in the class to be asked to the cinema by a boy (not a boy and his parents, but a boy acting under his own auspices). But then the telephone rang and she knew, by some inexplicable sixth sense, that it would be Duncan. It was. Contact had been made, he said, and they should go to Rutland Square the following morning at nine-thirty. They should be on foot, and they should walk round the square until they were contacted further.

Jamie, who had been able to overhear this conversation, said nothing, but looked disapproving. Once Isabel had put down the phone, he said quietly, "Rutland Square?"

"Yes," said Isabel. "Apparently so."

"Why there?"

She had no idea. "The picture won't be there. We'll get instructions."

"Promise me one thing," said Jamie. "Promise

me you'll phone and let me know where they've told you to go."

"I promise."

She suddenly remembered the cucumber sandwiches. "She promised cucumber sandwiches," she said. "But they never appeared."

"She must have forgotten."

Isabel had to concede that was possible. "It's a ridiculous thing to resent something like that," she said. "I know I shouldn't, and so I shan't." There were so many bigger moral problems connected with food—our duty to help the hungry, the implications of genetic manipulation of crops and so on; these dwarfed all those smaller food issues that were really not much more than questions of etiquette. And that reminded her—"Jamie?"

"Yes?"

"What do you think of this? Somebody told me the other day that they had invited friends round to dinner and they had agreed that the couple who had been invited would bring a course. It was that sort of casual, kitchen-supper arrangement in which everybody contributes."

"So?"

"Well, the guests—a husband and wife—brought a casserole dish of stew. The hosts provided the starter and the pudding."

"All right."

"Everything went very well," Isabel continued. "The guests, though, had brought too much stew. There were only four people at the table and their stew would have fed six. So there were two portions left over. The hostess noticed and thought, **Good, that'll do for our dinner tomorrow. I won't have to cook**."

Jamie listened. "Stew improves, doesn't it? I think it tastes better the next day."

"So do I," said Isabel. "Perhaps one should always eat leftovers. One would cook everything a day in advance and not touch it until the next day. But that's not the point of this story. The point is this: at the end of the meal the guests took the leftovers away with them."

Jamie looked pensive. "It was their casserole dish. That's reasonable enough."

Isabel had thought of that. "Yes, they had to take it back. But the stew had been taken from their casserole dish before the dinner and put into the host's serving dish."

Jamie frowned. "So they put it back into their casserole?"

"Yes. At the end. They all cleared up and she—the guest—spooned the stew back into its original casserole, which she then took away with her."

Jamie did not hesitate to condemn that. “Way out of line,” he said. “The stew belonged to the hostess from when it was transferred to her serving dish.” He paused. “But it was also mean.”

“That’s what I think,” said Isabel. “The whole case becomes complicated because of the casserole dish. It would be simpler if it had been breakfast they were having and the guests had brought, say, eight croissants—two each—and people didn’t finish them.”

“Four left?” suggested Jamie.

“Yes. Four. Let’s say they’ll be sitting on a table still in their brown-paper packet.”

“That’s where they should remain,” said Jamie firmly.

“I agree,” said Isabel. “It’s a gift, isn’t it?”

“Yes, of course. And you don’t take gifts back, do you?”

Jamie wondered whether that was an absolute rule. Could there not be circumstances in which it became apparent that a gift was not appreciated or not being used? Surely you could ask for it back in such a case? Isabel thought you could not. “You have to put up with it,” she said. “You might hint. You might say something like: ‘Remember that china tea service we gave you for your wedding? We love that pattern, and it’s such a pity they're not making it any more. I'd do anything—anything!—to get my hands on more like it.' " She smiled. "And then you might add: 'You're so wise, keeping it in a cupboard, unused.' "

"Not very subtle," said Jamie.

"No. Perhaps not. But there are times when subtlety just won't work, don't you think?"

"Perhaps you should have been less subtle yourself," he said. "Perhaps you should have mentioned cucumbers."

"Just dropped them into the conversation? Perhaps as an expletive. **Oh, cucumber!** Expletives don't have to have a meaning. 'Cucumber' would do fine—like that marvellous Italian expression, **caspita!** It doesn't mean anything at all. It's the equivalent of saying 'heavens.' "

"But 'heavens' does mean something," Jamie objected.

Isabel said nothing.

"And 'cucumber' means something too," Jamie continued.

Isabel rose to her feet and crossed the room to the fridge in the corner. "I know we've just had dinner," she said. "But all this talk of cucumber is just too much. I'm going to make myself a cucumber sandwich." She turned and looked over her shoulder at Jamie. "Want one?"

He did, and a minute or two later they were seated at the table again, a small plate of thinly cut cucumber sandwiches in front of them. "Heaven," said Isabel, as she began to eat. "Singular. Heaven."

AS ISABEL LET DUNCAN into the house the following morning, she could see that he was nervous.

"I'm sorry that I'm so early," he said. "I was worried what would happen if there was a delay on the roads."

She reassured him that it made no difference to her, as long as he would not mind entertaining himself for half an hour or so. "I have to take my son to nursery school."

He made an apologetic gesture. "Of course, of course. I'll be fine."

She left him in the sitting room with a copy of that morning's newspaper. She had started the crossword over her breakfast cup of coffee and had not got very far. She enquired whether he did crosswords. He did. "Eight down," she said. " 'A dirty child will not like this command.' Four words. It begins with an **o**."

He took the paper from her. His hand, she saw, was shaking. He glanced at the crossword and then looked up. "Order of the Bath," he said.

Isabel laughed. "Yes! Why didn't I think of that?"

"I'm sure that you would have," he said.

"It's such an odd name for a chivalric order," mused Isabel. "I gather it was something to do with the fact that medieval knights were washed to purify them. Rather like baptism."

Duncan made a polite expression of interest, but she could tell that his mind was elsewhere.

"Not that people bathed very much in those days," said Isabel. "Do you know that a Venetian ambassador expressed surprise that Queen Elizabeth I took a bath every month—even when she didn't need one."

He did not laugh.

"You're nervous," she said.

He looked down at his feet. "Very."

"I don't think there's any danger," she said. "All these people want is money. I don't think they're violent criminals or anything like that."

"It's not that I'm worried about," Duncan said. "It's my painting I'm worried about. It could get damaged if they're carting it around. These people will know nothing about how to treat a painting." As he spoke, his anxiety gave way to anger. "It means nothing to them. It's just a way of extorting money. They don't care about anything else."

Isabel put a hand on his forearm. “There’s every chance we’ll get this back,” she said. “They have no interest in damaging it.”

She wondered why she was trying to persuade him out of his anger. People had a right to be angry when they were the victims of ill-treatment. We automatically tended to calm them down, but perhaps we should let anger run its course. It had its function, she imagined, which was . . . What exactly **was** the role of anger? Self-protection? Did anger serve the purpose of encouraging us to avoid harmful situations in the future? Did it show us who our enemies were?

She looked at her watch. Jamie had been dressing Charlie upstairs and she needed to relieve him: he had to be at the Academy in forty minutes for his pupils, and he was planning to call on Grace later. She left Duncan with the newspaper, inviting him to tackle the crossword if he wished. Upstairs, Charlie was now ready. “Tiffin box,” he said. “Don’t forget tiffin box.”

She led him downstairs, collected the tiffin box from the kitchen and made her way out of the front door, Charlie walking beside her, his hand in hers. He was wearing a pair of red shoes of which he was inordinately proud. “Red shoes go fast,” he announced.

“That’s right, they do, darling,” said Isabel.

She squeezed the tiny hand that was holding on to hers, and the tiny hand squeezed back. She imagined what it must be like to have Charlie's mind—to believe that red shoes are faster than other shoes; to believe, as he did, that ducks could drive fire engines and that pigs built houses of bricks and straw. There were plenty of people who weren't three-and-three-quarters who believed equally implausible things . . . and went to war over them.

They made slow progress, as Charlie's steps, in spite of his red shoes, were small. A few yards away from the house Isabel noticed a car that had been parked in one of the parking bays pull out into the road. She had not been paying particular attention to it, but she glimpsed the driver briefly before he made off. He was vaguely familiar; somebody from a neighbouring street whom she had seen walking in to Bruntsfield or in the delicatessen, perhaps? Or had she met him somewhere else? Her gaze followed the retreating car: she could just make out the back of the driver's head now; nothing more than that. And then it dawned on her. It was Patrick, or somebody who looked very much like him.

She stopped in her tracks.

"Why we stopping?" asked Charlie.

"Because I've just seen something, Charlie. I've just seen something odd."

They resumed the journey, but as they did so, Isabel went over in her mind the possible explanations for Patrick's presence. Coincidence led the list. Patrick might have a friend in the area and might be visiting him; there was no law against visiting your friends first thing in the morning. Or he had spent the night at a friend's house and was now going back to his flat. Or it was not Patrick at all.

Those were the innocent explanations. The less innocent included the possibility that Patrick was watching his father, or, and this made Isabel's heart skip a beat, that he was watching **her**. If Patrick were in some way mixed up in the theft of the painting, then he could be expected to have a close interest in the outcome of today's meeting. The thieves would be concerned about the police coming to the meeting, and so they would naturally want to be warned when Duncan came into town to pick up Isabel. That could explain Patrick's presence—if, indeed, it was Patrick whom she had seen.

After she had dropped Charlie off at the nursery, Isabel returned to the house, where she found Duncan immersed in the crossword.

"It took my mind off things," he said. "Not that I've made much progress with it—apart from this." He passed her the newspaper and she looked at the clues he had filled in. Order of the Bath had helped him to get **The sea sounds like a man** (brine) and **A plucked instrument says Italian yes to group of notes; it has a keyboard** (harpsichord).

"Very clever," she said.

"Not really."

She looked at her watch. They could walk to Rutland Square if they had time—it was only twenty minutes from Isabel's house to the west end of Princes Street, and Rutland Square was only minutes from there. But it was now nine o'clock and they could not afford to be late. Isabel telephoned for a taxi and suggested that they wait for it at the gate. "They don't take long," she said. Duncan nodded; he was still distracted, she noticed, and she thought that she could make out beads of sweat across his brow.

"It's going to be all right," she said, as she locked the front door behind him.

He swallowed. "Yes, thank you. Thank you."

They stood under the large tree at the front of the house. Somewhere in the foliage a bird moved; that tree was popular with doves. Charlie was fascinated by them. "Doves got bedrooms?" he had asked.

She looked up the street, attentive now to any cars that were parked nearby. For the first time, she felt what she realised was fear. The people they were about to meet did not belong to her world; they came from a world in which the rights of others did not matter. She had assured Duncan that they would not be violent, but how did she know that? The answer was that she did not.

In the taxi, Duncan sat quietly, not attempting to make conversation but staring out of the window at the houses and at the cluster of shops at the top of the road that led down to the canal. They passed a church on which a large banner had been hung. **We must love one another**, it said. We must, she thought. And Auden came to mind, again, as he did in the most unexpected circumstances. It was "1st September 1939," the poem that people in New York read and sent to one another after that fateful September day in 2001. They found comfort in it because it was about the ending of a world and the despair that this will bring. He had originally written: "We must love one another or die," and had changed it to: "We must love one another **and** die." Auden disowned the poem, considering it mendacious; but it had a grave beauty about it. Things that are not sincere can be as striking as those that are, and insincerity, thought Isabel, can—curiously—end up being sincere.

She turned to Duncan. The taxi had stopped at the lights outside the King's Theatre; the traffic was moving slowly. "Your son," she said. "Your son, Patrick. I thought I saw him."

He looked puzzled. "You met him?"

"I did. At a concert. I thought I'd told you that when I came out to Doune."

"Did you? Perhaps you did. I can't remember, I'm afraid."

"I thought I saw him," she said.

He frowned.

"I mean, I thought I saw him this morning. In a car. On my street."

He took a handkerchief out of his pocket and dabbed at his brow. "You probably did."

Now it was Isabel's turn to look puzzled.

"He drove me to your place," said Duncan. "I called on him this morning. I wanted to leave my car near his flat. You can park up there. Your area has these regulations."

Isabel felt relieved. The innocent explanation meant that she had not been imagining things—

it had been him—and at the same time served to defuse the awkward possibility that Patrick was somehow involved in the theft of the painting.

"He knows what's happening this morning?" she asked.

"Yes," said Duncan. "I told him." He looked down at his hands. "My son and I are, regrettably, not close."

She said that she was sorry to hear that.

"Thank you. I'm afraid that he's something of a disappointment to me."

He looked at her as he spoke, and she felt that he was asking something of her. Did he want reassurance? Did he want some sort of comfort?

"I suspected that," she said.

"Why?" There was a note of surprise in his voice.

She chose her words carefully. "I formed the impression that you might . . ." She faltered. What did she want to say? That he and Patrick inhabited different worlds?

"Go on," he said. "Please go on. Tell me what you think."

She had not imagined that she would discuss it with him, but now he was asking. "I can understand how it's sometimes difficult," she said.

"It is," he said. "It is difficult."

"I have a friend whose son is gay," said Isabel. "She found it hard at first, but she realised that what really counted was his happiness, and he was happy. She . . ." She trailed off. Duncan was staring at her in incomprehension.

"I really don't know what you mean," he said.

She struggled to find words. It had suddenly dawned on her that either he did not know or that she had been mistaken in her conclusion that Patrick was gay. Perhaps the assumption was misplaced—one cannot read the lives of others on a cursory meeting.

Duncan now looked confused. "My son . . . ," he began, and then, looking down at the floor of the cab, he lapsed into silence.

"I'm sorry," said Isabel. "I really don't know your son."

He did not meet her eyes. "There is a political difference between us," he said. "My own views are liberal—middle-of-the-roadish. I'm not particularly political, I suppose. But he . . . he's an extremist, I'm sorry to say. He's in with a very leftish bunch—not the Labour Party or any of the other mainstream options of the left, but the real hard left—a small outfit in Glasgow. He gives them money. Castro is his hero, as far as I can make out. I try to point out to him that Castro took many prisoners of conscience over the years, but he won't hear any of it. He even laments the passing of the Soviet Union. He forgets about the Gulag, the KGB, the millions who perished under Stalin."

Isabel listened. Had the traffic not been so slow, they would have been at their destination by now; as it was, they were stuck in a line of cars outside the Usher Hall. "People change," she said. "The scales may fall from his eyes. And . . ." She hesitated, unsure whether to broaden the discussion, but decided to do so. "And if you look behind the party allegiance, you may find some fine sentiments. The left generally want people to have good lives, don't you think? They want people to have their material needs satisfied, to be lifted out of poverty. Perhaps your son—"

He interrupted her. "We all want that." He sounded vehement. "Who doesn't want hospitals and schools and all the rest? It's how we achieve the material satisfaction that's the issue. He thinks you can have it by taking everybody's property away from them and having state ownership of everything. He really thinks that."

"No," said Isabel. "That wouldn't work."

He looked at her now. "I'm a farmer, and I know that if you take land out of the hands of individual farmers and collectivise it, you destroy agriculture. Every single historical example has shown that to be the case. Yet Patrick, my own son, told me that I had no right to the five hundred acres I farm. He said that if I leave the farm to him, he'll treat it as a collective." He snorted. "Collective agriculture? How long would that work? A month?"

The traffic had started to move again and they were approaching the end of Lothian Road. To their left was the Caledonian Hotel, a great edifice of red sandstone, while on the other side of the road St. John's Church marked the end of Princes Street Gardens. The church was displaying a line of flags on its forecourt: the Scottish flag, the Saltire, fluttered above flags of the various European countries and a flag on which the word **Peace** was sewn in great black letters. **We must love one another and die**, thought Isabel.

The taxi turned and began to make its way down the short road that led to Rutland Square. "You could drop us right here," Isabel called out to the driver.

Duncan reached for his coat. "We can talk about Patrick some other time," he said; he spoke in the tone of one wanting to shelve an awkward topic.

• • •

ISABEL KNEW RUTLAND SQUARE for two reasons. Her friend Lesley Kerr had her legal office in one corner of the square, and she had occasionally called there to collect her for lunch. And on the other side, in a three-storeyed Georgian building looking out over the gardens that made up the centre of the square, was the Scottish Arts Club. Isabel went to dinners there from time to time, and parties too—the club had long had a reputation as the most hospitable of Edinburgh clubs, with its talks on the arts, its Sheeps Heid dinners, its Burns Nights. Isabel sometimes had lunch there with another friend, Lucy Mackay, an artist known for her portraits and wispy, whimsical watercolours. That was her Rutland Square, a place with predominantly positive associations but which Isabel was now visiting in a very different context.

Duncan paid off the taxi and the cab shot off to its next assignment. His nervousness had now returned, and he looked about him uneasily. "What now? We walk around?"

Isabel took his arm. "Yes. To all intents and purposes we are just two people out for a walk."

She pointed to a man walking two black Labradors on their leashes. "Like him."

They began to walk round the square. Isabel glanced discreetly at her watch; in spite of the traffic delays, they were still at least ten minutes early.

"They could be watching us," said Duncan.

"They probably are," said Isabel.

They continued their walk in silence. There was not a great deal happening in the square, which was tucked away from the busy thoroughfares of Princes Street and Lothian Road. Now, in midsummer, the trees made an island of green, their leaves sibilant in the warm morning breeze. "The winds must come from somewhere when they blow" . . . it was among the most beautiful of lines. WHA again, even here, she thought, when I'm about to enter the murky, unpleasant world of theft.

They reached the western end of the square and began to make their way in the direction of the Scottish Arts Club. The lights were on in the drawing room; somebody was reading a paper, enjoying a cup of coffee. And on the other side of the club, in a house now converted to offices, she saw a man and a woman talking in front of a window—the ordinary world of legitimate business: a world in which people did not hold one another to ransom; a world in which rules, like hidden, powerful electrical fields, governed the affairs of men.

She was suddenly aware of Duncan's hand on her arm. He was whispering something that she found it hard to catch.

She whispered back, although there was nobody about to hear them. "Yes? What is it?"

"There's somebody parked up ahead. He's looking at us."

She switched her gaze to the vehicles parked up against the garden railings. She saw a large grey car that had been carelessly parked and was protruding into the road; an old Morgan, lovingly tended, its silver trimmings worn almost to the base metal below from the rubbing of generations of polishing cloth; both were empty. But then, behind the Morgan, parked hard up against it so that the bumpers must almost have been touching, was a black van with a long crack in the windscreen. There was a man at the wheel.

"I think that must be them," said Duncan out of the side of his mouth.

"We'll find out soon enough," said Isabel. She was not sure; there were building works going on in one of the buildings in the square and the man could have had something to do with those—there were other builders' vans in the square, disgorging planks of wood and other mysteries of their craft.

Isabel slowed her pace. She found it hard to pretend to be casual in the face of observation, particularly from somebody who was probably either a builder or a thief. Some builders took it as their right to watch women with an appraising look that was frequently nakedly intrusive; they still wolf-whistled and called out—as Italian men used to do before they suddenly grew up. Why did men think they could behave that way? What satisfaction did they get from wolf-whistling? It was about power, thought Isabel. It was about being able to assert themselves publicly and to objectify women. It was a direct denial of the idea that men and women should treat one another with courtesy and consideration; it was a nod to the days of strutting men and meek, passive women.

Thinking of builders helped to take her mind off being watched, with the result that when the window of the van was suddenly—and noisily—wound down, she was not paying full attention to it.

"Over here."

The tone of the voice was peremptory; the vowels were those of the east of Scotland. Isabel looked. He was staring at them through the open window of the van: a man in his early thirties, or thereabouts, with lank, mousy hair and a chin that was covered in heavy stubble.

She stepped off the pavement and began to cross the road towards the van with Duncan following behind. "Quick," the man called out. "Get a move on."

Isabel, offended by his rudeness, regarded him with disdain as they approached the van. She saw that there were two earrings in his right ear—two small studs, one of which was red. It was a code, she imagined. What had Eddie once said to her about men and earrings? Left: right; right: wrong.

He stared at them through the open window. "Get in the back," he said. "The door's open."

She smelled something on the man's breath: stale alcohol. She saw that his eyes were bloodshot and that the skin around them seemed to be puffed-up. He was not sober, she thought, but then some men like this never were.

"Why?" she asked.

"Do you want to see the thing?" His voice had become a sneer.

She felt her heart beating within her. She

would remain calm; she was determined to deny him the satisfaction of seeing her riled.

Isabel kept her voice level as she replied, "Yes. That's why we're here."

Duncan now stepped forward. "Is my painting in the back?" he asked.

The driver stared at him for a moment or two before answering. "No, it isn't, Pop. I'm taking you to see it. But only if youses shift yoursels and get in." He used the demotic plural of **you**, a common feature of speech in Scotland. Isabel had always rather liked it, just as she liked the complimentary Texan plural **you-all** that her mother had told her about. "It assumes that nobody would be unfortunate enough to be on their own," she used to explain. "Hence **you-all**."

There was something in the driver's answer that made Duncan start. She looked at him and he shook his head, as if to put her off saying anything now.

"I think we should probably do this," Duncan said to her. "Do you mind?"

Isabel weighed the possibilities. It was no small step to get into the back of a strange van, especially one driven by so patently unpleasant a person as this; but what was the alternative? If they declined, then the whole arrangement for the recovery of the Poussin—and the painting—could be in jeopardy.

She nodded to Duncan, and they walked round to the back of the van. Duncan opened the doors hesitantly.

"I'm not sure," he said. He stopped. A man dressed entirely in black, his face half covered by a football scarf, his eyes obscured by sunglasses, was crouching on the floor of the van. Gripped on either side by his gloved hands was the Poussin.

Isabel gasped. Her hand went to her mouth.

"See this," said the man, jerking the painting towards them but still keeping his tight grip on it. "See?"

Isabel noticed the sky, saw the intense Poussin blue, saw the clouds; that was her abiding impression—the clouds. Absurdly, she wanted to say something about the painting, even now, in this threatening, tense situation—she wanted to say something about the beauty of the painting. **We don't react in the right way**, she thought; **we think the wrong things, as I am doing now**. She had read of people who found themselves facing death and who subsequently survived and of how they had spent what could have been their last precious seconds thinking about some matter of no real consequence—whether they had paid the newsagent's bill or licensed the car or something like that. It was the same with last words, which were no doubt mostly banal and often inappropriate, although some, at least, managed a memorable final statement, as did Charles II. He had apologised for taking so long to go: **You must pardon me, gentlemen, for being a most unconscionable time a-dying.**

There came a growl from the front, as the engine started. The man holding the painting looked over his shoulder through a small window that gave on to the cab. Then he looked back and jerked his head. "That's it," he said. "Out."

He laid the Poussin down on the floor and reached forward to close the doors. Isabel backed off, but Duncan did not. She looked at him in alarm, concerned that he might try to snatch the painting.

"My painting . . . ," he stuttered.

The man pushed him out of the way, not roughly but firmly. "Sorry," he said. "Show's over."

The door slammed shut and the van pulled out sharply on to the road. They watched as it sped away; it barely slowed down to negotiate the difficult bend that would allow it access to the back lane behind the square.

Isabel turned to Duncan. She saw that he was about to cry, and intuitively she reached out to embrace him, to comfort him.

"I'm very sorry," he said, struggling to compose himself. "I find this very upsetting."

"Of course it is. And there's nothing to be embarrassed about."

She patted his shoulder, as she might pat Charlie when he hurt himself and ran to her for the embrace that could so miraculously relieve the pain. It was understandable that one might cry in the face of something like this, not only out of frustration at seeing a beloved object treated in this way, but for what the whole unpleasant little episode represented. So one might cry for everything that was wrong with the world, for all the injustice and crudity and cruelty, for all the things that are stolen from people.

CHAPTER THIRTEEN

EDDIE CRIED, too, later that morning. It was in very different circumstances—not publicly, in Rutland Square, but in a small clinic room, with the antiseptic smell so characteristic of such places, the smell of cleanliness. On the wall behind Eddie's head, tacked on to a noticeboard, was a poster with dietary recommendations: **Five pieces of fruit and vegetables a day for a healthy life**. Isabel, seated beside Eddie, wondered briefly: Do they mean five pieces of fruit and five pieces of vegetable, or five in total? It was five in total, she knew, because that was the message that had been drummed into people's heads over the last few years—except for some heads, particularly in those Scottish cities where the diet tended to greasy food and no vegetables at all and, according to legend, deep-fried chocolate bars. Jamie confirmed that he had seen them served and had even tasted one after an evening at the Glasgow Concert Hall; not that they sold them there, he hastily added, but they had found somewhere nearby that did. "When in Rome," he said, smiling. In Rome, of course, they did nothing so foolish as eating deep-fried chocolate bars, but courted disaster in their own ways, as all people do. We each have our own way of behaving self-destructively, thought Isabel; we each have our folly, and for the Italians it was . . . What was it? Their Mediterranean diet was famously healthy, with all its tomatoes and fish and olive oil, and although they liked wine, there was evidence, much proclaimed by topers, that two glasses of wine a day was positively beneficial. They took siestas—if they could—and that was also good for health. So what did they do that was self-destructive? They drove too fast; that was all she could think of.

She held Eddie's hand as the nurse behind the desk referred to the file in front of her.

"Everything's fine," said the nurse. "All the tests are clear."

Isabel thought at first that Eddie had not understood. He gasped as the nurse spoke, and half turned to Isabel. Then he started to sob.

"It's fine, Eddie," Isabel said. "Listen to what she said. It's fine."

Eddie turned back to face the nurse.

"Yes, it's all right," repeated the nurse. "Negative. Everything's fine."

"It takes a little time to sink in," said Isabel, pressing Eddie's hand gently.

"So . . . ," Eddie began, but stopped.

"So, you're fine." Isabel pressed his hand again. She looked at the nurse, who nodded.

The nurse began to say something about counselling and being careful; Isabel looked away, as she did not feel that it was appropriate for her to listen at that point. But it did not last long. Eddie said, "Yes, I know, I know," and the nurse did not persist.

They went outside, into the sun.

"That's that," said Isabel. "Happier?"

Eddie nodded. "Very," he said.

Isabel looked at the sky. On the same day, within little more than a few hours, she had seen two men cry, and had comforted both. She could not help but reflect on the differences between these men: Duncan, middle-aged and wealthy, the product of an expensive education and a family that was perfectly assured of its place in the world; Eddie, whose life had been far harder in every respect, whose horizons had been so much more limited, but who had a future before him. Would Duncan exchange lives with Eddie if, by some miracle, he were given the chance? It was a peculiar thought experiment that Isabel liked to engage in occasionally. Would one choose youth—and years—rather than comfort and the security of being oneself? Would the elderly millionaire change places with the indigent twenty-one-year-old?

They decided to walk back to their side of town. Isabel had a book to collect from a bookshop on South Bridge and Eddie said that he would accompany her. "I just want to walk," he said. "I don't think I could focus on anything right now. I actually want to fly, you know, but I can't, and so I'll walk."

She smiled at him.

Eddie continued: "I was worried for so long. I put things out of my mind and then every so often it would come back to me and I would go all cold."

"Anybody would," said Isabel.

They made their way along Hanover Street and then up the Playfair Steps at the back of the National Gallery. Below them, the railway lines caught the afternoon sun until they were swallowed by the tunnel under the Gallery.

"When I was very young," said Isabel, "I

thought that the tunnel down there was Glasgow. I was told that the trains went to Glasgow and I saw them disappear into that tunnel. I thought that it must be Glasgow."

Eddie laughed. "When I was seven, something like that, I used to go through to Glasgow to see an uncle," he said. "But he was never in. We went several times, but I don't think he was ever there."

"What do they say? It's better to travel hopefully than to arrive?"

"Do they?"

"Yes," she said. "They do."

They climbed the remaining steps in silence. Isabel thought about Eddie's saying that he wanted to fly. We all did. Who had not imagined themselves flying; who had not dreamed that they could fly? The dream interpreters spoiled those dreams of flying, which they said were not about flying at all. But they were; that, or freedom, perhaps, but not about sex, as they insisted. Everything, they said, was about sex except . . . perhaps sex itself. Isabel smiled: a dream about sex was really about flying—what would they say to that?

They paused at the top of the steps and looked back over the New Town, now lying below them.

Isabel noticed that although neither of them was breathless from the exertion of climbing the steps, Eddie's face had coloured. She wondered about exercise: he came to the delicatessen each morning by bus; perhaps he should be encouraged to walk to work. But that was none of her business. You did not tell your friends to get fit or lose weight. They made that decision themselves and then you complimented them on the effort.

After collecting the book, Isabel treated Eddie to a cup of coffee in the bookshop coffee bar. Eddie had cream on the top of his, and she found herself pointing to the topping—rich, white, fatal—and saying, "You can't, Eddie!"

He looked at her in surprise. "What's wrong with cream?"

"Everything," she replied, then thought again. "Well, no, not everything, but you see, we have these things called arteries and . . ."

He was grinning at her. "Yes?"

"Another time. I don't want you to think that I'm trying to run your life."

His grin widened. "Unless I wanted you to."

She toyed with the small packet of sugar—destined to be unused—that had come with her coffee. "Which, of course, you don't want."

"Who says?"

The conversation had started lightly but there was now a tinge of seriousness. Isabel frowned as she wondered where it was leading. He was Eddie, the young man who worked in the delicatessen; she was his employer's aunt; he was in his early twenties and she was in her early forties. There were not quite twenty years between them, but the gap was almost that large. He was damaged, and was hesitantly feeling his way towards recovery; she would help in that—of course she would—but it would not be a good idea for him to replace whatever had been missing in his relationship with his parents with some form of substitute provided by her.

He answered his own question quickly. "I say . . ."

She looked away.

"I mean," he continued, "that there's something I really want you to do for me, Isabel. Will you do it?"

She looked back at him. His expression was imploring. Whatever he had in mind was important to him, and she could not simply brush him off.

"It depends, Eddie. Obviously it depends. You know that I'm happy to help you but I can't do everything."

"I know that. And this isn't everything. It's dead simple."

"What is it?"

He sniffed.

"Do you need a hanky?"

"No. I'm all right. Sometimes there are things that make me sniff. Something in the air. Pollen maybe. But not here, I suppose."

"You were telling me about this thing you want me to do."

He sniffed again. "You know I've got this girlfriend?"

"Yes, Diane. I met her the other day at the deli, remember?" She paused. "Is everything still all right there?"

"Yeah, yeah. Fine. No problems with that."

She said that she was glad to hear it. And then he went on, "Her parents are the problem. They hate me."

Perhaps it was an exaggeration to say that they hated him, but Diane had told Isabel herself that her parents disapproved of him, considered him beneath them. And for Eddie, the difference between hate and disapproval in such circumstances surely seemed slight.

She tried to reassure him. "Hate is a very strong word, as we know, Eddie. Parents often don't see things the way their children do. They have their own ideas about who are suitable boyfriends or girlfriends for their sons and daughters. They may have ambitions for them—"

He cut her short, his anger now surfacing. "They think I'm no good."

She wondered how to respond to that. He evidently understood exactly how they felt.

"I'm sure they don't think you're . . ." She searched for the right word. "Bad. I'm sure they don't think that. You're not involved in drugs or anything like that."

"I could be, the way they talk about me . . . So, if it's not that, then what is it? Because I'm not from their group or whatever? Is that it?"

She nodded. "To be frank, yes. People are like that."

He shook his head in frustration. "So what do they expect me to do?"

She considered his question. It was, she thought, exactly the right question to ask, as it exposed the moral flaw in Diane's parents' position. You can only blame people for that which they have chosen to do—Aristotle spelled that out clearly enough. And that meant that you should not hold it against somebody for being what he **is**. A person's background, then, was the classic example of something for which he can never be judged adversely.

"They shouldn't expect anything of you, Eddie. There's nothing wrong with being who you are and you have nothing to be ashamed of or to reproach yourself about. Nothing."

"So why do they hate me?"

They wished him to be something different, she said, and that was impossible, and wrong. If they knew him properly, then they would surely realise that there was nothing wrong with him; that he was a perfectly good choice for Diane.

He was alerted by what she said. "If they knew me properly?"

"Yes. I'm sure that if they knew you better they'd see your merits. You're kind to Diane, aren't you? You treat her well?"

"Of course."

"And the two of you are happy together?"

"Yes. Really happy. That's why we want to live together, which they don't want." He paused. "But listen, you said that if they knew more about me, they might not be so hostile. That's just what I want you to do for me. I want you to talk to them."

"Diane's parents?"

"Yes. Talk to them. Tell them that I'm OK. Tell them that there's no reason why we shouldn't get this flat. Tell them—"

She stopped him. "I'm not sure, Eddie. I don't think I should interfere."

He looked incredulous. "But Cat says that you're always interfering. She says that you get mixed up in all sorts of things and that you help people. She told me. And everybody knows it. They know that if they need something sorted, they can go to you."

Isabel looked at her watch. "You have to get back to work," she said. "Cat's expecting you."

"But you haven't answered me."

She picked up her coffee cup. The coffee was almost too cold to drink. "Give me some time to think," she said briskly. "I need to think about it."

"Do you think you can? Do you think you can speak to them?"

She put down her cup. "I don't know them," she said. "How can I go and speak to people I don't know?"

"You do that for other people," he muttered.

She knew that what he said was true. She spoke to people for other people. But she also knew Diane's difficulties over setting up home with Eddie were not simply to do with parental opposition.

"I'll think about it," she said, picking up the

plastic bag that contained her book. It was a book she had ordered a week ago, Scanlon's **What We Owe to Each Other.** She needed it for an editorial she was writing on contractualism in moral philosophy and . . . she smiled; she needed it for her life.

"What's so funny?" asked Eddie nervously.

She wanted to cheer him up. Half an hour previously he had been talking about wanting to fly; now he seemed morose. "What's so funny? Life," said Isabel. "Come on, Eddie. Let's get going."

SHE WAS BACK at the house in time to collect Charlie from nursery. Jamie was at home, practising, in case Isabel should be late and he would need to do the Charlie collection. Her return liberated him; he had promised to see a friend about a recital they were planning and he needed to get away. He was anxious, though, to hear about Isabel's morning.

"You saw the painting?"

She nodded. "Yes. Can we talk about it later, though? I'll have to go for Charlie."

He looked relieved. "Did you see them—the thieves?"

"Yes." She stopped. Were those men the thieves or the intermediaries? Did it make much difference? "I saw the people who had the painting. I didn't see very much of them, though . . ."

Jamie's eyes widened. "They were masked?"

"Nothing so melodramatic. It all happened rather quickly—and they were wearing scarves. I couldn't really give you a description of them. Thirty-ish? One had earrings. There was a certain amount of tension and aggression, but we weren't hurt." She turned. Talking about what had happened made her feel somehow queasy. Was this how people felt after a traumatic experience? Weak at the knees, sick, fearful perhaps? Or even dirtied? She had heard about how people who were the victims of assault could sometimes blame themselves for what happened. Was that happening to her?

To change the subject, Isabel asked about Grace. "Will you tell me about the peace mission? Later?"

Jamie's face fell. "Some messages of peace fall on stony ground."

"Oh."

He nodded. "I'll try again."

She wanted him to do that. The house seemed empty without Grace. And it would be dustier too and Jamie's shirts would be unironed and she would miss hearing about the latest goings-on with the local council and their iniquities, and the failings of the bus service, and the spiritualist meetings . . . There was so much that Grace brought to her life, as any friend or colleague does. That, Isabel thought, was what made the texture of our lives: the doings, the little ways of those about us. We defined ourselves socially as much as we did individually, perhaps even more so, and that, or course, meant duties to others . . . including to people like Eddie. But I can't, she said to herself; I can't go out and interfere in the lives of people I've never met, who would not thank me for giving them my opinion on a matter that is no affair of mine. No, I can't. And yet Eddie has asked me to do this and if he has no claim on me, then who does?

CHARLIE WAS BREWING a cold and would not settle to any activity that afternoon. By the time that Jamie came home at seven in the evening, Isabel was ready for a glass of wine. Charlie had been put to bed and had dozed off quickly in spite of his runny nose and incipient cough.

"Should I be worried?" she said to Jamie. "I

really want a glass of wine, and that makes me wonder whether I should be concerned."

"Anybody can want a glass of wine," Jamie reassured her. "I'd be worried if you wanted a whole bottle."

"Sometimes . . ."

He had never seen her the worse for alcohol. "I don't believe you," he said, handing her a glass. "And here's the remedy from New Zealand."

The wine had a delicious fruitiness. She let it linger in her mouth. "Oh, well," she said. "My day."

Suddenly, and with so little warning that she surprised even herself, she felt tears well up in her eyes.

Jamie put down the glass he had poured for himself. "Isabel . . ."

She fought it for a moment or two, but then yielded. "It's been . . ."

He took the wine glass from her hand. "It must have been."

". . . horrible."

"Yes. I know."

She spoke between sobs, the words jumbled. "Eddie too. Poor Eddie."

A cloud passed over Jamie's face. "Bad news?"

She shook her head. "No. Good news."

He stroked her cheek gently. His hand was wet with her tears. "I'm glad. I thought it could be different."

"He asked me. He asked me to speak to . . . you know, that girlfriend of his has parents who disapprove of him and he wants to live with her . . ."

"You said something about that. But listen, don't worry about all that."

"And those people, those people who stole the painting . . ."

He said nothing.

"It was an attitude of disregard," Isabel went on. "We were nothing to them."

"There are plenty of people like that," said Jamie. "Plenty of people disregard others. Plenty of people hold others in contempt. Turn on the television and see it."

She was beginning to compose herself. She reached for her wine glass; he dropped his hands from her shoulders. "Here's to those nice New Zealanders," she said.

"At least there are plenty of those," said Jamie.

Isabel was thinking. "I've been trying to remember the details of what happened. I've been trying to piece it together."

"Tell me then," said Jamie. "Describe it exactly

as it happened, moment by moment. That might help you to remember."

They sat down at the kitchen table. "We were walking in Rutland Square, Duncan and I."

"Yes. Then?"

"Then Duncan drew my attention to a van parked nearby. I saw a man in the driver's seat. He was watching us, and he put the window down and called us over."

"What did he say?"

"Something like 'Come here.' No, it was 'Over here.' Just that."

"And what did he look like? Picture him."

"His eyes were puffy and bloodshot. He had a thin face. Earrings. Two rings in one ear. One of the earrings was red. I noticed that and thought it might be a code of some sort."

Jamie shrugged. "Piercings mean nothing. They mean you've been pierced—that's all."

Then Isabel remembered something. It came back to her with clarity. "He called Duncan 'Pop.'"

Jamie looked puzzled. "Is that important?"

She did not answer immediately. She was thinking. Pop. Why would that be significant? She felt that it was, but she could not work out why this should be so. It was the sort of thing that somebody like that might call a middle-aged man if he wanted to show contempt; a casual, sarcastic equivalent of "Granddad." And then she remembered. That was what Patrick had called his father; he had said, "Pop is very unworldly."

She explained this to Jamie and asked him what he thought. He looked doubtful. "Anybody might call somebody that," he said. "I don't think that proves anything."

"But it could," Isabel insisted.

"Yes. It could. But that's not the same as saying that it does. Could and does are different."

She conceded that. But now that she thought about it, it was quite possible the painting had been stolen by Patrick. He had the knowledge and obviously he would have the opportunity. But what about motive?

"Imagine for a moment that Patrick did it," she said. "What would his motive have been?"

Jamie returned the question. "Why does anybody steal anything?"

"Money, usually. Either that, or they want the thing itself."

He nodded. "Does he need money?"

"According to his sister, yes. She said something about expensive habits."

Jamie made a gesture that said: Well, there you have it.

"So what do I do?"

Jamie made another gesture. This time it said: Don't ask me. Then he expanded on the theme. "I really can't suggest anything, Isabel. And, frankly, I don't see what you can possibly do. If the insurance company wants the painting back, then they're going to have to pay. It may stick in their throats, but I can't see what else they can do."

"Unless . . . ," interjected Isabel.

"Unless what?"

"Unless the person who stole it were to have it made known to him that we know who he is. We might then give him a chance to return it, failing which . . ."

"Yes? Failing which?"

"Failing which, the police are informed."

"On the basis of what evidence? Your hunch?"

He was right. They knew nothing more than they had known a few days ago.

"I think I should see him again," said Isabel. She was speaking half to herself, half to Jamie.

"Who?" he asked.

"Patrick."

Jamie frowned. "And confront him with your suspicions?"

"I shall be more subtle than that," said Isabel.

Jamie looked away. "I doubt if you'll achieve anything," he said.

She suspected that he was right, but she felt that she could still try.

"You know something?" she said. "I sometimes feel that lies are tangible. When they're being told, they seem to hang in the air, almost so that you can touch them. It's very strange."

Jamie looked bemused. "I think it depends on the liar," he said. "A good liar doesn't create that impression; a bad one does."

She knew what he meant. Her metaphor was probably based on no more than a reading of body language—those small clues that people give to what is in their mind. And guilt was a powerful creator of such tell-tale signs: the flushed expression, the avoidance of eye contact, the shifting of limbs; all these revealed inner discomfort springing from simple guilt. A liar could show these signs just as surely as he could show any of those physical signs that triggered a response on a polygraph: the heart rate, respiration, the reactions of the skin. But what if the liar is psychopathic and feels none of that? What if he feels not in the slightest bit guilty? What if he is proud of his lie? Patrick might feel that if he had acted out of a sense of entitlement, or because he believed that he was redistributing what he saw as his father's ill-gotten wealth. The children of the rich can feel strongly about that, Isabel knew; there is no fervour like the fervour of those who have been raised in the bosom of those they despise.

"I'd like to try," she said. "I'll see him and say things that might provoke a reaction—one way or the other."

Jamie was curious. "What things?"

She could not answer because she did not know what she was going to say. Sensing her uncertainty, Jamie laughed. "You're the most unlikely Sherlock Holmes," he said. "But very kissable."

"Don't condescend," she said. "Don't speak down to me."

"But I don't," he protested. "Everything I say to you is said from down here to up there. You're up there. I promise. I promise."

"Let's have another glass of wine," she said.

He reached for the bottle. "A bad day can always end well."

"Yes."

He passed her glass. She took it and smiled at him. She had everything. A few years ago, a day that had brought two men to tears and then had ended with her crying too would have been irredeemable. Now it could be salvaged. Completely.

They went through to the music room and he played the piano while she sat on the stool beside him. She put her hand on his knee. He played at random, as he could do for hours, moving from one melody to another. She thought she recognised something from Verdi. "**La traviata**?" He nodded. And then a complete change; a shift of mood and style as he suddenly started to sing "Shoals of Herring," all about a young man on a fishing boat pursuing the herring. Isabel closed her eyes. She imagined Jamie as that young man. Or Charlie, when he was older. Her little boy—a fisherman, battling the North Sea. She thought: I love all these men. I love the men who went to sea and led that hard life. I love them. But how strange to think and say that.

CHAPTER FOURTEEN

❖

YOU WANT my brother's number?" said Alex Munrowe.

At the other end of the telephone, Isabel detected a note of satisfaction in Alex's voice.

"If you don't mind. I didn't want to disturb your father."

"I don't mind at all," said Alex quickly. "May I ask . . . no, perhaps I shouldn't."

There was an expectant silence. Isabel felt she had to explain. "I feel I should discuss the matter with him. That's why."

Now satisfaction was replaced with concern. "You won't mention the conversation we had the other day, will you?"

Isabel thought: Perhaps you shouldn't accuse your brother of theft quite so readily if you don't want it to get back to him. But she did not say that;

instead she reassured Alex that she would not dream of mentioning it. “I regard what you said to me as confidential. I promise you that.”

“Good. Maybe I shouldn’t have been so explicit; it’s just that the thought crossed my mind that if there was anybody who could think of doing something like this, it’s him.”

“You don’t have a very high opinion of your brother, if you don’t mind my saying.”

Alex laughed. “He has his good points. And he is my brother, after all. I’ve never forgotten that. And I’m not sure that he would actually stoop to theft. Yet . . .”

It seemed to Isabel that Alex was blowing hot and cold. If she suspected him of the theft, then she should state her grounds for doing so.

Isabel changed tack. “May I ask you something? If your father discovered that Patrick was behind this, what would the effect be?”

“What do you think?” expostulated Alex. “He’d be devastated. He worships my brother.”

Isabel kept her voice level. “Really?”

“Yes. Pop thinks he’s marvellous—he always has.”

Isabel noticed the use of “Pop.” It was natural that siblings would each use the same name for their father, but it meant that if anything were going to be read into its use by the thieves, then this would throw suspicion on both Alex and Patrick—not just on Patrick. But what puzzled Isabel now was the suggestion that relations between Patrick and his father were good; that was the direct opposite of what Duncan had said to her. This raised the possibility that Alex simply did not know what her father's real feelings were, which could be the case, she decided; children thought they knew what their parents felt, but they could be wrong about that—sometimes dramatically so.

She brought the conversation to an end even though she felt that Alex would have liked to prolong it. There was something irritating about her manner, thought Isabel; it was as if she enjoyed being mischievous. She may have disliked her brother but to suggest, as she had, that he was behind the theft carried with it a feeling of sourness. Disloyalty was like that, Isabel thought: It left a sour taste in the mouth.

By the time she rang off, Isabel had reached a decision. The allegations against Patrick were meretricious and highly unlikely. She would see him, though, because she felt that she had to do something to justify her involvement in this matter. She would talk to him simply to confirm her view that Alex was an idle troublemaker pursuing some sort of petty squabble with her brother—a squabble that probably had its roots in the jealousies of childhood. Somebody had enjoyed more parental attention than somebody else; somebody had been able to run faster or been better at playing the piano; somebody had won more prizes at school . . . there were so many reasons why one sibling might resent another and carry the resentment well into adult life.

She lost no time in dialling the number that Alex had given her. It was a mobile number, and when it was answered Isabel could hear the sound of voices in the background. Patrick was in the office, possibly in a meeting.

"Yes," he said, his voice lowered. "I'm with people. Who is it?"

"Isabel Dalhousie. Sorry to bother you. Could I call back?"

There was a brief silence. The voices in the background seemed to fade. Had a door been closed?

"No, it's fine. You can speak now."

"I wondered if we could meet soon. Not for a long meeting. Half an hour maybe."

She heard him breathing. "Yes. If you need to. How soon do you want to meet? Today?"

She had not expected that, and had to think quickly of her schedule for the day. Without Grace, Charlie became more of an issue. Jamie was in, though, and had not said anything about going out.

"If you could manage today," she said, "that would suit me perfectly well."

"Lunchtime?"

That was two hours away.

"That would be fine," she said. "You suggest a place."

He explained that his office was in the financial quarter just behind Lothian Road. There was a restaurant in the Lyceum Theatre, not far away—did she know the place? She did, and they agreed to meet there at one.

"What do you want to talk about?" asked Patrick.

Isabel thought quickly. "Your father. How he's coping with all this."

Patrick made a noncommittal sound. "He's tougher than you think."

"Well," said Isabel. "We can talk about that too. Sometimes it's hard for men to be tough."

She thought this was true: yesterday she had seen two men cry, and for every two men in this world who wept, she suspected, there were twenty who wanted to but couldn't.

SHE ORDERED a plate of tagliatelle with chopped smoked salmon and a sauce that was creamy, but not too thick. All that one needed, she felt, was a hint of cream. **A hint of cream . . .** It could be the title of a song, something that Jamie could sing perhaps. It would be about how life should be kept simple, but the addition of small treats, small self-indulgences, could make all the difference.

Patrick ordered a salad, and when it came she noticed that he separated out the various ingredients, pushing them to different corners of his plate. Tomatoes went in one place, lettuce leaves in another, spring onions elsewhere. She was fascinated; she had never seen anybody do that before, and she wondered what it said about him. Was he obsessive-compulsive—one of those people who make sure that everything is neatly arranged; who line the cutlery up in scrupulous parallels, who fold the towels in the bathroom into perfect squares?

He saw her watching. "Sorry," he said. "I've always done this."

She looked away guiltily.

"You see," he went on, "I worry that if I don't, then something will go wrong."

"That sounds like a superstition," she said. "I take it you won't walk under ladders?"

He smiled. "Who does?"

Isabel thought: I don't.

"There's nothing wrong with a bit of superstitious behaviour now and then," she said. "In fact . . ."

He looked at her expectantly, his fork poised above a slice of tomato. "Yes?"

"In fact, I've read somewhere that research . . ."

He laughed. "You aren't going to tell me that superstitions actually **work**?"

She remembered her conversations with Jamie about childhood superstitions, about ambulances and touching your collar and your toes. "No," she said. "Not all of them. But some superstitious behaviour, apparently, can have positive results. If you believe that doing something will bring you good luck, then you may do better if you do the thing in question."

"Carry a rabbit's foot?"

"Yes. Or you might wear one of those odd-looking charms that they wear in southern Italy—those things that look like peppers. You know the ones?"

He did. "Swarthy types wear them round their necks on gold chains."

She nodded, picturing hairy chests and open-necked shirts and the charms against the evil eye. "If you have your lucky rabbit's foot in your pocket when you write an exam, then you probably feel calmer. If you feel calmer, then you do better in the exam. **Post hoc, propter hoc**."

He speared the tomato with his fork and began to eat his salad. "Latin," he mumbled.

Isabel apologised. "I'm sorry," she said. "I didn't mean to sound pretentious. **Afterwards and therefore caused by . . .** It doesn't sound quite as effective in English."

"I had a lot of Latin at school," Patrick said. "I never want to read or hear it again. It represents everything I hated about that school. Everything. Latin allows you to obfuscate. It allows you to dress up a system that puts people down."

"Does it? I thought it could have a certain beauty."

He shrugged. "**Quot homines, tot sententiae.**"

She laughed at this. **There are as many opinions as there are people**. "You brought yourself to utter it."

He saw the humour in the situation. "My Latin teacher liked boys."

"Did he?"

He held her gaze. "Yes."

"I'm sorry." She was not sure what to say. Was this the issue?

"However, he behaved scrupulously correctly. He never touched us."

"Then he was a good man," said Isabel. "He must have resisted a lot of temptation."

Patrick seemed to relax. "You know, I think you and I might be on the same wavelength. People are so quick to condemn. They don't think much of the private battles that others have."

"But I do think of that sort of thing," said Isabel quickly. "I think of it all the time."

He looked at her intensely. "Really?"

"Yes." She paused. "Since this conversation is becoming quite frank, I might as well tell you that I do have an inkling of some of your own battles."

There was nothing in his expression to warn her off, and so she continued. "I don't like to intrude, but I suspect that you have considerable difficulty in being who you are—in the sense of where you come from—and who you are in the sense of what you think."

He smiled. “Maybe.”

“Yes. You come from a certain sector of society—a privileged one, if I may describe it as such—and yet you don’t identify with all that. In fact, you identify with the opposite. So you reject inherited wealth, but at the same time you know you’ve benefited from it. And your father . . .”

She saw him stiffen slightly, but the moment quickly passed.

“Your father is everything you don’t want to be. And yet you’re fond of him.” She hesitated, but only a second or two. “You want him to love you, but you think he doesn’t.”

She stopped. Patrick was looking down at the tablecloth; his salad was barely touched. He spoke suddenly. “Pop doesn’t like me. That’s the problem.”

She reached out across the table and touched his arm gently. “I don’t think that can be true.”

“It is. He doesn’t like me because I’m gay. Did you know that? He can’t bring himself to accept it.”

“Perhaps he needs time.”

“He’s had a long time. Since I was sixteen and told him.”

“He may need longer.”

"He hasn't got longer."

She wondered what he meant.

"His heart," he said, pointing to his chest. "He has a condition. He may be all right, but he could drop dead any moment." He paused. "Put it this way: he wouldn't get life insurance."

"I see."

She wanted time to think of the implications of this. If Duncan was unlikely to survive very long, then the issue of the fate of the painting became rather more pressing. So, if somebody wanted to stop the Poussin going to the nation, then he might think it necessary to act sooner rather than later. Her pasta was beginning to get cold. "I should tackle my lunch," she said, twisting a couple of strands of tagliatelle round her fork.

"Of course." He was watching her. He seemed on the point of saying something, faltered, and then spoke. "Why do you suspect me?"

The tagliatelle, made slippery by the sauce, unwound and fell off Isabel's fork. She thought: Sensitive conversations and difficult-to-manage food do not go together.

He was staring at her now with a look that seemed to combine challenge and reproach. "I don't know why you think that," she muttered. I'm being disingenuous, she realised; I know why he should think this. This self-reproach shamed her, and, after a brief hesitation, she continued: "Yes, I did think that. I considered the possibility, that is . . . And now, I'm not sure . . ." She trailed off.

She found herself thinking about his political position. If that were as it seemed to be, then he would have no interest in preventing the Poussin from going to the nation—in fact, that was exactly what he would want. Unless that same political position could prompt him to relieve an insurance company of whatever sum might be payable as a reward . . . The doubt resurfaced.

"Well, I can tell you something," he said. "It's not very nice being suspected of stealing from your own father."

"No," she said. "It can't be. And look, I'm sorry: all I said was that I had considered the possibility. That's all. I'm not accusing you of anything."

He sat back in his chair. "My life's a bit of a mess," he said. "I accept that."

She asked him why.

"Emotionally," he said. "I've had bad luck

with a relationship. I love somebody, you see, who can't love me back. It can't work."

"I'm sorry about that."

"Thank you. I've loved him for a long time. Fourteen years, in fact, which is almost half my life. Since I was fourteen."

She was silent.

"I've tried to do something about it. I've tried to forget. But I keep thinking of him, and all I want is to be with him. That's all. That's it."

She felt a pang of sympathy. She had loved John Liamor, and for a few years after that had come to an end she had felt the same way. But she had recovered, as most people in that position do after a while. Time does its work; a scab builds up over the emotional wound and protects it. Only if you scratch does it bleed again. Was he scratching at it? she wondered.

"Do you mind?" he asked.

"Mind? Mind about what?"

"Mind about my speaking of this."

She was quick to reassure him. "Of course not."

He closed his eyes briefly, as if to deal with some pain within him. "I was sent to boarding school. That's what they did—still do—that class. It was thought to be the only education worth having."

"I know," said Isabel. "It's hard to believe that now."

"I went to a place up north. It takes girls too now, but in those days it was just boys. It was, I suppose, quite good academically, but it had this big thing about rugby too. We all had to play. I hated it."

"It's not for everyone," said Isabel. "We had to play lacrosse, which is equally not for everyone."

He smiled. "Those places . . ."

". . . are behind us," said Isabel. She had been happy enough at school, and she felt vaguely disloyal now to be suggesting otherwise. "I wasn't really unhappy," she corrected. "I suppose I resented the restrictions on freedom, but what teenager doesn't?"

Patrick was silent for a moment. Then he continued. "I don't know why I should be telling you this. I don't normally talk about it."

She encouraged him. "If you don't normally talk about it, then perhaps it's something that wants to be talked about."

He looked away. "Yes. This person I fell in

love with. He knew. I never told him—never dared—but he knew. And he was very kind. He didn't tell me to get lost or anything, he just gave me his friendship. That was all. He couldn't reciprocate what I felt, but he said to me that I was his best friend. He said that when we were fourteen, and I thought about it and thought about it. Not a day went past, not a day, but that I remembered what he said."

He paused. "Do you mind if I go on?"

She shook her head.

"You see, I don't know if other people get this. People don't necessarily empathise. I feel that you do, though. You seem the type to understand, if I may say so. I suppose that's why Alex persuaded my father that you would be the person to help him."

The remark might have passed unnoticed. Isabel's thoughts had begun to drift; she had been thinking about the other boy, trying to envisage him. She saw two boys on a cross-country run, against a backdrop of the Scottish hills, their hair soaked by the rain, shins streaked with mud; and she saw, for some odd reason, a deer that was watching them from the edge of a forest. The deer had a look of frightened interest, the look that would precede its bounding off into the covering darkness of the trees; and one of the boys had a heart that ached, and the other was looking up at the sky, at the veils of gentle rain, like thin muslin curtains across the landscape, and . . .

She gave a start. "Sorry. You said . . ." She collected her thoughts. The deer had bounded off, the boys were gone. "You said that your sister persuaded your father that he should speak to me. Did you say that?"

He was surprised by her interest. "Yes."

"How did you know that?"

He shrugged. "Martha told me. I saw her a couple of days ago. Or rather, she saw me and came and buttonholed me about the Cockburn Association—she's a big supporter and she knows that I approve of them."

"Martha told you," Isabel half muttered.

"Yes. She said that Alex was very keen to get you involved. She was the one who pushed for it once she mentioned your name."

"Who mentioned my name?" asked Isabel.

Patrick looked at his watch. "Martha did," he said. "But look, I have to get back to work. We've got a meeting. Some company's coming to make a presentation to us."

"Wanting money?"

He nodded, and signalled to the waitress for the bill. "Everyone wants money."

Everyone wants money, thought Isabel. Yes.

She suddenly felt emboldened to ask him, "Why do you work with money if you have such a low opinion of the financial world?"

He was clearly surprised by her question, but not offended; he smiled before he answered, "I needed a job. Simple."

"Not because you wanted a job that paid well?"

He shook his head. "I live pretty simply. And the job involves investment in products that make people better. Should that be a problem?" He looked at her, as if working something out. "My sister said something, didn't she?"

Isabel had carefully avoided passing on Alex's comment, but Patrick had divined what lay behind her question. He did not wait for her to confirm or deny it. "She accuses me of being venal, but you know something: when people accuse others of something, it's because they see themselves as being guilty of that precise thing. Yes?"

Isabel agreed. She had often observed as much.

"She's the one who's interested in money,"

Patrick said. "Her fiancé—I don't know whether you've met him, but he's had two marriages already and three children. He was cleaned out financially—completely cleaned out, and the kids are at fee-paying schools, so that's thirty thousand all told a year, out of taxed income. He must be pretty hard up, and Alex earns nothing, or more or less nothing. I suspect she secretly can't wait for my father to go. She'll want to get her hands on anything that's not actually nailed down."

Isabel listened carefully. If she had been looking for a motive for Alex to be behind the theft, then she could not have hoped for a clearer statement of it.

The bill had been brought to the table, and Patrick was extracting his wallet.

"Please let me pay," said Isabel.

He put his wallet back. "That's kind of you," he said. "Thank you."

She had one last question, and she put it playfully, as if she were not quite serious about it. "She wouldn't be behind it, would she?"

He frowned. "Why do you say that?"

"Because you've just described to me how she needs money. She might also be unwilling for the Poussin to go to the National Gallery. After all, that's a loss to your father's estate of several million pounds." She watched for the effect of her words.

He shook his head vehemently. "Definitely not. No. She wouldn't. I know her, and she wouldn't."

"Or her fiancé?"

He was equally adamant. "No. Not him. Definitely."

He stood up. "Thank you for what you've been doing for my father," he said. "He and I may not be close, but I love him, you know."

She shook hands, keeping his hand for slightly longer than one would normally do with a handshake.

"I suspect he loves you too."

He looked at her wryly; disbelievingly.

"And there's another thing," she said, lowering her voice. "You told me about your feelings for the person you loved. You told me about your efforts to forget. I had exactly the same problem, you know. I was married to somebody who didn't love me or, if he did, had an odd way of showing it. I got over him eventually, but it took a long, long time. I didn't forget him, though. That's not the way to do it—"

She had not finished, but Patrick was already beginning to move away. He does not want my advice, thought Isabel, because he's not ready to stop loving. Love was a bit like alcohol in that way: the alcoholic would not listen to advice until he was ready to stop drinking. Love was a little bit like that; not always, but it could be.

CHAPTER FIFTEEN

◆

THEY LAY IN BED late the next morning, Charlie sleeping between them. He had awakened early and Jamie had played with him for half an hour or so before bringing him into bed with them. The early start had caught up with the child, and now he had dropped off again, clutching a teddy bear and the already threadbare blanket he liked to drag around with him.

"Look at his eyelids," said Isabel, her voice lowered. "He's dreaming."

Jamie propped himself up on an elbow and gazed at Charlie. "How strange that we made him," he said. "This infinitely complex collection of cells is our son. We made him."

Isabel smiled. "Or facilitated him. The spark comes from somewhere else."

Jamie looked into her eyes. "And becomes Mozart."

"In Mozart's case, it did," said Isabel. She frowned. "We haven't sorted out the mathematics problem."

Jamie shook his head. "I went to see her again, but let's not talk about it just now. She's hard to read. Tell me about yesterday."

He had been back late from a concert in Glasgow, and Isabel had already been asleep when he had come into the bedroom shortly before midnight. They had seen one another briefly in the afternoon, when Charlie had been handed over.

She sighed. "I had lunch with Patrick."

Jamie looked blank. "Patrick?"

"Duncan Munrowe's son."

"Oh yes." He remembered now. He stroked Charlie's hand gently. The small fingers moved, gripped the teddy.

Isabel told him about the meeting. "He's certainly not behind it," she concluded. "I don't think he has any reason to be."

"Whereas his sister has?" said Jamie.

Isabel nodded. "Yes, every financial reason. Her fiancé has two expensive divorces behind him. She doesn't work."

"Being hard up doesn't make you a criminal," Jamie pointed out.

"Of course not."

"And you said that Patrick was adamant that it couldn't be her. He must know his own sister."

Isabel thought about this. "Unless he was protecting her." It was an idea to be dismissed as soon as it was raised. "Which I think is unlikely."

She waited for him to say something, but he was silent. Charlie shifted his limbs slightly, but was still fast asleep. Jamie looked at the boy, then at Isabel, and smiled.

"However," Isabel said. "However . . ."

Jamie looked at her expectantly.

"However, he said something else which struck me as being very significant."

He raised an eyebrow.

"He said that Martha suggested me in passing but that it was Alex who really pushed for me to be involved. She was the one."

Jamie shrugged. "I don't see what difference it makes," he said. "You. Martha. Duncan. What's the difference?"

Isabel lay back on her pillow and stared at the ceiling. "I think it all adds up. Alex wanted to have suspicion focused on her brother in order to deflect any suspicion that might otherwise be attached to her. So what does she do? She gets somebody else involved—somebody into whose ear she can pour poison."

Charlie stirred now, his eyes opening. He half turned towards Isabel, before turning to Jamie and reaching for his hand. Jamie said: "Look, he's taken my hand." But Isabel's mind was elsewhere. It could be that Patrick had asked Martha to invite her to intervene. Then, to throw suspicion on his sister, he would say that she had recommended Isabel's involvement. And as for his firm rejection of the possibility that Alex was behind the theft, that again could be a deliberate deception. He might think that Isabel thought that he was deliberately covering for his sister, thus increasing the level of suspicion under which Alex laboured.

Or neither of them was involved. Both could be completely innocent. Isabel remembered her university logic classes all those years ago. She had been taught to deal with possibilities in a rational, ordered way. Formal logic dictated that you moved from what you knew to what implications may flow from your knowledge. It required one to weigh evidence and reach conclusions on the basis of those implications. Applied here, the principles of formal logic led to the conclusion that in the absence of any further evidence, responsibility for the theft of the painting could be attributed to neither Alex nor Patrick.

Isabel closed her eyes.

"I'm getting up," said Jamie. "I'm going to give breakfast to this wee man."

"Lots of breakfast," said Charlie. "Lots of egg. Lots of egg. Egg and Marmite toast."

"Egg and Marmite toast," agreed Jamie. "A very good choice." Marmite, that salty yeast paste so adored by Britons and so vigorously disliked by Americans, was not the first choice of the average child, but was craved by Charlie, just as he relished olives and, more recently, garlic.

They left the room and Isabel lay alone in the bed. She stretched out her left leg, lazily, and felt the warmth of the sheet where Jamie had been lying: his heat shadow, as she thought of it; like the heat shadows of those unfortunate residents of Pompeii who were consumed by the lava but who left the outline of their forms on the stone. She had lived with him now for a sufficiently long time to forget, or at least find it hard to remember, what it was like before him, before this young man had moved into her life and into her home, possessing both; so that she dreamed of him and felt his presence about her, a cloak of comfort. And when he was not there, when he was in Glasgow rehearsing or, as occasionally happened, he went abroad for some concert—he had been the previous month to Amsterdam, to play at a music festival—she felt his absence keenly. She always knew where he was, she realised; which made her think of how important it was for us to know what others are doing. When we met friends, for instance, and asked them what they had been doing, we really did want to know. But why? It was, she thought, because of our sense of **being** with others; our need to anchor ourselves in a network of friends and acquaintances. This was our bulwark, our dyke against the sea of loneliness that we were only too aware washed about us.

She got out of bed, showered and then dressed for the day. She was under the shower for longer than she had intended—it was not good for the skin, she believed, but it was certainly good for thinking, just as walking was. And under the shower that morning it occurred to her that there was a further motive for the theft that she had yet to consider. She had assumed all along that what the thieves really wanted was money—the reward from the insurance company. But what if the real object were the Poussin? What if the person who stole the painting had no intention of collecting the reward but actually wanted the painting for itself? If that were true, then the negotiations for the reward could be just a smokescreen—to make it look like a financially motivated theft.

At first she dismissed the idea. People did not steal well-known paintings in order to hang them on their walls—it was far too risky. Nor, she imagined, were many paintings stolen by apocryphal South American collectors who could display them with impunity in their remote Amazonian villas.

The idea seemed unlikely, and yet, as Isabel thought about it under the stinging water of the shower, she remembered that Alex had said, "I loved that painting . . . I adored it." Was it not possible to love something so much that you would do anything to get it—even if it meant that the pleasure derived from possessing it would be a solitary one? If Alex adored the painting, and felt possessive of it, then she was likely to be strongly opposed to its being given to the National Gallery after her father's death; in which case, the solution was obvious—the painting could simply be removed from Munrowe House and hidden in the flat in Edinburgh until Duncan's death. Alex would hardly be able to hang it on a wall where it might be seen by visitors, but she would at least have it in her possession, which might well be enough for her. It would be important, though, to mask the whole exercise as a theft. That would require elaborate subterfuge—and accomplices too: the solicitor and the men in the van, who might also have been the ones who removed the painting in the first instance. It was possible; yes, it was possible. However, the problem was that for those who live in the normal world—a world in which people did not steal beautiful objects from family members purely for the aesthetic pleasure they might bestow, did not defraud them in that way—such actions seemed vaguely improbable.

She stepped out of the shower and wrapped herself in a towel. Jamie had come back upstairs, and he now walked into the bedroom. He hesitated at the bathroom door; they still respected each other's privacy in spite of their common life.

"I've finished," she said. "I stood in the shower for ages—thinking."

He raised an eyebrow. "About?"

"About the Poussin."

He nodded. "Well, here's something else for you to think about."

She slipped past him. The bedroom carpet was soft underfoot; her hair was wet upon her shoulders. It was summer, but only a Scottish summer, and goosebumps could still make themselves felt. She turned to face him. He was smiling.

"What am I to think about?"

He spread out the palms of his hands, as an illusionist might do. "Grace—she's back." He seemed pleased with the look of surprise—and gratitude—on Isabel's face.

"Oh."

He came towards her and kissed her lightly on the cheek. She shivered—from the cold, from the contact.

"Apparently everything is normal. She said nothing about having resigned, and she's already cleared the dishwasher. She said something about ironing my shirts."

Isabel smiled. "I'm glad." She looked at Jamie enquiringly. "What shall I say to her? Sorry?"

He shook his head. "You have nothing to apologise for. Just say nothing. It's always better, I think, to say nothing. If things sort themselves out—as they have done here—then why say anything?"

She was not sure he was right that saying nothing was always preferable. Not always: there were occasions when it was clearly unwise to remain silent—when there were misunderstandings, for instance, or suspicions; where a few words could explain something or defuse ill-feeling. There were occasions, too, when those few words might be words of apology—short, potent words that could erase whole landscapes of resentment, undermine entire edifices of anger or hatred. But perhaps he was right; although Isabel would have preferred to resolve her disagreement with Grace by talking things through, Grace had her own way of coping with disagreements, which involved pretending that they had never occurred. And if that worked for her, then Isabel was prepared to let it be.

"All right," she said. "I'll act normally. I'll pretend she didn't resign."

"Good," he said. He reached out to touch her, laying his hand gently on her forearm. His skin was warm against hers, which was chilled by the evaporation of the wet from the shower. She wanted to hold him; she wanted to take him in her arms, but the towel was precarious and there was always an awkwardness between the clothed and unclothed body. So she simply looked at him, and saw the colour of his eyes, and the light within them, and the shape of his brow.

"I'll tell her again how much we appreciate what she does," said Isabel. "We do, don't we?"

"Of course. And I think she knows that."

While Isabel dressed, Jamie went back downstairs and when she made her way into the kitchen he could be heard in the music room beginning a session of practice: scales, arpeggios, the technical limbering-up that even the most experienced professional musician must undertake; musical press-ups, Isabel called it.

She entered the kitchen unannounced. Grace was seated at the table, a piece of paper in front of her, and Charlie was perched on her lap.

"Four," said Charlie. "No, six. Six, Grace! Six!"

"Six," said Grace. "Yes, six." And then she turned round and saw Isabel, and she immediately lifted Charlie off her lap and stood up. Isabel did not see what happened to the piece of paper; it was there and then it was not there, vanishing so quickly that she might have doubted that she had seen it in the first place.

She felt her heart race. Mathematics! Grace had been teaching Charlie mathematics. It was blatant and it dismayed Isabel, because she did not relish conflict and she did not want to have to speak to Grace again, not so soon after the row that had led to her resignation. Grace was quite capable of resigning again, and Isabel could not face that. So she turned away and simply said good morning to Grace as if nothing had happened; as if there had been no resignation, no mathematics.

She walked to the window and looked out. There was no reason to look out of that particular window, which had no view to speak of. She was not looking out of it to see what the weather was like, nor was she looking out of it to see whether Brother Fox might be lurking in the rhododendrons which could be seen—just—if one craned one's neck slightly to get a sight of what was happening alongside the house. She realised that she was looking out of the window because she did not have the courage to look in the direction in which she should have been looking. **Blind eye**, she thought. **Turn a blind eye**.

And that thought changed everything. To turn a blind eye was morally reprehensible; it was an affront to the whole concept of seeing—and it was the beginning, in so many cases, of significant failure. No, she would not turn a blind eye. She would not allow herself to be a moral coward.

She turned, her heart hammering within her. "I'm sorry, Grace," she began. "The last thing I want is for you to be upset. But please see it from my point of view. With this mathematics . . ." She paused. The solution had come to her. "Look, I think that it will be fine for Charlie to develop his mathematics. But why don't we wait? How about waiting a couple of years and then, when he's six or so, we can look at it again. Both of us. We can go and talk to somebody about it and do the thing together. I'll read that book of yours then and we might even be able to work from it. How about that?" She paused again. Grace was looking down at the floor. "Are you listening to what I'm saying?" asked Isabel.

Charlie answered. "Charlie listening," he said solemnly.

Isabel bit her lip. She wanted to laugh. **Charlie listening**. Perhaps she might say that in the middle of some discussion with Jamie: **Isabel listening**. It would be so comic, so disconcerting. It would derail anybody.

She could not suppress her amusement, even in this grave moment of challenge. She smiled. And Grace did too.

"Mummy is shouting at Grace," said Grace to Charlie.

"I wasn't exactly shouting," said Isabel.

"Well, I heard you well enough," muttered Grace. "And that sounds fine by me. Now I've got to go upstairs and start the washing."

Isabel felt the tension flood out of her. Her heart returned to its normal beat.

"I really do understand why you wanted to do it," said Isabel. "And we appreciate that—both Jamie and I. We both appreciate it."

Grace acknowledged the thanks. "That's fine," she said. "It's probably a good idea to wait anyway. He'll be even better then."

She stood up, straightening her skirt. Isabel noticed that it looked creased and rather worn in the front, although Grace normally looked smart and attended to that sort of thing. She felt a pang. She paid Grace generously—she always had, as had her father before her—but by the very nature of things she had so much more than the woman who worked for her, and she did not want there to be any sense of a victory having been won.

"Another thing, Grace," she said. "I'm sorry if you've been upset."

"Doesn't matter," said Grace. And then, in a quieter voice, "My fault."

"Not Grace's fault," said Charlie suddenly. He had picked up the tension in the room, and he now slipped his hand into Grace's and squeezed it.

"Look," said Isabel. "He loves you."

Grace looked down. She hesitated, and then bent down and kissed Charlie on his brow. She stood up. "Washing," she said, and moved towards the door. Then she added, "One of Jamie's shirts is missing two buttons. Two! I'll replace them this morning."

"Thank you," said Isabel, adding: "Men!"

It was a curious, inconsequential thing to say. Men lost the buttons on their shirts, as did women, but there was no evidence, not one scrap, to show that men lost more buttons than women did. However, Isabel suspected that they did, and this comment, this single word, made her belief quite clear.

"I agree," said Grace. She sighed. "Men."

AFTER THAT DRAMATIC START, the rest of the morning went smoothly. With the return of Grace and the resolution of the mathematics question—**quod erat demonstrandum,** Isabel could not stop herself from thinking—she was able to concentrate on her work. The **Review** imposed many deadlines, not just those that loomed when it was due to go to press. There were deadlines for the receipt of papers; there were deadlines for the obtaining of reports on articles submitted for peer review; there were minor, self-imposed deadlines for Isabel to answer letters and emails. Those two categories differed, of course. Electronic mail, that pervasive, intrusive means of communication that could penetrate, like the most sophisticated of missiles, the thickest bunkers of privacy, had to be answered within three working days; letters could be left one week before an answer was sent. Or so Isabel had decided, knowing that these periods were arbitrary and, in the case of electronic mail, quite out of kilter with expectations. Many people, she understood, expected emails to be answered within hours, if not minutes, and judged others accordingly. One would-be author of a paper on environmental ethics had actually complained to Isabel one afternoon that she had not answered his email of that morning. **I contacted you some time ago,** he wrote at four o'clock, **and I was wondering whether your reply has been lost. I've looked in my spam folder, but I don't see it**. His original message had arrived at ten that morning, which meant that he considered six hours to be more than enough time for a reply to be formulated, typed and sent.

Isabel had drafted a reply. **Dear Professor Grant, Your message was received this morning. I have read it but have not yet had time to reply. I'm so sorry to test your patience in this way. I know that six hours can seem a very long time, but please be assured that I shall reply to you when I have had time to think a little bit about what you said in your**

message and to give your remarks the weight they undoubtedly deserve. Yours sincerely, Isabel Dalhousie (Editor).

She had not sent this message because she had felt, quite rightly, that it was cutting. It was easy to cut; too easy sometimes, and so she had sent back a simple message: **I received your email. I'll get back to you as soon as possible. I.D.** Doing the right thing, she knew, was often not as enjoyable as doing the wrong thing. The wrong thing often made for a better story, but it was still the wrong thing—nothing could change that.

The deadline that morning had nothing to do with letters or emails, nor with anxious printers waiting to press the buttons that would set their presses rolling. Rather, it had to do with the gathering-in of reports on several papers on which an editorial decision had to be taken. Isabel took this process very seriously, being only too aware of the anxious state of those awaiting her response: researchers, post-doctoral fellows, junior lecturers in neglected and unfashionable universities and colleges in obscure places; the unrewarded infantry of the academic profession, who needed publication in order to hang on to their poorly rewarded jobs. And behind these people there were wives and husbands, partners, boyfriends, girlfriends, who were waiting at home and who might ask at the end of the day: "Have you heard from her yet?" The **her** was Isabel. That weighed heavily.

Already she had one letter of rejection to write, and would have to do it that morning. She had received three reports on a paper submitted for a special issue of the **Review** that would be concentrating on the ethical issues surrounding adoption. These issues were manifold and more complex than one might imagine. There was the right to know parentage, widely accepted now and the subject of a very good paper from someone at Lenoir-Rhyne University in Hickory, North Carolina. They would publish that, and she would write a response to this effect later that morning. That was easy.

Then there was a paper on surrogacy and the finality of the mother's consent. Should a surrogate mother be allowed to change her mind after the birth of the "commissioned" child? Could she refuse to hand over the child fathered by one of the prospective parents? Isabel imagined the scene and had made her mind up on that. Of course she could: you could never snatch a child from its natural mother, no matter what pieces of paper had been signed while the child was in utero. No, you could never do that. But, asked the author of the paper, what of the rights of the father, or indeed of the child? Teleologically speaking . . . Isabel sighed. No, one could not obscure the issue by bringing in teleology. Mothers were mothers, and being a mother meant that you had a right against all the world in respect of the baby that had been part of you, within you, for months. No amount of philosophising could change that fundamental, bedrock fact.

This paper was provocative and well argued, and both reviewers had agreed that it should be published. So that presented no problems; but . . . Isabel picked up the file that she had been subconsciously avoiding since entering her study that morning. The topic was difficult, and one that had been the subject of some debate in the newspapers. That fact alone meant that it deserved a place in the **Review of Applied Ethics** which was, after all, heralded by its very title as being involved in the day-to-day world. "Should children be placed with families of a different ethnic group?" Isabel's initial reaction to the question had been one of puzzlement. Surely there was no reason why this should not be done: loving homes and families had nothing to do with ethnic groups.

But then the complications, and the doubts, introduced themselves. What if there were two sets of prospective parents—each belonging to a different group—or, more likely, the choice was between remaining in a children's home or being adopted by parents from a different background? The solution, Isabel thought, would be to ignore ethnicity altogether and concentrate on the home life that the child might expect. Love was love, no matter in what social context it was offered. But not everybody felt that, it seemed, and there were those who argued that taking a child out of its community was to deprive it of a heritage; more than that, it could imply that one group was actually preferable to another.

The paper on this subject was well presented and the argument was cogent. It defended the implicit rejection in many parts of Canada of the adoption of native Canadian children into non-native families. The previous taking of native children out of their communities was a form of cultural genocide, the author argued, and was responsible for cutting off many children from their culture and roots. Isabel was aware of that shameful past and could see the argument against allowing its continuation, even in an attenuated, less culturally arrogant form. She saw that, but the two reviewers did not, and one of these was Professor Lettuce.

Does the author of this paper really suggest, his report asked, **that it would be better for a child to stay in an institution for its entire childhood—as happens, I believe, only too often—rather than be given the chance of a life in a non-native home, with loving parents and all the benefits and chances that go with having loving parents? If he does, then I disagree most profoundly and would recommend strongly against the publication of a paper with such a heartless message at its core.**

The other reviewer had been less bombastic, but had still been against publication. **I'm not impressed with the author's conclusion that the appalling schemes of the past, where native children were snatched from their parents, have much bearing on modern, child-centred adoption regimes. Nobody is taking these children from their mothers or communities. They are taking them from children's homes. Should ideology stand in the way of a child's happiness?**

Isabel read and reread the reports. She found herself inclined to ignore Lettuce simply because he was Lettuce, and she disliked him intensely, and with good reason. Allowing her mind to wander, she thought of Lettuce as a small lettuce being transplanted from a bed of lettuces into a bed of cabbages, and not flourishing at all because the cabbages had thicker leaves and were more vigorous in their growth. She smiled. It was such a childish thought, but so vivid, and so satisfying, and surely one could allow oneself the occasional reverie, the occasional dream of revenge.

She reread the paper itself, and after doing so went to make herself a cup of coffee in the kitchen. She returned with the cup and held the paper lightly in her hand, as if weighing it. Its tone was assertive and there was an air of grievance in it. That had clearly registered badly with the reviewers, but her job as editor was to be dispassionate and also to ensure that the pages of the journal were open to unpopular views. And if there was an air of grievance, it might be that grievance was understandable: injustices had really occurred, even if an effort was now being made to make up for them. Victimhood, however, should not last for ever; the Highland Clearances had been a great wrong to Scotland and to Gaelic culture, but she was not sure that the Scots should continue to regard themselves as victims, even if there were people whose purposes it suited.

She looked at the author's biographical details. He was affiliated to the University of Manitoba and was a graduate of the University of Toronto. There was no further clue to where he came from. He sounded as if he was writing from the perspective of a Canadian aboriginal, or a member of a First Nations group—the terminology, Isabel knew, was sensitive and she was never sure exactly what was considered appropriate and what was not. But he did not **say** he was a member of such a group. And, anyway, did it make a difference to his argument?

She imagined what the author would say if she rejected the paper. "There! Proves it! Bias. Prejudice. Silencing of the challenging view." No, she would not allow herself to think of that, because it was irrelevant to her decision, or should be. The real test was whether this was a defensible, well-expressed view—and it was both of those. And she was certainly not reaching that decision because she wanted to overrule Professor Lettuce. That would be very satisfactory, but it was a pleasure that should have no bearing on her editorial decision. What the paper presented was uncomfortable, perhaps, and the author's conclusions might seem harsh and unsympathetic, but it was representative of a viewpoint that had found considerable support in Canadian officialdom and could hardly be dismissed on the basis that it caused discomfort. **In,** she thought. **Publish.** Lettuce will be **green** with anger, but that is not why I'm doing it, she hurriedly told herself: the pleasure of flouting Lettuce's opinion was a collateral benefit, nothing more. No, she reminded herself; I must not think that. I must rise above **Schadenfreude** and such pettiness. I must do the right thing because it is the right thing, and for that reason alone. She got to her feet. The window of her study was half open, and she could pick up the scent of summer—the smell of vegetation, of humidity in the air, of a world of humming insects and mulch, of life.

She gazed out of the window. It was close to midday and was not a time when Brother Fox usually showed himself. Foxes liked the watches of the night, or the early hours of a summer morning when the human world was silent. But now he was there, poised halfway between a tunnel of old lavender bushes and the sheltering panoply of a late-flowering rhododendron. The rhododendron provided his heartland, the vulpine headquarters from which he planned his raids. Now he was briefly out in the open and seemed, for a few moments, to be enjoying the sun on his back. He lifted his head and sniffed, and then, quite suddenly, dropped to the ground and rolled over on to his back. Isabel gasped, thinking she had witnessed a death, but it was not that—it was a roll, a brief, hedonistic revelling in the sheer joy of being in the sun, of being warm and of being alive. Within a few seconds he was back on his feet and had resumed his journey; the dappling shadows had him now; he was gone. She felt disappointed. She wanted him to stay; she wanted him to engage with her. But she knew that he would not. She was nothing to him, even if he understood, as she hoped he did, that she was not an adversary. We are often nothing to the things that fascinate us, or the things we love; she was well aware of that. Charlie, though, did not know that; the world loved him, he believed, because he loved it. Trains loved him, toy cars loved him, long-suffering stuffed toys loved him too, just as he loved them. It was an example of perfect mutuality that would end soon enough—when he discovered that the world did not centre upon him, that it was sometimes cruel and that love given was not always reciprocated. When would that be? When he was six? Eight? Or did that realisation come much later, in adult life, perhaps, when the first big disappointments struck, when it first dawned upon us that we were not, as we secretly believed in our youth, as deserving of love and success as we had previously imagined? Charlie, dear Charlie, she whispered, may you be protected from that until the last possible moment, and even then may it seem a small cloud on your horizon, a tiny shadow on your landscape. May that be your fate, my darling, my darling boy.

CHAPTER SIXTEEN

THE IDEA OCCURRED to Isabel later that day, shortly after she had collected Charlie from nursery school. It came as she was walking home—a short journey in her steps but an odyssey in Charlie's—an odyssey that was interrupted by stops to examine objects found or spotted: a piece of paper lying in the gutter, a twig from one of the trees whose boughs overhung the garden walls along the road, a feather from a seagull. The gulls, unwelcome guests in the neighbourhood, occasionally conducted aerial battles, mewing and screeching in outrage over some infringement of territory, some obscure gull slight. Charlie, who for some reason could not manage the word **seagull,** called them **seagirls,** and Isabel now did too, in the way in which we take from our children their special words, their mispronunciations, which strike us as such fitting, attractive neologisms.

"Seagirls cross," said Charlie, looking skywards.

Isabel, however, did not hear this comment, as the idea had dawned on her and it seemed to her that this was the obvious thing to do. It was an unlikely thing to do, of course, and it might not survive close examination, but she could try it. Why not?

"The seagirls . . . ," Charlie repeated, looking at his mother for support.

"Yes," said Isabel. "The seagirls." But she did not expand. "Come on, Charlie. Let's hurry."

He tugged at her hand. "The seagirls . . ."

She picked him up. "Let's just go home, Charlie. The seagirls will be all right. I don't think they need us." She paused. "Chocolate pudding."

It never failed: the ultimate, fool-proof bribe. Even so, Charlie sought confirmation. "Chocolate pudding?" he asked.

"Yes," she said. "When we get back."

He was silent for the rest of the journey, thinking, perhaps, of the treat that lay ahead. And when Isabel arrived back at the house, she found that Grace was only too happy to take Charlie into the kitchen and prepare the treat for him.

Grace indulged Charlie, and would have willingly provided chocolate pudding in vast quantities, had Isabel permitted it.

She went into her study and took three pieces of writing paper from the stationery drawer. Sitting down at her desk, she pushed aside the small pile of papers on which she had been working that morning—the papers on the ethics of adoption—and began the first of the letters. The wording, she had decided, would be identical: the only difference being the name in the salutation. She wrote first to Duncan: **Dear Duncan, I have found out what has happened. Obviously, I need to talk to you privately about this, as the last thing, I imagine, that you would want would be for it to become a public matter, with all that it would entail for the family. I assure you I shall be discreet. With kind regards, Isabel Dalhousie.**

She looked at the handwritten letter and reached for another sheet of notepaper. **Kind regards** was wrong. Not only did it sound slightly contrived, but she was not sure that regards could be kind: they could be warm regards, they could be best regards, but kindness, surely, was something that would be in the heart of the person sending the regards and it would be unduly self-congratulatory to impute kindness to oneself. Perhaps it would be better to write **With all best wishes,** but then she thought: Does this letter really come with all best wishes? It did not. **Yours aye** was an appropriately Scottish ending to a letter, but it meant **Yours ever,** and it implied long and loyal sentiments. These were not there. **Yours** was best, then—the simple contraction of **Yours sincerely** or, indeed, of **Yours faithfully** or **Yours truly.** What had she been taught at school? Isabel remembered those lessons in that stuffy classroom where Miss . . . what was her name? . . . McLaren or Maclaurin had taught them the etiquette of correspondence. "Don't forget, girls," she had said, "you will be judged by your competence to write a letter. So remember the rules. Never, ever write **Yours sincerely** in a formal or business letter. We are not sincere in such letters, girls; we are, by contrast, faithful." At which Amanda . . . what **was** her name, the first girl in the class to report on experience with a boy? (**experience** being the term used darkly by the teachers to warn of the consequences of such things)—she, that Amanda, had sniggered and whispered, "Speak for yourself!" Amanda . . .

Amanda . . . Isabel looked up at the ceiling. Amanda Weir—that was her name. She was two divorces down the line now, Isabel had heard, both because she had gone off with somebody else, and that was presumably because faithfulness had meant so little to her. Amanda Weir had grown into unhappiness because she did not realise that happiness came from sticking at things—things that often seemed mundane, prosaic, boring, unglamorous.

Isabel rewrote the letter in exactly the same terms as her first attempt, inserting only the deliberately perfunctory **Yours, Isabel.** She reread the letter, and then wrote an identical one addressed to Alex and one to Patrick. Next, she addressed the envelopes, wrote **Strictly Personal** on the top left-hand corner of each, and went into the kitchen to inform Grace that she was going out briefly to the postbox. A scene of chocolate chaos greeted her: chocolate smeared around Charlie's mouth, chocolate on his hands and across the front of his shirt. Grace smiled guiltily. "I tried," she said. "I'll put him in the bath afterwards."

Isabel returned the smile. "Such happiness," she muttered.

• • •

AFTER SHE HAD POSTED the letters in the small postbox on the corner, Isabel stood for a moment and considered what she had done. She often did this after consigning something important to the post; she stood and reflected. Posting something was a simple act, but it could be the first of a sequence of important events that changed one's world, or somebody else's. The letter of application for a job that might take one far from home; that might result in one's meeting the person with whom one would spend one's life . . . A letter could change so much, could create just as much as it might destroy.

Isabel imagined what the effect might be of the letters she had just put through the mouth of the postbox. What if she changed her mind? Could one ever recall a letter after posting it? It would surely be impossible. Letters lay in the postbox until the next collection—which she noticed was barely an hour away—and then they were removed by the postman when he passed by in his van. One might stand by the postbox and ask him for the letter back, but surely he could never accede to such a request. How would he know that the letter was yours? And once a letter was handed over to the postal authorities they were, she presumed, the legal custodian of that letter until it was handed over to the intended recipient. But they did not **own** it, she thought, because the letter and its contents remained your property until it was given to the person named on the envelope. So surely you could ask for the return of your own property? No, she decided, you could not; it was not that simple.

For a few moments Isabel wondered whether she had made a bad mistake. She had claimed that she had found out what happened, but it was simply not true, and if she were to be asked to expand on it, she would have nothing to say. But that was the whole point, she decided: she hoped that **two** of the three would ask her what had happened, while the third would not. And the reason for that was that the third would know and would not need to enquire. Unless, of course, all three asked, which would suggest that all were innocent. Yet the guilty could affect ignorance; there was that to consider, and sometimes the guilty were adept at it—more adept than the innocent might be in the assertion of their innocence.

She moved away from the postbox. It was too late: the stone had been thrown into the pond and all she could do was to return home and wait for the ripples to break—if there were to be any. As Isabel walked back down the road, the seagulls' cries were now a Greek chorus, or so it seemed to her. She looked up at them as they circled overhead. Their earlier dispute resolved, their mewing was now less strident, but some, at least, appeared to be directed at her. **Behold the fowls of the air: for they sow not, neither do they reap, nor gather into barns . . .** And then there were the lilies to be considered; they neither spun nor weaved and yet Solomon in all his glory . . . She stopped herself. The wisdom of Solomon. Would he have written such a letter? Possibly, she thought. Possibly.

JAMIE WAS TEACHING that afternoon and returned in a bad mood. This was unusual for him, and Isabel knew that it would not last; Jamie's temper was equable, and although he might manage a few minutes of silence, he seemed incapable of sustained grumpiness. Cat was the past master at that: she could sustain a huff for days on end, sometimes to the extent of forgetting—Isabel suspected—the original cause of her annoyance. Isabel had often thought that much the same thing happened in those puzzling animosities between whole nations: although there might be fresh aggravations to keep relations on edge, the original **casus belli** of many of the great historical dislikes were shrouded. The Greeks and Turks disliked one another, and each could provide chapter and verse for why this was so, but behind many such recited wrongs there lay ancient animosities based on incidents that really were forgotten. **Greeks and Turks** . . . she remembered now. When she was six, or thereabouts, there had been a boy who lived in the next street whose parents had been friendly with hers. This boy, David, was brought by his mother to play with her and spent long afternoons in her company. His favourite game, which she tended to tire of well before he did, was one of his own invention, or so she believed, and it had been called "Greeks and Turks." The memory of this game always brought a smile to Isabel's lips, as the rules had been so simple. One person was the Greek and the other was the Turk. The Greek chased the Turk and then, on catching him or her, became the Turk, to be chased in turn by the Greek. There were no further implications to the game—it continued until either the Greek or the Turk fell over and grazed a knee, as sometimes happened, or decided that endless running around in pursuit of another was of waning interest. That conclusion was more frequently and more quickly reached by Isabel than by David, and reflected what the young Isabel was to discover as she became older: that boys and men were content to chase things while girls and women saw no point in such behaviour.

Jamie's bad mood, such as it was, had been caused by one of his pupils.

"I don't like that boy," he said as he came into Isabel's study. Charlie was having a nap, and Isabel was in the middle of a rare tidying session. There was so much paper, so many piles of books, that had she thought about it she too might well have decided to indulge herself in a bad mood. But in general, in the average marriage there is room for only one bad mood at a time and on that afternoon Jamie was there first.

She shifted a pile of papers from one surface to another; the guilt that a pile of papers may induce can be so easily dissipated by a small move, she decided. "What boy? Thomas?"

Thomas was a pupil of whom Jamie had spoken more than once—a boy, he complained, who persistently came to his music lesson without some important part of his bassoon—usually the crook, but often the reed or the sling. Jamie would always have a spare crook that he could lend him, but he disliked providing reeds, which had to be placed in the mouth. He had told Isabel about how he had tackled the subject with Thomas, telling him that one's saliva was, as a general rule, best kept to oneself. Thomas had stared at him uncomprehendingly and had forgotten to bring his reed to the following lesson as well.

"No," said Jamie, flopping down in the armchair beside Isabel's desk, "not Thomas. Barry."

Isabel picked up an unopened letter that had somehow escaped her attention and examined the postmark. "Barry?" The letter was postmarked two weeks earlier, and she winced.

"He's fourteen," said Jamie. "And he has the most ghastly mother. He's ghastly himself, but his mother is really seriously ghastly. And the father's ghastly too. They're nouveaux riches and wear really flashy clothes. Barry had this sort of shiny shirt on today and a belt made out of some endangered species. His father came to collect him and he was wearing sunglasses—very designer—and endangered shoes."

Isabel smiled. "They probably weren't actually endangered. Some of these things are imitation crocodile, or lizard, or whatever it is. They're just plastic."

Jamie was having none of this. "No, they're not. Not in this case. You could tell that the father goes for the real thing. He probably shot his shoes himself."

Isabel raised an eyebrow. Jamie was usually tolerant in his views, and rarely vituperative. And surely it could not just be Barry to set him off like this. "Anything else happened?" she asked casually.

He was silent.

"Nothing?" she asked.

Jamie sighed. "There was a letter. It had been delivered to the flat. I told them—I told them two or three times that my mail was to come here, but these people are hopeless, just hopeless. You may as well save your breath."

Isabel said nothing. It was clearly nothing to do with Barry or his father's shoes; it was the letter.

"What was it?" she asked gently.

Jamie spat the word out. "Tax."

"Ah."

"They said that I underpaid last year. They said it was my mistake."

Isabel was about to say "It usually is" but

realised that this might not be the moment. So she said instead, "They're **ghastly** . . ." It was, she realised, a curious echo of Jamie's complaint about the unfortunate Barry and his family; a word, as often happens, can be like a musical worm in the mind and invite repetition. But it slipped out. Tax inspectors were not ghastly, she thought; they were simply doing their job, and they did it, she imagined, fairly well—for the most part. They had to contend with all sorts of dishonesty and rudeness on the part of taxpayers, who were, no doubt, quite capable of being particularly ghastly in their dealings with tax officials, and so . . .

"You can say that again," said Jamie. "Why do they have to wait until now to tell me? Why didn't they sort this out earlier? Six months ago?"

Isabel shrugged. "They have a lot of tax to collect. And the public itself can be ghas—" She stopped the word in its tracks. And holding her unopened letter, she was hardly in a position to bemoan the inefficiency of others.

"How much?" she asked.

Jamie closed his eyes. "Eight hundred and fifty pounds."

Isabel looked out of the window. She would have to handle this carefully. "Are you all right for that?" she asked. "I could . . ."

He looked up at her. "I'm all right. It's just that . . . well, I don't want to pay."

"No," she said. "That's understandable."

He sighed. "Oh well."

She could see that the bad mood was already wearing off.

"I've had an interesting day," she volunteered.

"Really?" His tone was almost normal now; the memories of Barry and the tax demand were clearly fading.

"Yes. I had an idea. A rather interesting one, as it happens."

He got to his feet. "I must have a shower. But what was this idea of yours?"

"You have your shower," she said. "I could talk to you about it later on. We could go out for dinner."

Her suggestion was well received. "Yes, why not?"

"No reason," said Isabel. "I'll book that place at Holy Corner. The something-or-other bistro. And I'll ask Grace to babysit. She offered earlier today. I think she wants to read to Charlie."

"Not teach him mathematics?"

Isabel laughed. "No, I don't think so."

Jamie nodded. "Good."

Isabel returned to her task of tidying. Jamie's

birthday was coming up. She would put a cheque for eight hundred and fifty pounds in an envelope and seal it with a kiss. He would accept it, she felt, because it was his birthday and such things were permitted on birthdays even if pride, however unreasonably, prevented them on other occasions. She would give him anything, she felt. Everything she possessed. But at least eight hundred and fifty pounds was a start.

JAMIE STARED AT HER over the dinner table in the Bistro Bia. "So," he said, "you wrote to all three of them and told them that you had worked out . . ."

"Discovered," interjected Isabel.

"Discovered what had happened. And yet you say that this isn't strictly true?" His intonation rose sharply at the end of the sentence, underlining his doubt.

"Not strictly," said Isabel. "Of course I don't want to rely on pedantry, but I could argue that the forming in my mind of a **theory** as to what happened amounts to a discovery. So that means I wasn't really telling a lie."

Jamie looked at her uncertainly. "You don't really mean that, do you?" he said.

Isabel gave a sheepish grin. She had not convinced herself; she had not even tried. "Maybe not. But the point is this—this letter of mine might just flush out the guilty party."

"If one of them **is** the guilty party," said Jamie. "And frankly, it doesn't seem all that likely."

"Maybe not to you," said Isabel. "But if you look at the evidence. One of the men holding the painting called Duncan by the name Alex and Patrick use . . ."

"And the name millions of other people use for their father," said Jamie. He saw her face fall, and he immediately added, almost apologetically, "But carry on anyway."

"Motive," said Isabel.

"Motives aren't evidence."

She bit her lip. "Do you want me to tell you what I think, or not?"

He was placatory now. "I'm trying to play the role that Peter plays when he quizzes you about something." Peter was Peter Stevenson, a friend who often acted as a critical sounding board for Isabel and whose advice she valued.

"But you're not Peter," she blurted out. "You aren't here to test everything I say like . . . like a judge. You asked me what I think and I started to tell you and . . ." She did not finish. Jamie had reached across the table and placed his hand gently on hers.

"You're right. I'm sorry."

She forgave him.

"All right," she said. "Motive: Alex needs money, or rather, her fiancé does. Same thing really. She loves the Poussin. She doesn't want it to be given away. There's also that very odd thing, not motive, I suppose, but back to evidence: the fact that she got me involved and then tried to shift suspicion on to her brother. Patrick may need money—we're not sure. Disagrees with his father on politics and farming and all sorts of things, I imagine, and there's no love lost between him and his sister." She paused. "I suppose his motive is probably the weakest—or at least it's the one we're least sure about. But then . . ."

"Yes? But then?"

"Then there's Duncan himself."

Jamie looked doubtful. "Surely not."

"What if he has financial problems?" asked Isabel.

"He could sell a painting. The Poussin could go down to Christie's and that would be it. Financial problems solved."

Isabel considered this. "Except that he might not feel able to sell something that he has promised to give to the nation." She looked at him enquiringly. "Would you? Would you sell something that you had promised to give to somebody in the future?"

Jamie took a sip from his glass of water. "I might—if I needed to."

"But you're not Duncan Munrowe. Remember, he's old-fashioned. He has his reputation to consider."

Jamie smiled. "But you're still suggesting that he might try to defraud an insurance company?"

Isabel shook her head. "No, you're right. I don't really think that he's behind this. It wouldn't be in character, and, for the most part, people act in character, don't they?"

"Almost always," said Jamie.

Isabel thought for a moment about her proposition that people acted in character. It was probably true, but if you were to use character as a means of predicting what people would do, you had to know their character very well. And that was the problem: most people had aspects to their character that they concealed—weaknesses, vices, and so on; not most people, she thought—everybody. Everybody had **some** flaws and these flaws could prompt them to do surprising things.

She looked at Jamie and thought: Was Jamie

capable of surprising her? Was he capable of doing something low or mean—something that she would think completely out of character?

"Why are you looking at me like that?" he asked.

She looked away quickly. "Was I?"

"Yes," he said. "You were looking at me in a very strange way." He seemed amused rather than unsettled.

"I was wondering whether you could ever do anything that would shock me. I suppose that's what I was thinking."

He gave her an injured look—but he made it clear that he was not serious. "Don't you trust me?"

"Of course I trust you. I was just thinking of cases where wives discover that their husband has been doing something shocking. It was mentioning character that made me think about that sort of thing." She paused. "I don't believe you would ever shock me, though. I really don't believe that."

As she spoke, she thought of all the women who discovered that their husbands were having an affair. It was a very common story—banal really, so frequently did it happen. But it was not those cases that involved the real shock: it was when the woman discovered something utterly out of the ordinary; for instance, that their husband had committed a serious crime. What would she do if she found out that Jamie had robbed a bank, or was a secret blackmailer, or had planted a bomb in a public place, or something like that? Isabel wondered. The men who did those things went back, she assumed, to their wives or girlfriends at night. Mafiosi had their families—they tucked their children into bed at night and exhorted them to do well at school. People who plotted the deaths of others bought their wives birthday presents and walked the dog and took the car to the garage. And they had their little tiffs and make-ups and went out for dinner in restaurants just like this one and talked about day-to-day things.

Isabel looked around the restaurant, at the couples at neighbouring tables. Just like us, but were there secrets at every table? There were, she decided. Yes, there were.

"We should talk about something else," said Jamie, picking up the menu that the waitress had placed before him. "Food, maybe." He ran his eye down the list of offerings. "One final thing, though: What do you expect to happen next?"

"I've already told you," she said. "Two of them

will be very keen to find out. Two will phone me. One won't. Or . . ." She hesitated. "All of them will get in touch."

Jamie laughed. "Oh well," he said. "Robert Burns."

"What's he got to do with it?"

"**The best laid schemes of mice and men,**" said Jamie. "Remember?"

"How could one forget?" said Isabel.

CHAPTER SEVENTEEN

THERE WAS NO PHONE CALL the next day, although the letters would have been delivered that morning—if the postal system worked as it was meant to do, which it usually did. Isabel spent the first part of the morning at her desk and the rest of the day at the delicatessen, standing in for Cat, who had a trade fair to attend in Glasgow. "All the food people will be there," she had said. "Miles of Italian sausage—miles. Tankers of olive oil. Everything."

"Then you must go," Isabel had replied. "I'll help Eddie. You go to Glasgow."

"Angel," said Cat, blowing Isabel a kiss.

"Well, I'm not sure . . ."

"But you are. You're a rock."

Isabel had wondered whether one could be both an angel and a rock. Angels were somewhat flighty; rocks were more . . . well, more **rocky**. What Cat might have said was that she was a brick; that was a compliment that people paid to those on whom they could rely, but the expression was dying out. Her father had talked about people being bricks—their mechanic, for example, had been a brick because he had been prepared to come and collect the car for its service when her father was too busy at the office to take it to the garage. That was the action of a brick.

She went to the delicatessen shortly after eleven, ready to help Eddie during the busiest period of the day, which was between twelve and two. There was time for a cup of coffee before she got down to work preparing bread rolls for lunchtime, and it was over a cup of coffee that Eddie mentioned Diane.

"Ah, Diane," said Isabel. "How is she?"

"She's going to London."

"Oh. And are you going with her? Have you been to London, Eddie?"

He shook his head. "I've never been there. I've been to America, but I've never been to London."

"Well, maybe you should go with her. How long is she going for, the weekend?"

Eddie reached for a jar of pickles. "No, she's going down there to finish her course. She's transferring to another college."

Isabel frowned. "But what about you, Eddie? Are you going too?"

He shook his head. "Not me," he said carelessly. "You wouldn't catch me living in London. Too big."

Isabel digested this. "So?"

"It's not a big problem," said Eddie. "We've finished. It's over."

Isabel put down her coffee cup. "I'm sorry," she said. "I'm really sorry to hear that, Eddie."

He shrugged, and then extracted a pickle from the jar with his fingers.

Isabel shook a finger. "You're not meant to do that, Eddie! Use a fork. You don't put your fingers in jars."

"Sorry." He put the pickle in his mouth. "It's only for me."

"But your fingers have been in the vinegar. You put germs from your hands into the vinegar. Now all those other pickles could be full of your germs."

"OK," he said. "I won't do it again."

She returned to the subject of Diane. "What happened?"

"I thought we should cool it," said Eddie. "So I did. She's cool with that."

Isabel was somewhat surprised by this abrupt

change of heart and was about to say something but stopped herself. She had not interfered before in the issue of the two of them living together and would not do so now. He was just too young.

"You'll miss her," said Isabel, largely out of a want of anything else to say.

"Maybe," said Eddie. "Maybe a bit."

Men don't miss women, thought Isabel. More women miss men than men miss women. That was probably right. It was depressingly right.

Work resumed, and it was not until three o'clock that things slackened off sufficiently for Isabel to telephone the house and ask if there had been any calls for her. Grace answered, and said that the glazier had called about a window that needed repairing but there had been nothing else.

She went home at five, leaving Eddie to do the last hour or so by himself. Again there had been no message, and there was no call either that evening. The next morning, though, shortly after eight, the telephone rang. It was Duncan.

"Astonishing news," he blurted out even before giving his name. "The Poussin's back."

Isabel started to say something, but was interrupted.

"This morning," said Duncan. "I went down

this morning and it was back in its place. Somebody had put it there last night. Astonishing. But it's safe—that's the important thing."

"Yes," said Isabel. "That's the important thing."

"I've told the insurance people," Duncan continued. "I woke that chap up, I'm afraid. I called him at six."

"I doubt if he minded," said Isabel. "It's rather good news for them."

"Yes," said Duncan. "He sounded pretty chipper. So that's it. Case closed. There's no claim from me, and that makes them extremely happy. Nothing more to be done."

Isabel had her doubts. "Do you think so? Surely the police will want to pursue the matter."

There was silence at the other end of the line.

"Have they said anything?" pressed Isabel.

"I haven't informed them yet," said Duncan. He sounded guarded.

"But you'll have to," said Isabel. She was thinking quickly; he seemed reluctant to inform the police and there had to be a reason for that. **He** was the one; that was the reason. Why else would he not wish to speak to the police? They would have to know eventually, but presumably he felt uneasy about talking to them himself. "After all," she went on, "this is a crime. A very valuable item was stolen. The police aren't going to want to let that go."

Again he was silent. Then: "I don't see what interest the police will have in dealing with something that's no longer a problem. They have better things to do with their time, don't you think?"

She did not get time to answer. Had she been able to say what was on her mind, she might have said that the issue was not so much theft as it was insurance fraud.

"Look," Duncan said. "Do you think you could come down here this morning? I know it's an imposition, but it would be much better to speak face-to-face. There's rather a lot to discuss."

Yes, thought Isabel. There was a great deal to discuss, but she did not see how she could discuss it with him. How could she? Would she accuse him of attempting to defraud his insurers? And if that was what she thought, was she not morally bound to go to the police with her suspicions?

She agreed to go. Jamie offered to accompany her, but she declined his offer. "It will be better for me to go by myself," she said. "I shall be perfectly safe."

She drove up to Doune in the Swedish car, not noticing the skies this time, nor paying much attention to the countryside unfolding on either side of the road. Her mind was occupied with what she might say to Duncan—that is, if she were to say anything, which was far from sure. Her earlier certainty that Duncan was responsible for the theft had been replaced by a measure of doubt. Now she thought: I really don't know. I know very little here, and I should simply leave the whole issue where it is. It was no business of hers to bring anybody to justice, nor to interfere in the affairs of a family that she barely knew and that had difficulties enough without her adding fuel to the flames of their dysfunctionality. By the time she arrived at Munrowe House, she had decided that her visit would be a brief one. She would listen to whatever it was that Duncan wished to say and then she would withdraw.

Duncan greeted her on the steps in front of the house. He was smiling broadly, and ushered her in warmly.

"Let's waste no time," he said. "Come into the drawing room. The painting is back where it belongs."

She followed him into the room, which was cold, in spite of the summer weather outside. Old Scottish houses were inevitably cold, she realised; it was the thickness of the stone walls. He saw her shiver. "I make a fire, even in summer," he said.

Isabel did not say anything; her eyes had gone straight to the Poussin.

"Back home," said Duncan.

Isabel walked forward and stood before the painting. She felt as she always did when she stood in front of a great work of art: a sense of marvel that she was so close to an artefact that was once worked upon by an artist of such stature as Poussin. He did this, she mused: he **thought** this painting, he touched this canvas.

She went a step closer. Duncan was now standing beside her. She heard his breathing. She felt his presence.

She turned her head, just slightly, so that she could see Duncan's face. His eyes were bright; there was joy in his expression. This man, it occurred to her, could not have engineered the disappearance of this painting. He could not be dissembling; he simply could not.

She looked at the sky in the painting. She saw the clouds, and behind them the blue of the void. Beyond the range of hills that the artist had painted in the background she could make out a glow in the sky that was the sun, and she remembered being in the Metropolitan Museum in New York and seeing Poussin's picture of Celadion standing on the shoulders of the giant, Orion, and guiding him towards the sun, that his sight might be restored. On the shoulders of great men we go towards the light . . .

"We should take a seat," said Duncan, indicating the sofa. "We can gaze at this lovely sight while we talk."

She sat down at one end of a chintzy sofa, with Duncan at the other.

He did not hesitate. "So you found out," he began. "Frankly, I wasn't surprised."

"No?"

"No, I'd dreaded it. I suppose I suspected it all along, but I didn't really want to face up to the fact that my own son could have done something like that."

She was still. "Your son?"

"Yes, Patrick. As I assume you've discovered."

"Why do you think it was him?" she asked gently.

He laughed. "Because it's obvious. The house was locked last night. This morning the painting was back in its original position, as if nothing had happened. There are four or five copies of the keys—mine, my wife's, my daughter's, my son's, and a spare set we keep in a drawer."

Isabel asked him where his wife was. He replied that she was in Paris and would be away for the next two weeks. He had spoken to her on the telephone, though—to give her the good news. "Needless to say, she's delighted."

"But I still don't see—"

He interrupted. "I assumed that you spoke to him after you discovered the truth."

Isabel shook her head. "No, I didn't."

"Then he must have realised that you knew."

She was not sure what to say. "Do you think so?"

"Yes."

He looked up at the painting. "He's gone on and on about redistribution—he's harped on about it for years. But I never thought he'd take his animosity to me and my concerns to such an extent." He shook his head ruefully. "Never. I would never have dreamed it."

"Are you sure it's him?" said Isabel gently.

He looked at her in surprise. "What do you mean? Who else could it be?"

"You have two children," said Isabel.

He laughed. "Alex? No, that's out of the question."

Isabel looked down at her hands. I could tell him, she thought. I could list the factors that pointed to his daughter: her financial need, her attachment to the painting, her deliberate involvement of Isabel through Martha.

Duncan now rose to his feet and took the few

steps that brought him close to the painting. He gazed at it, his back to Isabel.

"Do you know something?" he said, without turning round. "When I asked Martha to contact you, I never imagined that you would be able to sort the whole thing out. I hardly dared hope. I expected that you would be a comfort to me in the whole business—as I told you—but I had no idea that you'd bring the matter to a successful conclusion."

Isabel sat where she was. "When you asked Martha?"

He seemed surprised by her question. "Yes. I got in touch with her. I didn't want to speak to you out of the blue. I suppose I'm afraid of rejection." He looked at her and gave a curious, self-deprecatory shrug. "Who isn't? We're all a bit weak, I fear."

"I don't think it was your son," said Isabel.

Duncan appeared to weigh this—but not for long. "You don't have to protect him, you know. I'm not going to do anything about it, as I told you. After all, he's still my son."

Isabel stared at him. "Do you love him?"

"Of course I do. In spite of everything. I'll get over this."

She was astonished. "So this will make no difference to your relationship with him?"

Duncan sighed. "Probably not. We are very far apart, you see, in many respects. And I don't think this was directed against me. The painting was going to come back—he was merely going for the insurance company. He hates people like that—fair game, in his view."

"What if I told you," said Isabel, "that it was definitely not your son? What if I said that it was somebody else altogether?"

He sat down again. She had his full attention. "Why? What do you mean?"

She closed her eyes briefly, trying to order her thoughts. "It was somebody else, but I cannot reveal who. I'm sorry. But I assure you that I am one hundred per cent sure that it was not Patrick."

Duncan looked confused. "Then who . . . ?"

"I can't reveal that," Isabel repeated. She had made her decision. It had all fallen into place and she knew what she had to do. "You yourself said that the important thing is that the painting is back."

He corrected her. "You said that."

"No, you did."

He looked doubtful. And Isabel thought: Did I say it, or did he? And if we can't remember who said what, then how could anybody be sure about who spoke to Martha? But one thing was clear: it was right not to tell him that his daughter was behind the theft. If she was, which Isabel thought was probable. Or perhaps not . . . "I think I should get back to Edinburgh," she said.

"I owe you a great deal," said Duncan. "I'm very grateful to you."

She had been about to stand up, but at this, she remained where she was. "Then I'm going to ask something of you."

He was guarded. "Yes?"

"I'd like you to make some gesture towards your son," she said. "You said that you loved him. Well, he doesn't think so."

He began to protest, but she cut him short.

"Yes, I mean it. He thinks that you disapprove of him."

"He disapproves of me," blurted out Duncan.

"Disapproval can sometimes be an act of self-defence," Isabel pointed out. "And in this sort of situation it's not necessarily a good idea for people to blame each other for starting things. You have to short-circuit all that. You have to forget about it. Tell him that you value him. Tell him that you are happy with what he is. Don't deny it. He's not going to change his nature, you know. Tell him that that's all right. Say it. Embrace him. Put your arms around him and say that you're proud of him and you love him."

He stared at her.

"Or lose him," she said.

She rose to her feet, glanced one final time at the Poussin and began to leave the room.

SHE WAS BACK in Edinburgh well before lunchtime. Jamie had been practising that morning—he had a demanding concert coming up in which he was playing Mozart's bassoon concerto, and he was working his way through that, ironing out difficulties, making sure that his playing was as polished as possible. Now he was ready for lunch, which he suggested they have in the garden as it was a warm day—one of the warmest of the year so far—and they could eat on a picnic rug on the shady part of the lawn. Isabel agreed, and prepared a plate of sandwiches and a jug of the slightly tart lime cordial that she had made a few days previously.

Sitting on the rug, she told Jamie about her trip to Munrowe House and about the conversation she had had with Duncan. "So who was it?" he asked.

Isabel picked at a sandwich. "Ham," she said. "You should have the ham ones and I'll have tomato. Who was it?"

He took the ham sandwich from her. "Yes. Who was it?"

She extracted a tomato sandwich from the small stack on the serving plate. "Who was it? Sometimes it's difficult to say. You think you know the answer, then you don't."

"But you must have some feeling about it," pressed Jamie.

"The daughter," said Isabel. "I may be wrong, but I think it was her. The last thing I wanted to do was to tell Duncan that. He is very fond of her, and I'm not sure that it would be helpful for him to know that she's dishonest. Frankly, I think it could even be the end of him—that knowledge."

Jamie understood. "So you kept that from him?"

Isabel nodded. "I did. I think I had to." She paused for a moment. "But it could have been somebody else. I'm not sure. It could even have been Duncan—I doubt it, he was so obviously delighted about having the painting back that I more or less dismissed the idea, but it's theoretically possible. Just."

Jamie was silent. He had started on the ham sandwich and was making quick work of it. Within a minute, it had disappeared, and he reached for another one.

Once their lunch was over, they lay down on the rug. Isabel, feeling relaxed and relieved that the Poussin was back in its home, reflected on the fact that the best solutions in life are sometimes the vaguest and least clear-cut. That was true, no matter how much we strove for certainty, for the cut and dried, for the harsh truth that admitted of no nuances, no qualifications. I am glad that I do not live in a world that requires such certainty of me, she thought. I am glad.

"Look at those clouds," said Jamie, gazing up at the sky. "Look at them."

"Yes," said Isabel. "They're very beautiful, aren't they? Clouds are very beautiful and yet so often we fail to appreciate them properly. We should do that. We should look at them and think about how lucky we are to have them."

She turned to Jamie, lying beside her. He was still on his back, his hands tucked behind his head, making a rough-and-ready human pillow. Had she been able to write haiku, she thought, she would write one to him now. **You beside me / The grass beneath / I think . . .** and so on. But she could not, and what she wanted to say to him now was all jumbled up inside her. She could kiss him perhaps; that might express her feelings every bit as eloquently as if she were to speak at length. But she felt a piece of tomato on her teeth and she did not want to kiss him until that had dislodged itself, or been dislodged.

"Look at the shape of the clouds," she said. "What do you see in those beautiful clouds, Jamie?"

She thought he might find a shape of the clouds that they could treat as an omen, a portent perhaps, but he did not. Instead, he waited for a few moments, waited until a bee that had been crawling on a nearby flower went on to something else.

"I see you," he said.

ABOUT THE AUTHOR

Alexander McCall Smith is the author of the No. 1 Ladies' Detective Agency series, the Isabel Dalhousie series, the Portuguese Irregular Verbs series, the 44 Scotland Street series and the Corduroy Mansions series. He is professor emeritus of medical law at the University of Edinburgh and has served with many national and international organizations concerned with bioethics. He was born in what is now known as Zimbabwe and taught law at the University of Botswana. He lives in Scotland.

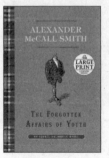

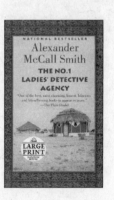